Calliope Street

Josh Hanson

MOONSTRUCK
BOOKS

ALSO BY JOSH HANSON

King's Hill

The Woodcutters

Cymbals Eat Guitars

Minotaur: Stories

Marshbank

Eucalytus: Poems

Moonstruck Books
Portland, Oregon
moonstruck-books.com

First publication 2026 by Moonstruck Books

ISBN (paperback) 979-8-9888154-7-1

Cover design and interior formatting by FZ Boda
Proofreading by Amber Finnegan, Finnegan Editorial

A NOTE TO THE READER

Be aware that this book contains graphic descriptions of violence, transmisogyny, toxic masculinity, animal death, abandonment, objectification, natural disasters, and other potentially triggering subjects. If you need help living, coping with trauma or harm, or staying sober, these resources offer support at no cost. Please reach out for help.

Suicide and Crisis Lifeline

988

The Rape, Abuse & Incest National Network (RAINN)

1-800-656-HOPE

The Trevor Project

1-866-488-7386

Alcoholics Anonymous

aa-intergroup.org/get-help-now

Adult Survivors of Child Abuse (ASCA)

info@ascasupport.org

415-937-1854

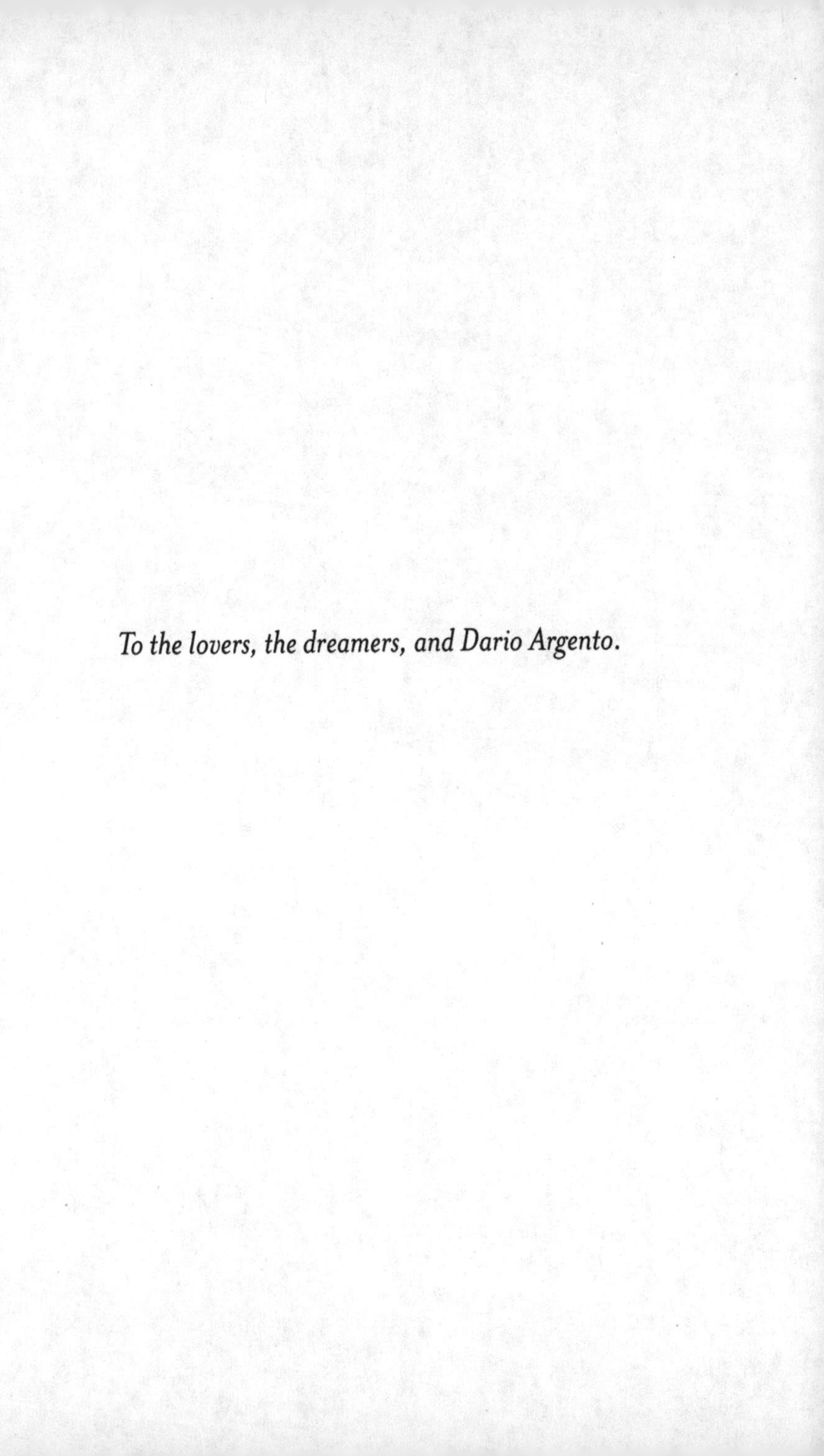

To the lovers, the dreamers, and Dario Argento.

Part I
The House on Calliope Street

1.

When Jack found the collage on the basement wall, he called out to Avery, who was still in the kitchen with the realtor. He heard her give some joking apology and move to the top of the basement stairs.

"What?" she called down.

"You've got to see this," Jack shouted, hands in his back pockets, standing back to admire it, his head tilted slightly to one side.

"I know what he's found," the realtor said, amused. "Go on down."

Dale, the realtor, was a tall, middle aged man with a booming radio voice and thick, rubbery features. He reminded Jack more of a car salesman, but he seemed alright.

He heard the clomp and creak of footsteps on the narrow staircase that hugged the basement wall and then made a weirdly tight, 180-degree turn before opening onto the laundry area. Jack was further back into the basement, with its concrete floor, exposed beam ceiling, and framed and plastic-sheeted walls that went in every direction. Clearly, someone had an idea for a larger project down here that had never quite come to fruition. So now it was just a labyrinth of semi-transparent walls, with the laundry room at one end and *this* at the other. A narrow basement window sat at the very top of the wall, half-darkened by leaves and trash that had fallen down into the window well. Below that was the collage. Jack stood, squinting beneath a bare bulb set in the beams, the white light glaring in the little square of concrete.

Avery came up behind him, looking over his shoulder.

"What the actual fuck?"

"Right?"

"I can't believe they didn't tear that out before listing, but they know what they've got. This place will sell in days. They're obviously not real motivated to put anything into it."

"But, like, what even *is* this?" Avery whispered.

It was a rhetorical question, and neither of them attempted to answer it.

The collage was a rough circle about six feet in diameter, composed exclusively of women and parts of women cut carefully from magazine pages. There were smiling women from advertisements, bikini-clad women, some almost-familiar faces of once-famous women, and lots and lots of exposed breasts. Nothing outrageous. Nothing hardcore. Lots of lounging, arch-backed headless bodies with full, natural breasts. Lots of big, unnatural hairdos:

teased bangs and frizzy perms that screamed 80s. The clippings were all overlapping, radiating out from the center of the mass, like a flesh-colored flower or a blazing sun.

The whole thing was built up into three dimensions, bulging from the wall, and it wasn't clear to Jack if there was something underneath the collage to give it this shape or if it was just layer upon layer of adhesive and paper. At the thickest point, right at the center, the mound probably stood out six inches from the wall. At its center was a hole. Dark and jagged, just wide enough for Jack to push his little finger into—though he wouldn't be doing that, thank you. The hole stared into him like a black and unblinking eye.

"You see all kinds of things in real estate," Dale said. "This is nothing."

"This is definitely something," Avery said, laughing. She clutched Jack's arms from behind, resting her chin on his shoulder. "Tell me we'll keep it forever."

"Who am I to argue with art?"

"So, you'd like to make an offer?" Dale said, his big radio voice filling the lighted space.

Jack and Avery both stared at the mass of women's bodies and faces, a thousand glossy eyes staring back—but mostly that dark one at the center, like a pupil shrunk to a pinprick. Jack suddenly had the idea that if he switched off the light above them, that hole would expand and dilate, the better to see them with.

He twisted his head around to see Avery's face, framed by her dark hair and severe bangs.

"Do we?" he said.

"We do, yeah?" Her expression said, *Obviously*.

Jack turned around, and Avery slid her tattooed arms around his middle, squeezing him. Jack looked past her head to Dale and smiled.

"We do," he said.

2.

They'd have been fools not to buy it, the house on Calliope Street. Half a mile from the university district, and just far enough away from the main traffic arteries, the split-level was in a quiet little neighborhood of modest one- and two-story houses with small yards and huge trees that turned the street into a green tunnel of overhanging branches. They were more than lucky to get it: the previous owner had died and the distant cousin who inherited it was old or in poor health or something. Jack and Avery didn't really know the whole story, but the upshot was that the sellers wanted it gone, so they'd listed it as-is and lowballed the price, and Jack and Avery had swooped in like a pair of osprey taking a trout.

But of course, nothing moved quickly, so it was late June by the time they got the keys. Jack felt a certain crunch for time. It was summer break, so Dylan was at his other mom's house, a thousand miles away, but he'd be back. And Jack would have to be back at school in mid-August for professional development and the usual nonsense; and then the students would be back; and then it would be only the occasional weekend devoted to the house, and he had enough self-awareness to know that that meant it would be *next* summer before anything of substance was accomplished.

Now was the time.

So he devoted himself to being Mr. Fix-It for the summer. He and Avery would do as much of the big stuff as they could right away, leaving the winter months for the cosmetic stuff, which Jack didn't really care about anyway.

There was a detached garage that opened onto the alley behind the house, and Jack filled it with his newly purchased table saw and cordless drill, a dozen sheets of plywood, another dozen of sheetrock, and a pile of two-by-fours. His plan was to start in the attic and work down, tackling the basement last, finally finishing those framed walls to make an office for him and a practice space for Avery.

The top floor was really just a converted attic, with steeply pitched ceilings that sloped almost all the way to the floor. It was a single room that ran the length of the house, with dormer windows at either end, one looking out toward the street and the other looking toward the yard out back.

The loft was cramped and hot, but they thought it would be a perfect spot for Dylan, who—at twelve—should love the hidey-hole nature of it. So, while Avery was at the salon during the day, Jack worked on adding built-in shelves around the front window, complete with space for the little TV and gaming system. This took longer than expected, and ended up requiring not one but two more trips to the hardware store, but in the end, Avery said it looked great, and that she'd paint them to match the ceiling that weekend.

They found a low bureau at the Goodwill, stripped it of its 70s-style brass knobs, and cleaned it up. It took both of them to get the thing up the narrow staircase, knocking a three-inch divot out of the plaster, but it fit perfectly under the back window, and the attic was all of a sudden looking like a living space. They brought up Dylan's bed, the tubs of toys, and all four cardboard long-boxes of comics books. Jack even installed a long rope of multicolored LED lights along the crown of the ceiling.

"He'll love it," Avery said, sitting cross-legged in the middle of the room, cycling through the rope light's colors with the little toy remote control. Jack watched the tattooed scissors on the back of her hand ripple.

"I'd have loved it," Jack said, approaching her with his head slightly hunched under the low ceiling.

"That's what I'm saying." Avery smiled up at him, her round face framed by straight black hair, bangs poking down into her eyes. "He'll love it, and he'll love that you did it for him." She pulled Jack by his belt, and he dropped to his knees beside her.

"Or, being a twelve-year-old boy, he will hate it on principle, like he hates me on principle, and it will all be for nothing."

Avery kissed him.

"Stop pouting. He doesn't hate you and you know it. And he will love this."

Jack was suddenly less concerned with what Dylan did or didn't like, as Avery pushed her hands up under his T-shirt. Her palms were hot and soft against his skin, and her mouth was at his ear.

"But not like I love you."

"Glad to hear that," he smiled, and just as her hands came back down to the buckle of his belt, there was a *CHUNK* from deep within the house and everything went dark.

"Um?" Avery said.

Jack let out a sigh of defeat. "It's the third time today. I really, really don't want to call an electrician, but it takes nothing to trip this breaker."

"I was hoping you might trip my breaker," Avery laughed into his ear. She was just a bluish outline in the dark room.

"Yeah, you're really not good at this," Jack teased, kissing her on the nose and groaning as he climbed to his feet. "I mean, 'blow my fuse' was right there."

"And you're leaving," she said, leaning back on her hands, as Jack went down the carpeted steps.

"It'll take thirty seconds," Jack called behind him.

"Not the flex you think it is, my dude."

3.

Jack laughed to himself as he went into the kitchen, pushing open the basement door. The lights were on down there, at least. He moved quickly down the steps and around the washer and dryer and opened the fuse box.

The various breakers were all labeled in pencil: *bedroom/bath*, *kitchen*, *attic*. But the switch for the basement had been scratched out and written over in red pencil. One word: *Shurpu*. He had no idea what language that was, and the strange word vanished from his mind as he groped for the breaker. He flipped the *attic* switch and heard a faint cheer from upstairs.

He slammed the fuse box door and moved to leave, but then he heard something.

In that moment, it was only that: a noise. Unidentified but vaguely familiar. His brain spun, trying to land on some connection, some label to affix to the sound. Then it would no longer be "a sound" but a known thing. The source was low to the ground, back beyond the plastic-sheeted walls, and he made his way through the empty frame of the doorway leading back that way. He could just make out the purple rectangle of the little window at the far end, but the overhead bulb was switched off.

The sound again, off to his right, definitely moving on the ground. His mind snagged on a name: *rat*. But he knew that wasn't quite right. There was something else there, too heavy, bigger. He thought briefly of the fuse box with its weird labeling. Maybe that's how rats moved down in *Shurpu*, after all?

He crept down the shimmering corridor, the light behind him reflected multiple times through multiple layers of six-mil plastic, and the purple glow of evening like a beacon in the distance.

And why such a distance? The whole basement couldn't be more than thirty feet long, but there in the half-dark, with his shadow cast weirdly before him, it felt much further. Of course, it didn't help that there was no straight line, but rather the twists and turns of the half-formed labyrinth.

The noise again, this time on his left.

It had to be a cat. An injured cat, dragging a broken leg. It had been hit by a car and crawled down here somehow, looking for a dark place to die. Jack's mind kept whirling, trying to find the right name to hang on the sound but instead he kept catching on the foreign word penciled inside the fuse box door.

Shurpu.

Suddenly he was sure that the penciled name labeled the thing that lived in this part of the house. Right now, the *Shurpu* was dragging itself along the edge of the wall, moving further back into the basement's shadows. And perhaps tonight, while he and Avery slept, it would rise up at the foot of their bed, long-toothed and scaly, extending its hooked fingers out toward their feet. Vaguely human in shape. Skin oily-black.

Jack laughed at himself, getting all worked up. This fear was probably primal, right? Moving underground through the dark, his reptile brain triggered by the unknown sound? His brain's own autonomic spook story unfolded behind his eyes. That was all beyond his control. What mattered was how he responded to it. And he would respond to it like an adult.

He reached the far end of the basement, where the dim light from the window illuminated that little square of space just enough to make out its shape. He reached for the string that dangled from the exposed bulb, and then the sound was louder, close, suddenly right at his feet, and he jumped to the side, lifting his right leg up high, and he gave a little yelp.

He saw a dark shape move into the deeper shadow of the wall ahead. It was long and moved swiftly, seeming to glide, and his reptile brain flashed *snake!* Even though it looked absolutely nothing like a snake.

Jack took a step backward, breathed, and reached once again for the string above his head. The light clicked on, too bright, and he squinted, his raised arm coming down to shield his eyes, and through the crook of his arm he saw it.

The thing (*Shurpu*) had made its way up the wall, over the collage of staring women. By the time his eyes adjusted, it slipped into the dark hole at its center, just a flash of movement that might have been the shadow off the swinging light cord, but he didn't think so.

He took another involuntary step back and looked around the concrete square where he stood. The light reflected bright off the plastic and threw barred shadows out into the depths of the basement, but his eye returned to that dark hole at the center of the collage. When he'd first seen it, he'd thought of it as a pupil, but now it seemed more threatening, like a mouth, a sphincter, an entranceway back into whatever was covered over by the magazine women.

He strained to hear any movement behind the paper, back inside the wall. Something had nested in there. That was obvious. Some weirdo had made this monstrosity, and the bugs had recycled it, made it a home.

That was no bug.

They should pull the whole thing down, whatever Avery had said about keeping it. What would Dylan think when he came home? A sick porno-hole in their basement. It had to go.

He knelt down, eye-level with the dark hole. It was too small for whatever he'd seen slipping inside. Had to be a trick of the light, the bare bulb's shadow enlarging whatever it had been. Some kind of millipede, maybe. Jack's rational brain was already soothing his lizard brain back into relaxation. After all, the light was on now. He would put down poison to get whatever was skittering around the basement, and he'd talk to Avery about that damned collage.

All the same, he moved quickly back through the twisting maze to the laundry area, where he fished through the wastebasket and pulled out a large blue-gray clump of dryer lint. Back at the collage, he pushed the lint into the hole, a piece at a time. Just for his peace of mind. Close it up until tomorrow. But no matter how much he fed into it, he couldn't seem to fill up the space. Finally, when the lump of lint was gone, he headed back upstairs to talk to Avery about it. She'd talk him down, convince him that he hadn't seen what he'd seen. And that's exactly what he wanted. He wanted her to gaslight him into calmness.

At the stairs, he looked back. He'd left the light on, not wanting to make that dark journey back again. From this far end, the basement looked like a glowing cube of light behind many shrouds, and though he couldn't make it out, he knew that the raised hump of the collage, with its thousands of eyes and breasts and parted lips, was there, staring back at him with its black pupil, perhaps breathing slightly, filled with many-legged things just waiting to spill out and come flowing in a chittering wave across the concrete floor.

He went up into the kitchen and closed the basement door.

He didn't say anything to Avery.

4.

The marriage was Jack's first and Avery's second. She had married young, back (she said with a wink) when she was another person, with another life. A recent college dropout with a lot of anger and a deep commitment to chemical substances of all kinds, she'd once been wild and destructive. Her first wife, Janie, had seen a sad man in need of comforting, and that had been the basis for their doomed relationship: Janie as savior-mother and Avery as broken boy.

It took three years and the birth of Dylan before it became clear that Janie wasn't going to be able to mother Avery out of her troubles; Avery wasn't anyone's sad, broken boy. She never had been. When she announced her plan to transition, that was too much for Janie, and the marriage quickly dissolved. Avery didn't blame her, and they were still friendly, but she didn't like to talk much about those years. They were too desperate, too dark. Her nadir. She remembered it as a time when, even more than her teen years, she had devoted so much of her energy into trying to be something she was not.

So Avery got clean. She went to beauty school. She moved west, settling into this little college mountain town with a genuine trans community. She joined a punk band where she played bass and screamed indecipherable lyrics. And she met Jack.

And that was the beginning of her real life.

La Vita Nuova.

When they met, Jack was a second-year teacher at the local high school and a music geek. He'd caught her band's gig in the parking lot of the local record shop. It was the same lineup as now, with Avery and her friends Em and Billy. They were going by Diss 4 Ya, which was a truly terrible name, but they cycled through names pretty quickly, so no damage done. Jack was quiet and lanky in a way that Avery liked. He really dug their show and complimented their set as they stood around the keg, and then he'd asked her out. Just like that.

He wasn't particularly good-looking. He had very little chin, which he tried to hide behind a scraggly goatee. Bad teeth. And he was so blind that his big plastic-framed glasses held thick lenses that warped his eyes, giving him a kind of frog-like appearance. And, last but not least, he had no ass. None, whatsoever. *Concave.*

But he was nice, and he was funny, and he had good taste in music. He was also wicked smart and had read everything, and he liked painfully stupid horror movies, so he was kind of perfect for Avery, really. And when he met Dylan, he'd been sweetly awkward but got right down on the floor with the kid, and the three of them just kind of clicked. And that was that.

Two weeks after moving into their house on Calliope Street, Avery came home from her evening at the salon and called out for Jack. He answered from the stairs leading up into the attic. She found him attempting to repair the chunk they'd taken out of the drywall when moving the dresser. It looked like he was just making a mess, though.

"How you doing?" she said, smiling up at him.

He sat down heavily on the steps, a putty knife in one hand and a little plastic tub in the other. His hands were smeared with what looked like gray mud. His skinny legs tapered down from his shorts into a pair of worn Adidas with no socks.

"I thought I could do this without buying a patch."

"How's that working out for you?"

"I'd like to throw myself into the sun."

"Understandable. Have you eaten anything?"

He shook his head and looked at the spot on the wall. It was built up with putty in a little hump that was too smooth to match the texture of the rest of the wall. In the center of the hump was a little indentation.

"Have you considered just covering it up with pictures of naked ladies?" she said, eyebrows raised, lower lip stuck out.

"I'm considering it now," he said, and set the tub down on the step beside him, resting the flat bladed knife on top of it. "Speaking of."

"Speaking of naked ladies?"

"Speaking of naked ladies, yes. I think we really ought to do something about that monstrosity in the basement." He crinkled his nose like he smelled something bad.

"You mean like track lighting and a little plaque, right? That thing is a work of art."

"Obviously, but I was just thinking about Dylan."

"I'm sure Dylan has seen tits before. Have you heard of the internet?"

"I'm well aware of what's on the internet, thank you."

"I just bet you are," she said. She wanted a shower. She wanted PJs.

"But that doesn't mean we need to—what?—put it out there for his consumption."

Avery raised a questioning eyebrow at him.

"You're not kidding. Are you turning into a prude, Jackson Todd?"

"I'm not being a prude. It's just creepy as shit."

"Would you cover his eyes if we went to an art museum? All those female-presenting nipples?"

"Okay, whatever, but that's nobody's art. It's some old dude's spank bank, and I think it's infested with bugs or something, and I think we should rip it out."

She shook her head in mock-despair. "This is so un-punk of you. I just want it said. You are turning into, like, the Man. If I'd known home ownership would do this to you, I never would have gone through with it."

Jack rolled his eyes and stood up, careful not to smack his head on the slanted ceiling.

"Okay, sure. I'm running to the store to get a patch for this thing. You want me to pick up food?"

"I'll make something as soon as I bathe," she said.

He came a couple steps down toward her, and she raised a hand up toward him. He dropped his hand into hers. She turned it back and forth, looking at the gray stuff covering his fingers and caked around his nails.

"Though, I do have to say: 'Mr. Homeowner' does suit you, setting aside your inevitable slide into ultra-conservative politics."

"Ya think?" he smiled down at her.

He could read his own name spelled out in ink across the fingers of her right hand.

"Definitely. If you were to, say, mow the lawn in your cut-offs, that would be porn. Pure prurient content. We could sell it."

"We might need to. Every time I step into that hardware store, I drop a hundred bucks."

"You'd show it all to keep us in spackle, yeah?"

"In a heartbeat."

He leaned down and kissed her, and she had a brief flash of the skinny guy at the back of the crowd that afternoon in the parking lot. She'd been drawn to him immediately. Maybe it was his eyes, enlarged by his glasses, but he'd seemed so intent, so focused, and she could feel his gaze on her, and it somehow didn't make her feel creeped out or objectified.

"You're gross, but I love you anyway," she said.

"I love you anyway, too," he said into her hair.

"And we should get a cat," she said. He could hear the smile.

"Ugh. Not yet," he said.

And then he was off to the store to do his manly shopping, and Avery took a quick shower. She preferred scalding water, but it was just too hot out for that, so she rinsed, patted herself dry, and slipped into her gray sweats and an oversized black T-shirt that hung on her like a sack.

Maybe we're both turning into dull home-ownery people, she thought. She pulled the shirt down and to the side to expose one shoulder, pushed her tits forward, examining herself in the foggy mirror. *Nah. Fuck that. I look good.*

She thought about Cash, the shelter cat she'd adopted when she'd first moved to town. She'd kept him secretly in her little apartment. He was pure white, a beautiful cat, and a scrapper, with scars and ragged ears and bobbed tail, and only one eye. She'd named him Cash after Johnny, after that song "Mean-Eyed Cat," even though Cash hadn't looked mean, not really, but the one eye kind of put you on your guard.

Cash had gone out one night to prowl and never come back. That was six, seven years ago now? She missed having a cat in the house, but Jack wanted to wait until all of the work was done. That was a trap, of course. The work would never be *done*.

Maybe she'd stop at the shelter tomorrow.
Just to look.

5.

She padded barefoot into the kitchen and instantly regretted it. Whatever psycho had lived here before them installed wall-to-wall carpet through the kitchen and dining room, and the kitchen floor was a horror show. The nap on the carpet was worn down smooth with traffic, and decades worth of cooking had left it stiff and discolored. She'd tell Jack to deal with that next. It made her sick to think of what might be growing under there.

And that made her think of Jack's comment about the basement collage. The old subterranean spank bank. He'd said something about it being infested.

She looked toward the basement door.

In the basement, the light was on at the far end, giving the whole space a weird, underwater feel, bars of shadow thrown across the floor, the light warped by plastic sheeting. Stepping into the basement, she once again wished she were wearing something on her feet. The concrete floor was cold and cracked, whole pieces heaved up a half inch. Cold grit bit into her soles, and somehow it made her feel naked, vulnerable. She wondered if it flooded in the spring. It didn't quite have that musty smell.

At the collage, she stood back a ways to take in all of its freaky glory. How many hours? Someone had meticulously cut out each of these figures and then pasted them into place. Using what? Her mind went to terrifying places, and she decided against touching it to see how it felt.

It was obviously made by a dude. Some lonely, obsessive basement-dweller. Literally. And it was a perfect emblem of how those dudes thought of women. Tits and a hole. She was surprised the eyes hadn't been scratched out. That would be some real serial killer shit. Instead, the faces all stared back. She didn't like it, all those eyes.

What was funny was, if a woman had made this, it would be a perfect feminist critique, without changing one thing. It was the male gaze made concrete. A giant eye reflecting back some idealized female form. The pupil shrunken to a tight, dark orifice.

What would it mean if she had made it? How would Avery be psychoanalyzed? Would the whole thing just be read as her demented mood board, with a place to stick her dick?

Suddenly, she was sure that that's what the hole was for. She couldn't quite believe it hadn't occurred to her before. The dude most definitely fucked this thing. No, that was too gross. And could it even feel good? She knelt down to look closer at the dark, ragged hole.

Maybe it wasn't meant to feel good. Maybe it was a punishment. A semi-religious penance for all of these dirty thoughts. Maybe he came down here, worshiped at his flesh altar, and then had to expiate his shame in some way.

She stepped back, feeling suddenly sick at the idea of what might be behind those endless images. They'd need hazmat suits to clean up that mess.

Yeah, Jack was right. It needed to go. There was no interpretation that she'd want to present to Dylan that would make this seem okay.

All of those eyes seemed to be pinning her to that spot, so she reached up and switched off the light, casting them all into darkness. It was less that she didn't want to see than that she didn't want to be seen.

She retreated quickly upstairs, and when Jack came home, she told him they had to do something about the carpet in the kitchen and, okay, he was probably right: they should take down the collage in the basement.

6.

As soon as Jack yanked up the first corner of the kitchen carpet, clouds of dust rose up with it. He was horrified to find a thick mat of what must be years and years of filth that had worked its way through, sometimes turned muddy with wet, and then dried into crumbling chunks. True to form, he needed to make another trip to the hardware store, this time for face masks.

Soon, masked up and sweating in his long sleeves, he was cutting the carpet into long strips, peeling it up into rolls, and tossing it out the back door into the yard. There was real hardwood underneath the mess, but Jack didn't know what it would take to get it into any kind of usable shape again. The area in front of the sink was the worst, where the wood was warped and discolored.

This is my life now. One stupid job that leads to two more stupid jobs, branching off forever, the expenses growing exponentially until I either die or file for bankruptcy. The idea of the new school year halting his to-do list seemed less like a problem and more of a blessing. He could only do so much.

He cut a clean line across the entryway carpet to the dining room and left that section alone, at least for today, and then set about cleaning up the kitchen floor. In some places he actually had to chip away at the filth, and when he tried mopping it up, the whole thing dissolved into silt.

By the time Avery came home, the floors were clear, and they talked about sanding them down and refinishing, which sounded great, though Jack had no idea how to do any of it, and he was pretty sure they needed to replace some sections by the sink where there was water damage.

They sat in the backyard in the early dark, the trees standing out black against the deep blue of the sky, a few stars already winking above. This was Jack's favorite time. Summer evenings, when the heat finally dropped off and sometimes a breeze crept through. He'd kill for a sudden thunderstorm. Soak the ground and drop the temp a few more degrees, leave the whole world smelling fresh and clean. As it was, he'd be blowing that rug shit out of his nose for a week, mask or no mask. West of them, there was already the haze of smoke from the encroaching wildfires.

The two of them sat in their folding camp chairs, plates on their knees, and listened to the crickets' rising chorus, and Jack was happy. He'd worked his body, and now it would rest, and he was sitting in the summer twilight with his one true love. In *their* yard, behind *their* house. All headaches aside, they were doing okay.

The next day, he started on the dining room carpet. He moved the table into the living room, stacked the chairs on top of it, shoved the other furniture into the kitchen and masked up.

The mess was somewhat less than in the kitchen, but it was still hot, dirty work, and he continued to take the fibers up in long strips, the easier to lug out into the yard. He was about halfway across the room when he found the chalk marks.

It was a pattern, large and curving. At first he thought it was kids' work, but it was too regular, too intentional, too careful. Foreboding rose up, a coldness that spread across his scalp. Somehow, he knew he didn't want to see the whole pattern. But still, he kept going, trancelike, removing the carpet and uncovering what lay beneath a one-foot strip at a time.

The circle revealed itself, another concentric circle within it, and Jack was fully prepared to find a rough pentagram from the heavy metal days of the mid-80s. Something he'd recognize from a thousand late night viewings of B-movie schlock. But what was there was somehow stranger. The double circle contained a whole string of illegible characters running between its borders. Greek characters, as well as Roman ones, though not making up any words he recognized. There were some crosses and squiggles, a few symbols that looked like stick figures. It was all carefully drawn out on the planks. In the center of the circle was a smaller circle, maybe two inches across, and there were a few lines bisecting it, but none of them formed anything like the five-pointed star he'd been expecting.

At one edge of the circle, spilling out beyond its border, there was a dark stain about two feet across, irregularly shaped. Like a shadow burned permanently into the wood. Something had spilled here. Wax, maybe? What's a ritual circle without candles?

But he knew it wasn't wax. His lizard brain told him.

Kneeling down, he wiped a fingertip across the chalk. It didn't budge. And then he saw why. The way the light came in the window, he could see the patchy edges of the sealant where the floor suddenly went dull.

He stepped to the edge of the dining room and tried to get a photo with his phone. In the end, he had to get up on a chair to get a good angle. He snapped a couple of shots and texted the best one to Avery.

"So, there's this," he texted under the photo.

It was ten minutes later when his phone buzzed. Avery had just sent a line of big eyed emojis.

"WTF?!" she typed.

"No idea."

"You can destroy the titty shrine but this absolutely has to stay. Amazing."

He laughed through his nose and went to drag the chunks of carpet into the alley.

7.

By the time cleanup was done, Jack was a sweaty, gritty mess. He showered and put on shorts and a T-shirt. He decided to get some chile verde going for dinner, and set about cutting up a pork shoulder, onions, and tomatillos. The kitchen seemed somehow bigger and brighter without the carpet. The dining room was positively cavernous. As he dropped chunks of pork into the dutch oven, the oil popped and sizzled, and Jack looked across the room, his eye continually drawn to the circles on the floor.

He was a no-nonsense kind of atheist. The supernatural had never even seemed like a possibility to him, let alone any kind of divine, guiding force. He didn't have strong feelings about religion, one way or the other. It just wasn't part of how he was built. He knew that Avery had some good old-fashioned religious trauma. Find a Midwestern queer kid who didn't. But he didn't think she really had any kind of religious convictions, either.

Demonic sigils were the kind of stuff from 80s horror movies, the ones with gratuitous nudity and outrageously grisly practical effects. Jack's happy place, basically. But the movies didn't bother addressing that demonic stuff in any meaningful way. It was just window dressing. Shorthand. The stuff teenagers played with, thereby inviting evil forces in. It was one step above an ouija board as a plot device.

Avery was right. The naked lady collage was unsettling, but this was just goofy. It was the perfect conversation piece for their weird little family.

He removed the browned pork from the pot and started feeding in the onions. The house was already filling with delicious smells and he realized he hadn't eaten anything. Just half a pot of coffee. Once he had the verde together and sealed and simmering under the heavy lid, he made a quick sandwich and went out to the yard, where he positioned a chair in the shade of a tree.

As he ate, he sent the floor pic to a couple of their friends.

Em responded immediately.

"Rock on!" she typed.

"Human sacrifice this Friday night," Jack replied.

He finished his sandwich, leaning back in his chair, looking up into the latticework of branches above him.

"Working hard?"

The voice seemed to come from above, as if the sky had opened up. Jack startled, straightening and looking around.

"Sorry. Just me." A gloved hand waved above the wooden fence that separated their yard from the neighbor's. He could see a sliver of face between the uneven boards.

Jack stood up. It was a woman's voice, older, and friendly.

"Hey. I'm Jack."

"Melanie. Looks like you've been pretty busy."

He moved toward the fence and peered over. Melanie was a short woman with straight gray hair cut bluntly at her shoulders. She was in jeans and a faded green T-shirt. She looked weather-worn and tough, but she was smiling up at him. He could see several pots at her feet and a big bag of soil spilling out onto the grass.

"Lots to do," he agreed.

"I bet. Arthur wasn't exactly known for his housekeeping."

"You knew him? The previous owner?"

Melanie spat out a bitter little laugh. "You could say that. Thirty years he lived next door. Pain in my ass, that guy. Never shoveled his walks. Always blocking the alley with his big-ass car. Not a friendly guy."

"Well, hopefully we'll do better."

Melanie waved a hand at him. "Already are. So good to see young people in the neighborhood. Bunch of dinosaurs these days. The girl, she's with you? The tough-looking one with the tattoos."

"Avery. Yeah. She'll be tickled you thought she looked tough."

"Kids?"

"One, yeah. Dylan. He's at his mom's house for the summer. Ohio."

She nodded knowingly. "It'll be even better to have kids around."

"Is it just you?" Jack said.

"Just me. Gary died three years ago. My long-suffering husband. He died quickly, don't worry. It was me he suffered from."

Jack liked Melanie. Avery would adore her.

He said, "I've got some dinner on the stove. More than enough. Would you like to join us? Avery would love to meet you."

Melanie blinked and looked at Jack closely, as if trying to see if he was pulling her leg.

"It wouldn't be any trouble?"

"None. I cook for six. Always. And it's just us two."

She considered. "Sure. Why not? What can I bring?"

"Just yourself. Seven o'clock?"

"Seven it is."

Jack put the dining room back together, though he kept the table a little off-center so that the circle wouldn't be completely hidden. And then he did a general pick-up, straightening up, even though they'd eat out back again. It was much more comfortable out there.

He texted Avery to give her a heads up about their dinner guest, and then he retreated to the backyard to read his book. He awoke an hour later when the sun sank beneath the branches he'd been shaded under, feeling as he always did after a nap: disoriented and stupid.

He went inside to finish making dinner and prepare for their first visitor.

8.

"That ghoul," Melanie said. She stood in the arch between the kitchen and the dining room, a beer in her hand, looking down at the complicated circle chalked onto the floor.

Avery stepped up beside her, shoving a tortilla chip into her mouth and talking around the crumbs. "You know who did this?"

Melanie gave her a hard sideways glance, and then—deciding she was serious—relaxed.

"You *don't* know who did this?"

Avery shook her head, eyes widened, mouth curved into a frown.

Melanie looked over her shoulder to Jack, who was ladling food into bowls.

"Was it that Arthur guy? Your nemesis?" he said.

Melanie gave a little laugh. "No, but he's the ghoul. I'm sorry, I was sure you knew the story of this place."

"Here we go," said Avery. "Time for some Amityville shit." She was laughing along, but Jack sensed that she was a little nervous, too.

"Are we haunted, Melanie?" he smiled.

"Haunted? Couldn't say. I'm agnostic on ghosts and spirits. But ghouls. Arthur Boorman was a ghoul."

"Who's that?" Avery said, looking back and forth between Jack and Melanie like a child, suddenly sure she was missing out on something important. Jack just gave a little shrug and came around the kitchen island to hand out bowls.

"I thought we'd eat in the yard," he said.

They all filed out the back door and took seats at the round plastic table Jack had set up in the center of the yard. He made a couple of trips back and forth, bringing out a bowl of tortilla chips, warm tortillas, and fresh drinks.

"Okay. This Arthur guy. Spill." Avery was already spooning stew into her mouth, looking across the table at Melanie.

"I'm not sure it's exactly dinner conversation," Melanie said, taking a tentative bite and then giving Jack an approving nod.

"We live for inappropriate dinner conversation at Casa Todd."

"This is accurate," Jack said.

Melanie shrugged. She said, "Arthur Boorman was a poet. He taught at the university for a hundred years. Bit of a big deal for about five minutes, when he was young. Won some big prize. A real golden boy.

Got the job here and basically stopped writing, as far as I know."

Jack turned his phone to show the women the photo he'd pulled up on Google. It showed a young man with a bushy mustache, his white shirt open, exposing a hairy chest.

"That's him," Melanie crowed. "Let me see that." She took Jack's phone from him and held it at arm's length, looking down her nose.

"Look at him," she laughed.

Avery took the phone from her and studied the picture.

"Mister Porno," she said, wiggling her eyebrows.

"You're not far off," Melanie said. "But we'll get there."

Avery handed Jack's phone back to him.

"That's obviously a very old photo, but I remember that guy. I do," Melanie told them.

"He won the Yale Younger Poets Prize?" Jack said with some amazement.

"That's the one," Melanie said, leaning over her bowl and taking a bite.

"Jack's an English teacher. Did he tell you that?" Avery said.

"He didn't." Melanie looked at him. "I taught at the university here for a lifetime," she said.

"What subject?" Avery said, delighted.

"Cultural anthropology. I taught two hundred freshmen every semester for twenty-three years."

"How have I never heard of this guy?" Jack said, mostly to himself.

"Like I said, he kind of disappeared off the map pretty quickly after his prize. I don't think he was very good anyway, but I don't pretend to be an expert."

"But he's a ghoul," Avery said, hoping to move the story along.

"Oh, God, yes." Melanie took a long drink from her beer.

The sun was low, caught in the trees, just slipping behind the distant houses, bathing them all in a golden hour glow.

"He bought this house because of what happened here. And then he milked it for everything. Wrote a movie under a pseudonym. Real B-movie trash."

"I adore B-movie trash," Avery said, sitting back and pulling one foot up onto the molded plastic seat of her chair.

Jack was furiously searching IMDb now, excited by all of this. A perfect intersection of his favorite things: poetry and schlocky horror movies.

"A. Darrio." Jack read aloud. "A. Darrio was the pseudonym of Arthur Boorman, American poet. Screenwriter for one low budget film in the early 80s that achieved mild cult status in later years."

"That's our boy," Melanie said.

"*House on Blood Street*," Jack said, looking excitedly at Avery.

"Hell yeah," she smiled.

"Like I said, a ghoul. He made that movie about what happened to the poor girl who lived here before."

"What girl?" Avery said, resting her soda on her raised knee.

Melanie set her spoon in her bowl and sat back. "Young woman. Don't remember her name. This was in the 70s. She did a little modeling and *acted* in some movies." She did air quotes around 'acted.' "And then she was killed. Right here."

"Like right here, right here?" Avery said.

"In what is now your dining room, yes. Once upon a time it was the master bedroom, I believe. Seems weird to remove a bedroom, but I guess no one wanted to sleep in there."

They both just stared at her. She went on, "Someone hacked that poor girl up inside the house. This was only five or six years after the Manson Family nonsense. Everyone was losing their minds. People thought for sure there was a murderous cult on the loose."

"On the loose? They didn't find out who did it?"

Melanie shook her head. "Never did. But there was that nonsense on the floor in there, and I guess they did some pretty … disturbing things with her body."

Jack was using every ounce of self control not to be plunging down an internet rabbit hole. He set his phone face down, determined to give Melanie his attention.

"So how does Arthur come into it?" Avery said.

"He bought the house a couple years after the killing. Cranked out his crappy little movie. *Blood Street* is basically his version of what happened here, though if I remember correctly, there's a lot of weird surreal crap thrown in. It's been thirty, thirty-five years since I've seen it."

"Well, I guess I know what we're watching tonight," Jack said.

"Ugh," Melanie sighed. "More power to you. Just remember, a real woman died in there." She pointed toward the house with her bottle. "That's true of basically every house, but still."

"No, you're right," Avery said. "But what about the collage?"

Melanie gave her a blank look.

"She doesn't know about the collage," Avery said, her face breaking into a wide smile.

"You're gonna love it," Jack said.

9.

A few minutes later, they were all in the basement, crowded around Arthur Boorman's titty shrine, and Melanie was leaning in, inspecting it closely, not quite touching it.

"That sick fuck," she whispered.

"Avery thinks it's art," Jack said.

Melanie looked back at them, her expression showing no amusement at all.

"This is terrifying," she said, straightening. "He was down here making this—what?—for years? Right next door."

"We're tearing it out," Avery said.

"I should certainly hope so," Melanie said.

And Jack felt the fun leach out of this presentation. Melanie didn't find it campy, quirky, or strange. She found it frightening and distasteful, and her judgment weighed heavy in the room.

"We didn't know," Jack said. "That there was, like, a whole thing."

Melanie straightened, stepping back from the shrine, and she favored them with a weak smile.

"Of course you didn't. Didn't mean to spoil your fun, but Christ." She gestured at the collage. "Gives me the creeps."

Jack nodded. "Yeah. Me, too."

A while later, they stood on the porch, saying good night, and Melanie shook both their hands. "I'm really glad you're here. I really am. And thank you for dinner."

"Our pleasure," Jack said.

"Alright. Well, just so you know, my friends all call me Mel. So, you should probably call me Mel, yeah?"

She looked very small on the sidewalk, down the two steps below the porch.

"Perfect," Avery said, and Mel moved out of the light of the porch and into the shadows of the heavy trees.

"Bad. Ass," Avery whispered as they watched her go.

"Right?" Jack said.

They went inside and closed the door behind them, switching off the porch light and leaving the night's accumulated darkness to press in against the house on Calliope Street.

10.

Jack and Avery made a cursory cleanup of the kitchen and retreated to their bedroom. It was still a disaster. They'd told themselves that they didn't want to *really* move into the room until Jack had done whatever things Jack was going to do to the room. But Avery thought she knew enough by this point to recognize that this would probably always be the "unfinished" room. They would simply close the door, the mess would grow, and they'd be stepping over piles of clothes and working around the dresser with the one stuck drawer until they died.

It was fine.

For the moment, the bed was just up on its metal frame, the headboard leaning against the far wall. Their nightstands were so heaped with unopened mail and papers they'd brought over from their old apartment that they were unusable.

They sat up in bed with their backs pressed against the cool wall, a box fan buzzing in the window. Jack's laptop yawned open in the middle of the bedspread.

They'd gone ahead and spent $2.99 to rent *House on Blood Street*, since it wasn't available to stream for free anywhere. The night was sticky, and they were both naked from the waist down, covered only by the thin cotton sheet. They shifted closer together as the opening credits rolled, ready to watch the crazy bat-shittery unfolding before them.

The movie was set in a neighborhood that looked nothing like the green and leafy wilds of Calliope Street. It was more rural, with hills rising up brown in the background. But the staged house was a pretty close replica for the real thing. Too modern-looking, but with the right shape at least. The first time it came on-screen, in an uncomfortably long establishing shot, Avery and Jack both looked at each other, and as the camera moved slowly in, Avery had felt a sudden chill, as if this were being filmed live, and there might be a whole crew of strangers in the street right outside. When the camera reached the closed door and seemed to pass through it, she found herself holding her breath, only releasing it when she saw that the room inside looked like nothing within their own home.

The movie interior was some kind of split level *Brady Bunch* bullshit, too big to even fit inside their house, and the irreality calmed her, allowing her the necessary distance to enjoy the movie.

And they did enjoy it. The two of them were connoisseurs of bloody schlock, and they'd expected *House on Blood Street* to be just another early 80s slasher. A cheap grab for the teenage market, not a single cinematic quality to be found. They both loved those movies, even as they mocked them. Mocking them was part of the enjoyment. But this wasn't like that at all.

The director had clearly been steeped in the Italian maestros. A little Argento, a little Fulci. Jack consulted IMDb. Jakob Spezialle. And *Blood Street* was his only credit.

The opening scene, which was a cliched presentation of a nameless actress's murder, was pure Giallo: sexy, stylized violence. The camera took a first person point of view, moving stealthily through the house. The killer was just a pair of gloved hands visible at the edges of the screen. His breathing was barely audible. Hunting. He hid behind a red curtain and watched as the woman moved around the kitchen in a sheer black negligee, smoking a cigarette and fixing herself a drink. The room was large and airy, and she swept through it, trailing her gown behind her. The whole scene glowed with a vaseline-tinged haze. The woman's hair was dark and permed in big, loose curls that fell around her bare shoulders, and the camera lingered to show the shape of her breasts through the black lace.

Was the driving synth meant to be part of the scene or simply part of the soundtrack? Could the woman hear its rising minor-key pulse? She disappeared off screen, passing through a beaded curtain, and then the camera—the killer—moved slowly forward.

The woman could be seen through the beaded curtain, moving around the bedroom, trailing smoke and sipping from her glass. She might be packing or laying out her wardrobe for the following day. The camera broke away from the killer's POV to a shot looking up at the woman from the bed. Her face was mostly shadowed by the light behind her, but her breasts thrust out, filling most of the frame.

"Yow!" Avery cried, laughing.

The next shot cut back to the kitchen as the gloved hand picked up the butcher knife lying beside half a lime.

Now, knife in hand, the camera pushed aside the hanging bead curtain. The woman turned toward the sound.

A close-up of her mouth, lips barely parted.

A close-up of one eye, wide and caked with mascara.

A flash of the figure, now a dark shape with the knife raised above its head.

And then a series of surprisingly effective practical effects, with the knife slicing down the actress' shoulder blade, leaving several dark stab wounds across her back, then finally plunging down behind her collarbone, leaving a dark mouth that slowly filled with blood when the blade was withdrawn. The blood was too red and too thin to be real, but looked good under the lights. The knife flashed up again and came down, leaving a slash down the woman's face, plunging directly into her exposed left breast. Another stab and another. Blood as bright as tempera paint looped across the ceiling.

A close-up of the woman's mouth, opened in a silent scream, teeth laced with blood.

And then, the title card—a bright red screen with black art deco letters—that came and went, almost too quickly to read. Finally, a surprisingly aesthetic shot of the bedroom, with the woman's nude corpse artfully arranged at the center of a chalked circle, candles flickering yellow against her pale skin, blood pooling around her head, a flowering branch tucked into one hand and the other positioned with its index finger extended. The chill of the shot was broken by a new woman pushing through the beaded curtain, taking in the scene, and screaming her horror movie scream.

The movie got weirder from there, with a circuitous plot involving the murdered woman's sister and a police detective who, together, try to track down the killer, who never reappears on screen. Instead, they investigate ever-deeper parts of the house, lit in pinks and purples, in increasingly surreal set pieces that don't seem to have any real narrative purpose.

Avery and Jack didn't care about the story. By the time the dead woman's sister was peeling at the wallpaper in the basement room, exposing a black ragged hole, they were rapt. Of course, she put her eyeball right up to the hole in a way no sane human being would ever do, and there was a tense moment where they were both certain that something would stab out and pierce her eye. Instead, the camera became her eye and she saw a vision of a woman silhouetted in red light.

"Sure you want to take down the titty shrine?" Avery said, running her hand up Jack's thigh.

"Very sure."

In a series of disconnected scenes, the sister awakened in the middle of the night and walked naked through the dark house. Each time, she paused before a closet door, barely ajar. This pause was uncomfortably long.

A close-up on the gap in the door. A thin bar of light on a scaly, ruined face inside.

The actress opened the door anyway, as if compelled, and the thing inside, with the dead eyes and blue skin of a Romero zombie, reached for her. She ran, the creature followed, and there was an unintentionally funny scene of the creature chasing the woman through the empty suburban street at night like some demonic Benny Hill sketch. The scene was later revealed to be a dream, which repeated with no discernable difference two more times in the film.

About two-thirds through, the camera made a wobbling first-person journey through the darkened house, down the stairs, and into the basement, and there on the concrete floor stood a fawn, spindly-legged and trembling. The shot cut up to show the sister standing pale and naked, staring down at the deer. In her hand—a kitchen knife.

The rest was done rather expressionistically, with lots of quick cuts and close-ups, but the scene ended with the camera close up on the sister's face, tears on her cheeks and blood on her chin, and as the camera slowly dollied back, a bizarre Pieta was revealed. She sat on the basement floor, the fawn cradled in her lap, knife hanging limp from her hand, blood pooling beneath them both from the deer's slit throat.

Nothing was explained, but this basement ritual seemed to kick something into gear, and the sister became more and more manic, and more overtly sexual. The detective fended off a particularly harrowing seduction in which she ripped her blouse and bloodied her breasts with her fingernails. Before the detective broke away and fled, the sister leaned in close and whispered into his ear, *I am the Red Witch.*

In the denouement, the detective found the house deserted and the basement wall ripped apart, leaving a black gap about two feet across. He climbed inside, seeming to believe the sister was within, and began a lengthy descent through a narrow rocky cavern.

Avery wasn't at all sure how they'd filmed this sequence, and it seemed like it must have cost more than the rest of the movie put together, but it was genuinely claustrophobic, and operated on a scale that wasn't even hinted at elsewhere. Strangely, in the film's most unreal moment, it felt shockingly real.

At the bottom of the basement rabbit hole was a kind of demon pit of writhing naked women, all welcoming the detective in. Psychedelic lighting with fisheye lenses and quick cuts, mixed with the soundtrack of high bells and snarling electric guitar. Was the detective being ripped apart or devoured or sexually assaulted? All three? And the women chanted: *Shurpu. Shurpu, Shurpu.*

The word tickled at the back of Jack's brain.

The film ended on two extended shots. First was the detective, his nude body arranged within the chalked circle in a perfect recreation of the original ritual murder. The shot seemed to go on forever, and Avery found herself waiting for something to happen, but there was no movement on screen. Instead, it cut to an exterior shot of the house, possibly the exact same establishing shot from the beginning. As the credits began to scroll shakily up the screen, the sister stepped out the front door and descended the steps. Gray smoke billowed out after her. She walked toward the still camera and turned to her right, smiling and walking with a kind of swagger until she exited the frame. The house burned slowly as the credits rolled.

Avery and Jack stared at each other. Everything felt as if it were expanding and closing in around them.

"What even *was* that?" Jack said.

"Three different movies slapped together."

"Were any of them good?"

"Shut your mouth. That was a masterpiece. And it's about our house. We need the movie poster for the living room!" Avery said.

"Not the dining room?"

"Don't be a ghoul, dude."

"Right, right."

Jack closed the laptop and set it on the floor beside the bed. Without the light from the screen, the room was very dark, blue-tinged, everything seeming to move with the air from the fan, or the slow breathing of the room around them.

"I'm kinda scared to take that thing down now," Jack said, and she knew he was thinking of the basement shrine.

"If there's a tunnel behind it, I'll shit myself," she said, sliding down into the bed.

"If there's a tunnel, we move," he said, and he was just a dark shape beside her. She could feel him, hard against her thigh.

"What if there's a pit of naked ladies at the bottom?" she whispered, wrapping her fingers around him and giving a little squeeze.

"Even if," he said, and he kissed her, pushing his hands up under her T-shirt. She was sweaty and hot, and his hands were warm, but she still arched her back at the feel of his palms sliding across her nipples, sending goosebumps shivering across her skin. And then his mouth was on her, moving its way down her belly, kissing at the crook of her groin and making her giggle and squirm, and then he was taking her into his mouth, and she closed her eyes and lay back, luxuriating in the sensation.

And the buzz of the fan sounded almost like the rhythmic pulse of analog synths, and she wondered if that sound was really here in the room or only in her head, or only in the soundtrack to this movie that was their lives, and then she clutched Jack's hair and her ears filled with the thrum of her own pulse, and she didn't care any more.

11.

Jack awoke at an indeterminate time in an indeterminate darkness, his brain sparking at some indeterminate sound.

His arm was thrown over Avery's middle, her ass pushed up tight against him, and when he moved, the places where their bodies had been touching were slick with sweat, chilled slightly by the air from the box fan in the window. He sat up, leaning back on his hands, sheet tangled at their feet.

It had been close by, the sound.

The thought of the insect thing from the basement—*it was no insect*—flashed across his mind and he discarded it without reflection. This sound was too big, too heavy. Another unbidden image rose up, and he tried to laugh it away. He imagined the insect thing—*no insect*—having grown in its nest in the wall, pupating into its final form. He saw something massive, no longer able to skitter anywhere but instead pulling itself along on its many legs. The size of a man. He thought of that dark hole in the basement, ringed by smiling women with full breasts. A kind of womb, raising up this monstrosity and then finally birthing it out through that ragged hole.

Had the magazine paper stretched and bulged as the creature pushed outward, its shiny helmeted head crowning, its pale mandibles clicking as it strained into life? He imagined the sound of its body falling heavily to the concrete floor, trailing amniotic fluid laced with black blood. A difficult birth. He heard the afterbirth plopping out wetly behind it, for the creature would be no insect, but mammalian—not quite able to rise up like a man, but too ungainly to move easily on its spindly legs.

In Jack's imagination, it dragged itself across the basement, its slick body rubbing against the plastic sheeting, leaving bloody streaks with its passing. Its umbilicus stretched out behind it, still attached, and the placenta hitched across the dusty concrete behind it, like a toy on a string. When it reached the basement stairs, it laid its full length across the steps and pulled itself up, beginning to feel the strength in its limbs, hungering for its first sustenance, alien senses already on alert, drawing it toward the front of the house, toward the room where Jack and Avery lay prone and exposed, so many soft places waiting for those cutting jaws to pierce and pull.

Jack blinked, realizing he had almost fallen back into sleep, upright as he was. He tossed the whole ludicrous image away. There were no monsters in the basement, but there was something close by.

There.

He was fully awake now, alert to the low, hollow sound, like something shifting on the floor outside their room. He felt like a fool, never locking up the house, but they'd both fallen into the same stupid complacency. Although the small town hadn't been a small town in decades, Jack and Avery imagined it as a place where no one locked their doors at night and car keys were in the glove box. The reality was, houses were continually being burglarized and cars stolen, and everyone's response was always, "I don't even lock my doors."

He was suddenly sure that someone was inside the house. His conviction lacked the same sensory richness of his vision—*dream?*—of the not-insect thing being birthed. It was instead starkly clear. A hulking man, not far outside the room, perhaps looking in through their partially open door. He came to steal what valuables he could find quickly, anything he could turn into cash to turn into methamphetamines to convert into a few hours of manic bliss. The figure was, for some reason, dressed all in black, including a black ski mask that exposed only his eyes. He held something heavy, made of iron, like a jack handle, and it was that jack handle scraping on the wood floor that had awakened Jack in the middle of the night, putting both his senses and his imagination on high alert.

Jack thought of the nine millimeter pistol he and Avery purchased a few years before. They'd taken it out into the woods and shot it once, just to be sure they knew how, that the gun worked right. It was so much louder than either of them had expected, and neither of them had found it terribly pleasurable, but the world kept getting more and more frightening, the fascist hordes growing more emboldened, and of course, Avery's very existence was taken as an excuse for violence by whole swaths of the population. For a brief while, they'd stockpiled non-perishables, bought a couple boxes of ammo, and told themselves they were ready for the worst.

But of course they weren't. The gun box was somewhere in the dresser across the room, locked up tight, and the key was... Jack had no idea. With the move, everything was even more disorganized than usual. And now, every moment Jack considered these facts was one more moment that the intruder was watching, studying, preparing how best to strike. Would he wait for Jack to come to him and hit him as he came through the doorway, or charge into the room and beat them both to death, there on the bed?

Jack could feel the stranger's eyes on his naked body. He slid from the bed, eyes on the strip of deeper darkness that was the doorway, and found his jeans crumpled on the floor. He stepped into them as gracefully as he could, not taking his eyes off the doorway. He felt as if his gaze were locked on those other eyes. They both knew what was coming. They both were just waiting for it to unfold. And hadn't Jack been waiting for it since early adolescence? This primal contest? Some chance to embrace the masculinity he seemed to naturally discard?

He pulled the door open a little more, bare-chested, breathing as calmly as he could.

The living room was lit by the streetlight through the sheer curtains, a television blue full of deep shadows. Empty. Jack waited, listening.

Then, there it was again: heavy and low, near the ground, but further into the house. Jack looked around for anything that could be a weapon. A black umbrella leaned in the corner near the front door. He picked it up, holding it like a baseball bat. It weighed nothing. It was ridiculous. He clutched it just the same.

He approached the entryway to the kitchen, its inky blackness almost solid, and he inched forward. To his left, the doorway to the basement. He thought of that recurring dream-like sequence in *House on Blood Street*, the sister opening the closet door and the creature bursting out, chasing her in widening circles through the streets. He would set the house on fire and run before he opened that door.

The anonymous sound again, now made known and familiar. No longer a sound but a distinct phenomenon. The back door was standing open, the breeze pushing it slightly inward, where it pushed against a fallen broom, the handle scraping slightly on the hardwood floor. Puzzle solved. Lives saved. Threat assessed and dismissed.

But why was the door open?

He sensed again the unseen eyes on him, on both of them, lying naked in the dark. He set the broom upright and opened the door, stepping out onto the back stoop.

It was another world outside the confines of the house. A summer storm was brewing up over the mountain, the trees rustling with the rising wind, and there was the sweet smell of the cooler air that would collide with sudden violence against the wall of heat and crack open in house-shaking thunder. But for now, it was just a thousand tiny noises, branches rubbing and leaves tumbling across the yard, fences shaking. A yellow sulfurous bulb burned over someone's garage down the alley, making everything seem frosted and unreal.

He went back inside, closing the door, pressing it hard until he heard the latch engage, then turning the lock. It was silly, but his heart was still beating a little harder than he liked to admit, and even symbolic safety was better than nothing.

He latched the front door, returning the umbrella to its corner, and moved into the absolute black of the bedroom.

"Everything okay?" Avery mumbled as he slid back into bed.

"Everything's fine," he said. He pulled her close to him again.

The window, propped open by the fan, was suddenly a block of pure white, a strobing flash that photographed the whole room and printed it against the back of his eyes, the whole house a camera obscura. And just as the image began to fade, the thunder rumbled down the hillside and washed over them.

12.

Somehow, June was over, and it felt like the summer was slipping away. The nights were punctuated by the sound of premature fireworks that left Jack jittery and tense. The wildfires were already bad and smoke drifted down into the valley and settled there, making the air bright and bitter.

Jack rented a floor sander and crammed it awkwardly into the back of their junky little Honda, tying the hatchback door down with a length of nylon rope. The open door alarm dinged the whole trip. With the trunk open, the sound of the traffic seemed too close, fake, like a canned sound effect piped in through the back of the car, hollow and blaring. He drove too slow along Reserve Street, cars and trucks rocketing by in the other lanes, and he thought of when he'd first come to town and this had all been cow fields. But the world crept in like blackberry vines, strangling everything, impossible to halt, twining itself into every nook and cranny. At least their neighborhood, the oddly situated blocks surrounding Calliope Street, was mostly unchanged. That was because the owners were all retired Boomers, just biding their time. And when they started dying off, it wouldn't be young people moving in to fill those houses—Jack and Avery were some kind of fluke—it would be the developers, the corporate landlords. It would be Airbnb assholes and house-flipping con artists. The whole area would be transformed.

He turned off the main artery to a street that would lead him into the center of town, away from the box-store sprawl, and found himself in a nightmare of endless townhouse apartments, each identical, telescoping out before him and in each direction like a carnival's house of mirrors. It was the kind of thing that made him want to turn terrorist, this creeping degradation of the place he loved. He cranked up the radio to block out the weird echoing sounds from the open hatchback and the ugly noise of the world that seemed to want only to chew things up and excrete them back out in the form of cheaply made plastic bricks. Iggy was singing about his T.V. Eye, the Stooges grinding through the song in their familiar, gloriously greasy garage pulse, the guitar snarling its way through an endlessly repeated riff. Jack beat out the rhythm on the steering wheel and smiled to himself, all of the filth of the world briefly flushed away in this cleansing wave of trash.

He had to run the cord for the sander all the way out to the garage, attached to the thick orange extension cord: if he plugged it in inside the house, the breaker tripped. He had no idea what an electrician would cost, but he was pretty sure they couldn't afford one.

The sander weighed a ton, and he could immediately feel the strain in his lower back and his thighs. He was out of shape. He would always be out of shape. Last summer he'd tried to hike the path up behind the university, a zig-zagging trail that was visible from anywhere in town, always dotted with little figures. He made it halfway up before having to sit down and just breathe.

He couldn't even attempt such a hike now, unless he wanted to pay for another day with the sander. So, he persisted, pushing the machine forward over and over again across the floor. He moved around the area with the circle sketched into it. They'd agreed to keep that, though since Mel's visit, the dark stain in the wood had come to unsettle him.

By noon he was slick with sweat, the armpits of his T-shirt blooming black circles, with wood dust clinging to his arms and face in a kind of chunky cement. His arms felt weightless as he pushed the machine back and forth across the water-damaged planks before the sink. Why did he think this was a good idea? Why did they buy a house in the first place? Why ever abandon hunting and gathering to be tied down to a chunk of earth?

Hours later, when he was trying to lift the sander back into the car, he felt too weak to even manage and stood hunched, hands on his knees, just looking at the open back of the car for a full minute.

"Need a hand?"

Jack straightened, turning toward the voice.

It came from a thin little guy with glasses, a scraggly gray beard, and hair sticking out in tufty wings off the back of his head. He wore a short sleeved button-up and khaki shorts that ended just above his knobby knees. His legs were remarkably bony. His sandals looked expensive, but they were also very worn.

"Karl," the man said, extending his hand.

Jack shook it and introduced himself.

"I'm across the street there. Been watching you. Glad you're doing something with the place."

"Trying. Even if it kills me," Jack laughed.

"Wait till you're my age, kid." Karl had a way of saying everything as if it were a joke but showing no humor in his face. He looked like he was continually awaiting an answer. "Well, let's get you loaded up here."

He moved around to the other side of the sander. They lifted it in, and Jack tied the door down again.

"Thanks," Jack said. "I was about ready to eat another day's rental fee just so I didn't have to do that."

"Next time, just come grab me. I'm almost always home."

"Well, thanks. I owe you a beer."

"I'll take you up on that sometime." Karl winced something approximating a smile and wandered back across the slight hump of the blacktop. He disappeared into his house with its neatly kept yard and covered boat in the driveway. A huge maple obscured most of the house, but it seemed as neat and trim as the yard.

When Avery came home, Jack was scrubbed clean and nursing a beer in the yard. The wind had briefly moved the smoke around, at least enough to make it tolerable outside.

"It looks amazing," Avery said, coming down the steps into the twilight shadows. She kissed him on top of his head, and fell into a chair across from the table. "When I can move again, I'll do the refinishing."

"Well, I got you something. Payment for all your hard work."

He raised his eyebrows at her, both wanting to make a joke about sexual payments but also too tired and sore to even really consider the idea. She read his look anyway.

"Not that, perv." She tossed a thin white book onto the table. The cover bore a crayon sketch from what Jack thought might be a Breughel. The vague shape of a plump woman in a funny hat. Arthur H. Boorman's *Incantations*.

"No way," he said.

"They had it at Fact and Fiction. I stopped in on my lunch."

"'Winner of the Yale Younger Poets Prize 1977,'" he read off the back cover.

"Maybe we can read it while standing in the magic circle and something will happen?"

"Poetry makes nothing happen," Jack quoted W.H. Auden's line in a sleepy drawl.

"Shut the fuck up," she snorted. "Did you eat?"

"Can't move."

"Sandwiches it is."

"Perfect. And thank you," he said, holding up the book.

"Well, I like you a little bit," she said, getting up and heading into the house.

"I like you a little bit, too," he called as the screen door rattled shut.

He opened the book. There was just enough light left filtering through the smoke from the fires and then down through the treetops to read by, but just barely. He read the first poem, "Incantation I." It was a dense thing that read like a kind of dramatic monologue from some cosmic loser, bent on cataloging his complaints. The language was taut and compressed, the voice surprisingly funny. The speaker sat high up in a locust tree, listening to passing voices below, all threading their way through the poem like random radio broadcasts. The tone was comic but decidedly dark. There was a self-effacing feel to the whole thing, and Jack realized he was excited in a way he hadn't been in some time.

The older he got, the more sure he became that he would never again experience the joy of sudden discovery. He had a clear memory of a late night in the university library, in the last year of his undergrad. He'd been avoiding the work he was supposedly there to accomplish, and pulled a copy of Rilke's *Duino Elegies* from the shelf. It had taken the top of his head off. He read it straight through and then turned back to the start, wondering how he could have walked around in the world for so many years without Rilke's words making up some part of himself. Like he'd been incomplete up until that moment. Hell, he'd been just a kid then. The older he got, the more his capacity for genuine, metaphysical shock seemed to ebb away. Everything seemed so *familiar.* It made him depressed to think about it.

But here was something brand new. A poet he'd never heard of, with a book of genuinely interesting poems. And he lived in that poet's house. Sure, that poet was also a weird pervert, but that was hardly a surprise. Kind of par for the course, really.

He read the next poem. And the next. He kept his eyes on the pages until the light finally grew too dim and Avery called him in to eat something, and he had to close the book on those sad, funny little verses, on the voice of a man underground.

13.

Avery opened up Studio M at nine. The salon was just a narrow room cut out of the old brick building a block across the river from downtown, but it was tucked between the fancy pizza place and single-screen indie theater, so there was plenty of foot traffic, and between Avery and Claire, they had a client list big enough to keep them going. Neither of them would ever get rich this way, especially with the cost of the lease in this neighborhood, but they were doing okay. Avery was glad to have Jack's income, too. And they were actually spending less on their mortgage than they had been on rent before they bought the house, which was totally backward.

She turned on the lights, and the shop flickered into life. One wall was all mirrors, countertops, and the shampoo station. Brightly lit, almost every inch of wall covered by photographs. The usual family photos: Dylan moving through a progression from chubby-cheeked little boy into lanky, sullen pre-teen. Photos of clients' hair in before-and-after shots. Random pages from magazines because the hair looked good or because the person looked good. Flyers from past gigs. Ancient *Far Side* cartoons. Avery dropped her bag onto the counter at her station and considered the wall. Not the same thing as Boorman's weird titty shrine. Not at all. Right? What made it different?

She crossed the room to turn on the bluetooth speaker, which was set up high on a little shelf between two standing plants. This wall was all exposed brick, with two low, uncomfortable couches pressed against it. The speaker bleep-blooped and gave a little chime, connecting to her phone. Sleater-Kinney's "Words and Guitar" picked up where it had paused in the car. She nodded along to the beat for a moment and then went to boot up the iPad, make sure the payment interface was working for once.

Her eye returned to the mirrors ringed with scraps and photos. Claire's station was the same, if a little neater. She had photos of her husband and their girls on the lake, holding up tiny fish. Her shrine to Florence Pugh and the other shrine to Madonna. Her twin obsessions.

But what was this magpie impulse?

The need to record and display what was important seemed borne out of adolescence. Once upon a time, Avery's walls had been all comic book posters and memorabilia. If she hadn't come to think of the comic pages as sacred texts, she almost certainly would have hacked them up and papered the wall in colorful panels. Her friends collaged their rooms with music magazines, ticket stubs, thumbnail-sized Polaroids. They decorated the insides of locker doors at school.

She slipped her apron over her head and tied it around her waist, checked herself in the mirror. She wore a too-small black tee that accentuated her shoulders, which she hated, but at least it showed off her tattooed arms to great benefit. Maybe a little flabby there on the underside? She held up her arm, made a weak muscle-man pose. Whatever. She'd always been the chubby kid, and while she was pretty much over that particular concern—having come to terms with significantly larger body image issues in her lifetime—sometimes it crept back in. Like with her upper arms or the little bit of skin beneath her chin that she thought hung down weirdly, giving it even less definition. But fuck it, she'd never been happier with the person looking back from the mirror.

She moved to the front of the shop and switched on the sign in the window. The traffic outside was heavy as always. Used to be the town emptied out a bit in the summer. Now it seemed to get busier. She laughed at herself. She'd been there less than a decade and was talking like old dudes did, about back in the day. The shadow of the building stretched out just beyond the sidewalk, and then the sunlight seemed almost too bright to look into. Across the road and its flashing, bright expanse, the crazy preacher—a local personality—was leading his flock toward the bridge, ready to make their semi-regular parade through downtown. An old man with shoulder-length white hair followed by five or six younger people, most of them women, shouting about the End Times. They were almost quaint, these nuts. Acting as if the apocalypse wasn't already here.

She pulled the shade down. Christ, she hated summer. She loved having Jack around, though, of course, she didn't see him much, because *she* worked all day. And mostly she missed her kid, who spent two months in Ohio with his other mom, Janie. Dylan sent Avery a text every once in a while, and she messaged him every night before bed, but she missed the physical presence of him, his baby-horse awkwardness and the way he still looked like a toddler when he slept, and even the way he left his messes through the kitchen after his late night feedings.

Mostly, she just missed talking to him. He was a funny kid. Smart, which he got from Janie. Softhearted, which he got from Avery, unfortunately.

She'd be happy when September lurched in. Autumn fell hard and sudden in the Rockies, and she loved that. She didn't think she'd ever be able to leave it. Let the temps drop. Let Dylan come home. Let the comforting routine of the school year settle in.

She looked back at the wall of photos and clippings. A flash of memory made her blink.

When she was a kid, she'd found a box of dirty magazines under her dad's workbench. Pretty tame, softcore stuff. Nothing compared to what was now readily available on the internet. They were old, like from the early 80s. Avery had slipped a couple out of the box and into her room. As she studied them, she knew they were supposed to make her feel a certain way, and they did that, a little. But mostly, she just examined the bodies, the curves, the ridiculously fake boobs, the gaudily made-up faces.

There was a continuum that she could now see. It ran from the drag shows she discovered much later in college, to the porn stars who displayed themselves in every imaginable pose. Both were a celebration of artifice. The dirty magazine wasn't anywhere as gleeful as the drag queens, though. In fact, there was something sad about these women who strained toward the camera, hair teased out, lips the wrong shades of red, brandishing their gravity-defying anime tits. She'd felt their sadness even then, at thirteen years old. It got mixed up with Avery's feelings about her own body. She didn't want to look like these women. Yet, she recognized that the body was a canvas, a thing that could be altered to fit someone's vision. Probably not their own vision, but still.

And here was the part that made Avery pause, now, in the middle of the salon, staring toward the lighted wall of mirrors: she'd cut those stolen pictures up. Those already-Frankensteined women. She'd cut them up and taped them onto the pages of a copy of *Marvel Fanfare*, in pieces. It felt like somehow just looking at them wasn't enough. She couldn't touch them. She couldn't be them. She had to *do* something with them.

How fucked up was that? Where did that impulse come from?

Of course, Arthur Boorman was a grown man, a teacher and decorated poet, and Avery had been a scared and confused kid preparing to slip into a six-year depression. Cut that kid a break already. But what was that need to cut and rearrange? Was it just magpie-think? Collecting pretty things? Or was it darker? The shrine gave serial killer vibes. What would someone think if they found Avery's old copy of *Marvel Fanfare,* pages stuffed with dismembered women?

The door swung open, sucking the cold air outward. Avery turned to smile at Claire, who was smacking gum and pulling her sunglasses from her head, her bleach blonde hair standing out in spikes.

"Hey-hey," she said. "You alright?" She dropped her purse into the chair at her station, gave a concerned head tilt.

"Yeah, just thinking," Avery unstuck herself from the spot where she'd been standing, staring, thinking. Framed in her stylist's mirror, surrounded by the photos and clippings, she was just another part of the collage. Just another lady on the wall. Taken apart and put together with hormone therapy, tattoo sleeves, carefully constructed outfits, and—of course—the hair.

No. Fuck that. She was nobody's Frankenstein, and Arthur Boorman had been a pervy old dude who couldn't get any. They weren't the same. His impulse was to consume. She could sense that. Hers was to *become*.

Or something. She picked up her phone, switched the music to the pop-punk channel, and got My

Chemical Romance right off the bat. Claire whooped from across the room.

The day began. She didn't think any more about the magazines or her collection of parts. All that was from another life. Now she was whole.

14.

Jack read up on the process for resealing their home's hardwood floors. It made him want to weep. So, instead, he moved on to other kitchen repairs. He spent a full day changing out the faucet in the kitchen sink. He wasn't proud of his creative procrastination, but there it was. Midway through the process, he cooked a microwave burrito, filled a mason jar with ice water, and took Boorman's *Incantations* out into the yard. The smoke was light enough that he could almost convince himself he didn't notice, but there was that tickle at the back of the throat.

Incantations was a thin book: forty-five poems, each about a page long, dense little runes. It turned out there was a whole cast of characters, speaking in monologue or in Beckett-like anti-dialogue. Jack's favorite was Anne-Jane, a childlike old crone who might be a bag lady or maybe some kind of witch. She could be both. Hers were the funniest bits, but also the most heartbreaking. Jack couldn't really pull out a clear narrative line. It wasn't that kind of book, but

Anne-Jane's constant references to absent people gave the impression of a damaged person drifting through a world made permanently strange by a cracked mind, and maybe by substance abuse. The unnamed main speaker—an obvious proxy for the poet—often observed this character from his perch in the locust tree, and his yearning for her was both comic and sad.

The book didn't exactly take Jack's head off, but it did that other important thing. It spurred a desire to write. It had been years since he'd really done that. Teaching seemed to drain too much of that part of his brain. He'd tried, but it always felt doomed from the outset, as if the tools were bad, so nothing good could be made of them.

Back when he was in school, he'd actually published a few pieces, and thought about going the MFA route, go all-in on something gleefully and obviously useless. But instead he'd blinked, and here he was.

Maybe this was the time? Jack had the rest of summer break to knock out some drafts, and there was no hurry. They could sit. He'd take Boorman's strategy of fragmented dramatic monologues and apply it to the house on Calliope Street. Let Becca Mays, the woman who died in this house, speak.

Was that too predatory? Or was there even such a thing as exploitation anymore?

He put the book down tent-like on his knee and drank off the ice water. These plans didn't matter, of course. It was all just a story he was telling himself. He knew full well he'd never actually write any poems.

Or if he did, he'd write two or three and then quietly abandon the whole thing. It was his modus operandi. No follow-through. Like the floors. Like the house itself. Come September, the house would still look like a construction zone, with a half-dozen half-finished projects. Only Dylan's room would be anything close to finished, because he had to over-perform for Dylan, and in his world, over-performing amounted to doing the bare minimum.

Jack wished he was different: more self-disciplined, better able to focus, a better partner. He'd be a better teacher, too. He was well-liked, he supposed, and he had lots of cool, creative ideas, but there was always this gap between the concept and the execution. A place where he just kind of lost steam. Realistic to a fault, he knew his limitations, and he knew this was probably as good as it got. He'd just keep making plans for creative projects that would never happen. Honestly, the planning was more fun than the work anyway.

He picked up the book again, feeling both chastened and sad by his own internal monologue, and read "Incantation XXII," which was an Anne-Jane poem. He was startled by a passage.

> *Sky, branch-shattered, thorn-pricked, red*
> *Witch-haunted, clears his throat: deeprumble.*

I am the Red Witch, the sister had said. In answer, thunder rolled down from the mountain.

15.

That night, Avery awoke to the sound of branches scraping the roof. Rather, she rose up from her bed and drifted like the mist in an old movie, sliding bare feet along the floor, seeking out the lowest point. Through the living room, where the light from the street lamp cut through the blinds and lay in yellow slashes on the floor, she moved like smoke. In the kitchen, she opened the refrigerator, drank from the orange juice carton, and set it still open on the counter. Her legs shone white in the light from the fridge, and she took this in like everything else, as if she were seeing it but also not seeing it—as if it were being described to her, whispered into her sleeping ear.

She moved to the back door, opened it, and looked out on the shadowed yard. The trees trembled, rattling in a light breeze. She turned, leaving the door standing open, just as she'd left the refrigerator open. She pushed the basement door open. Light from deep within the basement illuminated the bottom of the staircase, and she moved toward it, downward.

At the base of the steps, she saw the room stretched out, the plastic sheeted walls like a series of semi-opaque cubes lit from within. The concrete slab was cold on her feet, so she was almost certain that she was awake here in this space, not asleep and dreaming, but she couldn't be absolutely sure. How could anyone ever be absolutely sure?

She moved through the twisting pathway of the loosely framed space, until she came through the last little square of light, to the flesh-colored mound on the wall. She saw the collage through her eyes, but she also saw herself as if from above. She looked around lazily for the camera, saw nothing, resigned herself to this reality. She was both subject and object, observer and observed. The dream's eye slid downward, taking in her body—object and subject—her tattooed arms a mass of blue-black ink that seemed to swirl in the harsh light of the exposed bulb.

The dream's point of view came to a rest at about waist level, looking straight on at her. Her oversized tank top fell just below her ass, barely shadowing her crotch, where this probing eye seemed to be focused with some intent. And then she realized that it was the collage itself: that dark eye, staring blankly out at her from the wall, trying to grope its way around her, to find her out.

She was holding her breath, she realized as she let it out in a wet gurgle, as if drowning. With the moment's certainty known only to the dreamer, she was suddenly aware of some danger lurking within that wall. She wanted to run, but she also did not want to turn her back on that eye's unblinking lens. To do so would be to invite the camera to follow her retreating form in a shaky shot that would turn into a chase, reducing her to one of the film's early victims: the stupid half-asleep girl who goes into the basement alone at night.

She stood, looking at it for some indeterminate time. Dream time. She wanted to turn, but she was frozen in place. Her breathing was heavy as she kept her eyes trained on that black hole at the center of the staring women. No. She was no object. Not here, in her home. She lifted one foot to move herself toward the exit, and as she did there was heavy *CHUNK* from deeper in the basement. She was submerged in darkness so thick it pressed against her, held her still. She was aware of the sound of her own ragged breathing and her feet planted against the cool cement floor, her nipples going tight against the fabric of her shirt. She couldn't feel her arms or see them in the dark, and was suddenly overcome by a fear that they were gone, as if her limbs were being stolen away in the dark by unseen beings. Before her brain could follow this avenue, a red light appeared, projected from the wall onto her legs and the dark screen of her nightshirt. The circle of light was about a foot across. She looked down at herself and saw movement ripple in the light, as if something was moving over her, climbing up her legs and under her shirt.

But the movement was not on her. It was within the light, projected shadows from within the wall, within the collage. There was a movie playing back there in the wall, and she was seeing only the shadows, as if she was behind the screen. And somewhere on the other side of the lit screen, there must be an audience. She imagined the darkened theater, its seats filled with row upon row of staring women, their nakedness dressed in the red light from the screen.

Finally, she broke away—but not to run, not to flee. She took a step toward the hole, toward the source of that red light. Bending down, she put her eye up to the hole. In the dark basement, the light felt very bright. She squinted, her eyelashes almost brushing against the curled edges of the magazine clippings.

As her eye adjusted, she saw that there was no theater. A larger room extended beyond the wall. It had rough sides, as if it had been carved out of the earth. The red light emanated from a fire burning in the center of that room. Just beyond the fire stood an old woman, naked and shriveled, looking back at her.

Avery gasped but did not pull away. The woman raised her hands over the fire, her palms bright in the flame. As she spoke, Avery heard her voice inside her head. She recognized that she'd been hearing the same word for some time, like an echo in a well.

She gasped, straightened, and turned away from the scene beyond the wall to stumble blindly through the dark basement. The word circled around her, sibilant and soft but somehow filling Avery with nameless dread.

She tripped against the bottom step, falling forward. The pain in her shins was bright and brought her swiftly back to the waking world. She scrambled up the stairs, hands grasping before her. She pressed her way out into the dim light of the kitchen and shut the door tight, leaning her back against it.

The air filling her lungs was sharp with the tang of smoke. It had all been a dream. But the pain in her shins was radiant and she was there in the kitchen. The old woman's word was circling around in her brain, wanting to slip out through her teeth, to body itself forth into this world. Somehow, Avery knew this should not happen.

She limped out of the kitchen, across the barred shadows on the living room floor and back into the bedroom, which was very dark. She navigated through the clutter and into the little bathroom, closing the door behind her as gently as she could before turning on the light.

The three bulbs above the mirror seemed to stab at her. Too bright.

She splashed cold water on her face, dried herself with the towel hanging behind her. She looked at herself in the mirror, looking somehow not at all like the woman she'd seen in the basement, that dream-self. Here, she was relegated to the state of pure subject. She couldn't even observe herself without recognizing that it was *her* self.

She leaned on the edge of the counter, looking at her face in the mirror, trying to find something, anything.

It was just her face.

She flipped off the light and opened the door.

Jack was just a dark hump in the dark room, making a hot breathing sound under the covers.

She stood by the bed and stared, trying to make out that slight movement of his lungs, but it was too dark. She could only imagine it.

She climbed into the bed and pulled the sheet up over her, pushing the rest of the blankets down to the foot of the bed. She curled up against the curve of Jack's body, placing a kiss between his shoulder blades.

He didn't respond in any way, his breathing regular and deep.

Avery smiled to herself, settling down. As she began to drift back into sleep, she whispered to her husband. She'd meant to say *I love you*. Instead, a single word slithered out.

"Shurpu."

16.

Jack smelled the smoke first. Its scent was sweet and sharp, pulling him from a deep sleep up toward the surface of waking too quickly. He sat up, disoriented but alert. Unmistakably smoke, which was nothing new. The whole of the west burned every summer, and the valley where they sat was routinely socked in with drifting smoke from the surrounding fires. But this seemed different. A sharper tang.

He got up, slipping out of the room. The house was filled with a gray haze, and his heart jumped to doubletime. Fire. There was a fire.

"Avery!" he called back into the room. "Call 911!"

"Wha—?"

"Fire!"

He ran to the kitchen, throwing open the cupboard under the sink. The extinguisher was just a thin little thing, but he pulled the pin and clutched it, moving quickly to find the source of the smoke. He recognized with some other part of his mind that there were no lights. No digital displays. They were without power.

Smoke billowed from beneath the basement door. Open it or not? He felt as if there were rules about this. He swatted at the handle, once-twice, and finding it still cool, grasped it.

Avery was beside him in the kitchen, talking on the phone and answering in monosyllables.

"They're on their way," she said.

Jack opened the basement door and a wall of yellowish smoke rolled up toward them. They both choked and coughed.

"You get outside and wait for them," he said.

"You're not going down there," she said, not a question, grasping his upper arm so tightly that he felt the bruises forming.

"Just gonna see if I can do anything." He shook himself loose, looked into her panicked face.

Not waiting for an argument, he pulled his T-shirt up over his nose and mouth and plunged down the stairway.

The basement was lit only by a strip of orange flame running up a beam just beyond the laundry area, creating smoke so thick along the ceiling that it was almost impossible to see or to breathe. Jack ducked into a crouch and, gagging on sour bile that filled his throat, hurried toward the source of the fire.

The fuse box.

The flames licked up from behind the place where the box was bolted to the wooden beam, and Jack suddenly understood what made the smell so distinct.

It was the acrid scent of hot electronics, of burning plastic and superheated metal.

He hit the fuse box with the spray from the extinguisher, which was much less dramatic than he'd expected. It seemed to do nothing. He traced the line of flame up to where it was already spreading out across the floor beams. Soon, he could see absolutely nothing, between the dark, the smoke, and the heavy fog of fire suppressant. But he could hear sirens in the distance now, and he sprayed the extinguisher toward the flames until he finally doubled over, hacking, unable to draw air. *Stupid. I'm going to die down here. Stupid.* And just behind the familiar self-recrimination came panic. *I'm going to die.*

Footsteps thudded across the floor above him, and soon they were banging down the steps, and then he was being rather forcefully lifted and pushed toward the stairs. He could hear muffled shouting behind him.

At the top of the stairs, the kitchen was still filled with smoke, but the difference in the air felt like heaven. Jack drew a deep breath, which in turn sent him on a coughing jag. As he was being guided toward the front of the house, two firefighters were dragging a heavy hose through the living room, heading the opposite direction.

Oh, shit. This was serious. Somehow, this was the first time it registered in his mind. Their home. Dylan hadn't even seen it yet. They could lose everything.

The firefighters led him through the front door. The heavy canopy of branches was lit from below by strobing blue and red lights, overlit and stark. He spotted Avery near an open ambulance, and he hurried toward her, not even conscious of the firefighter's hand on his upper arm steering him in that direction. They'd slipped into a stock shot from the end of every 90s neo-slasher: the survivors wrapped in blankets, bloodied and shell-shocked, waiting for the credits to roll.

Avery threw her arms around him and he could see that she was crying, and he tried to tell her he was okay, but his throat was filled with something thick and foul as tar. He gagged, choked, and vomited on the concrete.

Through a cotton haze he heard Avery screaming. The panic had found her, too.

The EMT directed him to the back of the ambulance. Soon, Jack was sitting down, an oxygen mask strapped onto his face. Jack looked around, saw neighbors out in their yards, watching, the lights transforming everything into a mechanical nightmare. And then he looked toward the house. *Their* house.

The front door stood open, and yellow-gray smoke slipped out from the top of the door, rising up into the night. The scene was so uncannily familiar that he shivered, a real physical reaction that ran from the back of his arms and down his body. He'd seen this before. Perhaps in a dream?

Avery sat next to him, draping part of the blanket across his shoulders. They watched the men go in and out of the house in their big beige space suits.

Jack felt a little high from the oxygen, or maybe it was from the smoke inhalation. He couldn't tell. Avery was okay, it didn't look like the house was going to go up completely, and the mortgage had included homeowners' insurance, so they probably wouldn't be completely ruined financially.

The firefighters were gathering in the yard now, the frantic pace of their activity subsiding, and Jack felt suddenly exhausted. He just wanted to lay down on the strip of grass that bordered the sidewalk and the street and sleep.

And then, it arrived. He knew why the image of smoke rising from the open door was so familiar. It was from the final scene of *House on Blood Street*, after the sister left the house. Even Jack's angle from the ambulance's tailgate seemed to match that of the film. He didn't know what to make of that, but it struck him, pulled him back to wakefulness, as if he had drifted off before the television and awakened to find himself lost within the movie. The world was plotless now, and all he could do was remain watchful, awaiting the next uncanny image, and the next. The next scene of horror.

17.

Soon, a man with a thick, buzzed head stood before them: the fire chief.

"We got the fire out before it could do much damage, and we really soaked it down. That's the danger. You miss one little ember and it springs up again. We're keeping an eye on it right now. Looks like it's electrical, but I'll come out in the morning to do a full report. I think it's actually pretty minor. You have insurance?"

They both nodded.

"Good. The sooner you get that info to me, the sooner I can get my report to them and you can get repairs started. I wouldn't count on being back in there for the next couple of days at a minimum. There's no power, obviously. Smoke damage may or may not be serious. You have a place to stay? I've got a Red Cross contact if you need to be put up somewhere."

Avery and Jack looked at each other.

"We can stay with friends, yeah," Avery finally said.

"Good. How about one of you makes that call, and the other comes into the house with me so that you can gather up some things, just a small bag of necessities."

"I'll go," Jack said, slipping the oxygen mask off of his face. It was definitely making him light headed.

As he stood up to follow the chief, their neighbor Mel stepped out of the periphery.

"If you need someplace to stay while you get things figured out, you're welcome over at my place," she offered. "I've got a spare room, and I'm up for the night anyway."

Jack looked around as if someone might tell him what to do, might direct him. Exhausted and dazed, he finally said, "Thanks. Yeah. We might take you up on that."

He followed the fire chief back into the house. Already, the smoke had dissipated but not the smell. Would it ever go? Or would their home remain marked forever? He looked wildly about the living room, as if convincing himself that it was still there. The usual mess was spread out around him, strangely comforting.

He gathered up their things.

Once the chief had given Avery his business card and rattled off several things that would have to happen in the morning, none of which Jack really followed, Mel led them down the street to her house.

Inside, she switched on lights and started coffee, Avery looked at the paintings and photos on the walls, while Jack sat on the couch in a kind of daze. Mel's house was almost a mirror of their own, but somehow more lush, softer. Outside, night loomed, but Mel's kitchen was clean and bright, with butcher block countertops and dark tile. Oversized ferns blocked out much of the back windows.

"Scary stuff," Mel said from the kitchen.

Jack grunted his assent.

"When I was ten, I burned down my family's garage. Playing with matches. Never told anyone it was me, but I'm betting they knew. Anyway, it was terrifying. Fire scares me to death." She held out a cup of coffee to Avery.

Avery sipped. "Me, too." Her hands shook. *This is shock*, she thought. *I'm in shock.* She forced them still. "Thank you. For everything."

Mel crossed the room and handed Jack the other cup.

"Not a problem. I barely sleep anyway. I'm usually up four-thirty, four-forty-five. And the offer stands. I've got a room. And you'd be close to the action, as it were."

It occurred to Jack that he had no idea what time it was. He looked at the wall where a clock hung above the television. Almost six? Almost light out. How many hours had gone by? It felt like mere moments. His chest hurt, and his throat burned, but it was his mind that had slipped a cog. It just spun and spun, never landing on any idea but one. *Our house*.

There was a knock on the door. When Mel opened it, there was Karl from across the street. "Bit of excitement, huh?"

"Coffee?" Mel said, gesturing him in.

Karl smiled, pushing the door closed behind him. "One way to meet the neighbors, huh?" he said, taking the cup from Mel's hands.

"I guess," Jack said.

Karl moved across the room, holding his hand out to Avery. Jack watched the older man sizing Avery up, could see the question in his eyes, but then it was gone. Jack relaxed.

"Kerl Hepner. I live across the street. I met your husband last week."

"Avery," she said. "Nice to meet you."

Karl sat himself down in a chair as if he lived there. Maybe he did, Jack thought. He and Mel seemed pretty familiar. Mel moved into the room and stood just behind Karl's chair, holding her cup to her chin.

It was a good room. Uncluttered in a way Jack longed for but could never quite manage. Solid, comfortable furniture. Framed art on the walls. A huge fern took up one corner.

"I was telling these kids about Arthur Boorman," Mel said to Karl. She turned to Jack and Avery. "I only ever knew Arthur enough to say hello, but Karl actually knew him."

"Really?" Jack couldn't help himself.

"For a brief time, way back. A strange story."

"Every story involving this dude seems pretty strange," Avery said. She sat down next to Jack and pushed up against him like a cat.

Karl nodded. "He was a bit of a character. We both taught at the university."

"Is this whole neighborhood some kind of teacher housing?" Jack croaked.

Karl laughed and sipped his coffee.

"Pretty close." Mel said. "There's me and Karl. And there was Arthur. Anne Stein died a few years back, and she lived just two streets over. She was Forestry."

"And you were what?" Avery said, squinting at Karl, measuring him up. "Psychology?"

"Not sure if I should be insulted or not, but you're close enough. Sociology."

"Cool," Avery said.

Jack felt as if he were not really present, like he was just taking in the conversation from some remove. The house had been on fire. Had that been real? Jack had run down the stairs like an idiot. He remembered the moment of choking panic, but it seemed like a story he'd heard, unreal. And now they were all having coffee?

"Sometime, I'll tell you the whole story. Arthur Boorman was a little wild."

"Jack's been reading his book." Avery nodded toward him, and Jack watched her hand shake.

"Ah, the *Incantations*." Karl's smile was hard to read. It was pleasant enough, but with some twinge to it. Jack couldn't tell if he was sneering at it or showing some appreciation. Oddly, Jack felt that it was important. He felt protective of the book, of the poems, and by extension, of their author.

"I'd never heard of him before we moved in," Jack said, his voice a rough whisper.

"He was top of the game for a little while. His real legacy was as a teacher, of course. Practically built the writing program here. A genuine character."

"Mel, thank you so much for this. We really appreciate it. This whole night has been just—" Avery waved her hands around her face, and Jack wondered if the others could see the panic just beneath the surface.

"Not at all. Let me show you to your room. You two must be exhausted." Mel glanced at Jack, he saw that, yes, she did see and understand, and he felt an instant love for the woman.

They followed her back into the house, Jack picking up their bags. In his chair, Karl raised a papery white palm and lifted his chin to them as they passed.

Mel pushed open a door at the end of the hall. The guest room was dark, wood-paneled, with a small desk and a typewriter at one end and a full-size bed at the other. Books were stacked along the walls in little towers.

"My son used to stay here when he'd come to visit. You're welcome to it."

"Thanks so much," Jack said.

"Towels are in the bathroom. Help yourself. Just let me know if you need anything else."

Mel pulled the door shut, leaving them alone in the little room.

And finally she broke. Avery's face crumpled, her mouth open in a silent howl, and Jack pulled her to him, holding her as she shook. Maybe this would come to him, too, this terror and grief, but for now he was still lost within the smoke.

She cried hard into his shoulder for four or five minutes, wetting his shirt with her tears and snot. She straightened, wiping her face with the back of her hand, and then took Jack's face between her palms.

"I love you, but you reek," Avery said, scrunching up her nose.

Jack was confused.

"Smoke, my dude. You smell like smoke."

He didn't even notice. It was part of him, soaked into his skin. He was changed.

"You okay?" he said, pulling her back to him.

"No. My house was on fire. You?"

"Peachy."

He fell backward onto the bed, arms extended in a Christ-like pose.

"Get off that bed and go clean up," Avery said, tugging him by the arm.

He kissed her on the forehead and went back out into the hall, a man half-asleep. He heard Mel and Karl speaking in hushed tones from the living room, and he stopped before the bathroom door to watch through the tiny window at the end of the hall. The sky was lightening to the color of a new bruise, the sun still locked up beyond the mountain. It turned out morning was coming after all.

18.

They took turns in Mel's corner shower unit, trying to scrub the smell of smoke out of their hair, running the water too-hot, lathering and scratching at their scalps, only to realize it was inside their noses, too. Inside their lungs. They slipped back into their room wrapped in damp towels, and Jack smelled bacon from the kitchen, heard Mel banging around.

Jack watched Avery stepping into her underwear, skin still damp, hair plastered to her head, and he smiled, pulled her to him again, kissing the top of her head.

"You can sleep if you want," he said. I've got a lot of calls to make this morning."

"I've got work," she said. "Ten a.m. appointment."

They clutched each other for a long beat.

"I have nightmares like that," she said into his shirt.

Jack thought of the vision he'd had, sitting on the ambulance's bumper: smoke billowing out of their home's open door. But it wasn't a vision. It was no nightmare, sparked by an image from a shitty movie. Real. It gave him the same kind of uneasiness as any cases of deja vu. Cause and effect were scrambled. There was a glitch in the Matrix. Reality was a sham.

"The important thing is that we both got out safe," he said.

"I'm just glad Dylan wasn't here," she said.

"You gonna be okay going to work? You can cancel, you know."

"It'll be better, honestly."

"So you can leave all of the house stuff to me."

"Exactly."

"You suck." He kissed her forehead.

"But you love me anyway."

"But I love you anyway," he smiled.

Out in the kitchen, Mel and Karl appeared to be making food for an army, scrambling eggs and pouring out pancake batter.

"Ah, here they are," Karl said, raising his spatula in a little salute. Jack thought they looked pretty comfortable together. Good for them.

The four of them stood or sat at the little counter nook, talking about things that had nothing to do with house fires, eating, and things felt almost normal.

Jack's phone buzzed.

"Mr. Todd? This is Chief Connor."

"Oh, yeah, hello."

"Just finished up the inspection over here at your house. Definitely electrical. Looks like it was arcing between the box and the main line real good. If you can meet me, I'll have you sign off on this, and I can give you the name of an electrician to get you up and running again."

"What time?"

"I'll be here for another half-hour or so. Otherwise, just call me, and we can meet."

"I'm right next door."

"Perfect."

They hung up without saying goodbye, and Jack pocketed his phone. He gave Avery the plan, put on his shoes and socks, and headed out into the morning. The morning was already hot, and the air burned his throat and lungs, but he felt good. The chief would tell him what to do, and he would do it. The house was okay. He and Avery were safe. They'd been through something and come out the other side, mostly unscathed. *Safe*, he thought. *Safe, yes. Safe, but changed.*

19.

The chief seemed somehow bigger outside of his fire suit. His blue T-shirt stretched across his barrel chest and his arms were bulging. He was efficient and kind and made sure Jack had his card, reminding him to call the insurance company first thing.

When he was gone, Jack walked the house, opening windows to air it out. It was dark inside with no power and the smell of smoke was strong and sweet. He went up into Dylan's room, untouched by the fire but also filled with the scent of smoke. He opened both windows, letting the cross-breeze through.

He stood at the top of the basement stairs and closed his eyes, gathering himself. The night before, he'd plunged down into the smoke and flames without a second thought. Now, he felt as if he were at the edge of some great precipice. He opened his eyes and descended the stairs.

In the basement, he used his phone's flashlight and looked at the damage. The fuse box was scorched, the plastic melted. The beam it was attached to was blackened and charred up to the ceiling, where black scorch marks radiated out about six feet. The flames had extended out in a couple of thin runners along the support beams, but the damage really didn't seem bad. Mostly cosmetic. Once they had power restored, they should be fine to come home. Jack wondered if they'd ever get the smell of smoke out of the place.

He swung the blackened fuse box door open and looked at the label affixed inside it. It was stained brown and yellow where the fire had brushed up against it, but the writing was still legible: that one word in red.

Shurpu.

He felt a shiver. That alien word tickled something at the back of his mind. He knew he should be able to reach it, but his brain was tired, stupid, and overwhelmed by the things that needed doing immediately. He snapped several pictures of the blackened beams and the tongues of black soot across the ceiling. He went back upstairs, into the bedroom to find the insurance paperwork included in the bulging folder of mortgage junk. Then the call to the electrician.

He opened the fridge. Its interior was still fairly cold, despite the lack of power. He pulled out a beer. He cracked it, took a swig, realized it was about eight in the morning, grunted, and took it and the folder to the yard. As he made his phone calls and sat on hold, that word kept rattling around, searching for the right hook to hang itself on. *Shurpu.*

He was in the middle of the call with the electrician, who—amazingly—was available immediately, when it clicked. *Shurpu*. He remembered now.

House on Blood Street. Boorman had labeled the basement based on language from his movie. Or was it vice versa? Maybe he'd found the word penciled in, just as Jack had, and incorporated them into his script. Jack made a mental note to look the word up later, and then he drove down to the Walmart to buy some air freshener and ice, so they might save some of their perishables.

It was a very long day.

20.

Around ten the next morning, they got the okay from the electrician; Avery had no morning appointments, so the two of them returned to the house on Calliope Street.

Jack had sprayed the hell out of the place the day before, so the smoke smell was really just an undertone, a sweetness at the back of the throat, like a sense memory of the Fourth of July. To be fair, the air outside wasn't much different anyway. In the basement, where the blackened timbers gave off a pungent campfire smell that filled the whole space, there was a brand new fuse box, shiny gray and space-aged, bolted right to the charred post. The electrician had said that the contractor would take care of the post, but Jack was trying to decide how not to call the contractor, in order to save what was bound to be more than a few bucks. They were still waiting on the inspector to come out and give an estimate for the insurance. All of it made Jack feel vaguely sick to his stomach.

The old fuse box was lying out on the concrete slab, cut wires protruding from a pipe at its top. Jack examined the label again. He'd done some googling and the word appeared to be real. *Shurpu*, according to Wikipedia, was an ancient Babylonian cleansing ritual, something like baptism. A way of expiating sins. It also translated as "burning," which gave him a little shiver as he read.

He wandered to the other end of the basement, to the collage. It looked the same as ever, staring back with a thousand eyes, watchful and waiting. What had its gaping hole seen when the flames were running up the beam, spreading across the ceiling? Had it been frightened or joyful? Did it fear or welcome the cleansing fire?

Shurpu.

It was a stupid sounding word, and it got lodged in his head like a piece of meat between his teeth. Worried and worrisome. A crazy old man's private language.

A scratching sound. At first, Jack thought it was coming from the collage, something back behind it. They needed to deal with this thing. Then he heard the sound again and convinced himself it was just Avery, upstairs, moving things around, straightening up.

But there it was again, and it was definitely nearby, down there with him.

He moved closer to the mound of clipped pictures. *A heap of broken images*. That was T.S. Eliot, the old fake, but it fit. A heap of broken women. *They died a myriad*. That was Ezra Pound, in a surprising pass at human feeling. *Quick eyes gone under earth's lid*. It was Jack's favorite poem by old Ezra, that fascist crackpot, lamenting the human cost of the Great War, all for a botched civilization. *Under earth's lid*. He thought of the scene in Arthur Boorman's movie of the man climbing through that hole in the earth, descending downward, Dante-like. Was that what this was? Was this the lid to the underworld? Was this the detour off the midpoint of life's road?

He kneeled down, coming closer to the shrine than he ever had. The hole at its center seemed bigger. Not obviously so, but definitely enlarged. A memory of something slipping inside it quickened in Jack's brain, and he hesitated. But then he moved again, bringing his face down, close to the hole. It was hard to keep his balance so close to the wall, so he braced himself against the collage with the tips of his fingers, pressing lightly into the layered clippings. They gave slightly, dry and crackling.

He tried to press his eye up against the opening, but his glasses were in the way. He pushed his glasses up onto the top of his head, leaned forward. Not that there was anything to see. Just dark. But maybe. His eye pressed right up against the ragged hole, rough paper against his cheek, and he strained his vision, sure there was something to see, some movement, some light, some sign of something more beyond.

A ringing bell jerked him back and up, his glasses slipping from his head and falling to the floor in a clatter of plastic.

It was the doorbell.

He rescued his glasses from the floor, examined them, found them undamaged, and put them back on. The collage looked as it always had: staring and mute.

Avery's footsteps moved across the creaking floor above him. He heard the door open, the muffled rumble of talk, and then steps across the floor again. He was immobilized before the collage, head cocked, listening. For what?

Avery shouted down the stairs.

"Jack? Karl is here."

Karl. He unstuck himself, glancing back halfway across the basement. The shrine stared. He wondered what it saw when it looked at him. He hurried up the stairs.

21.

Avery and Karl were standing in the kitchen, a white casserole dish on the island between them. Flowers and little figures of people ringed the dish in fading greens and yellows.

"Karl brought it."

The man gave a dismissive wave.

"I figured you'd have lots to do around here, and cooking should be the last of your worries. It's not much."

Jack was genuinely touched. He shook the older man's hand, not knowing how else to show his gratitude, and then instantly felt ridiculous. How many places had they lived with neighbors who either pretended they didn't exist or were outwardly hostile? Now, their neighbors were people who welcomed Jack and Avery into their homes in the small hours. Who made casseroles. It almost had to be a *Rosemary's Baby* scenario, right?

"Thank you—I mean it. Thank you. Really," Jack said.

"Get you something to drink? Coffee, tea, water, beer, soda?" Avery was moved by this little sign of neighborliness, too.

"I'd take a cup of coffee if it's already made," Karl said, looking around the kitchen, taking in the floors and kindly ignoring the mess. "You've been busy."

"Not busy enough," Jack said, pouring a cup of coffee for each of them.

Once again, he led them all out into the yard. It was easily Jack's favorite part of the house, despite the now-omnipresent wildfire smoke. Green and almost wild, open to the sky but still enclosed. They all sat down around the plastic table.

"The yard's still a mess," Jack said.

"Well, I doubt Arthur did much to keep it up," Karl said, sipping his coffee, looking around the yard.

"Did you know him well?" Avery said.

"Depends on what you mean. We crossed paths. A particularly interesting path, actually."

"Okay, spill. We need your Arthur Boorman story," Jack was smiling, but he also found that he was oddly invested. He wanted any crumb.

"Well, I did promise. You've both seen his movie?"

"We have indeed," Avery said.

"I'm not much of a horror buff. I think it was more than a movie to Arthur. It was more like a personal statement, maybe an extension of his poetry."

"An incantation," Jack said softly.

Karl grinned. "Maybe. Whatever it was, all of that magical mumbo-jumbo? He was really into that stuff. At least I think he was. Hard to read, old Arthur was."

"What's the story?" Avery said.

Karl took a drink of his coffee, set the cup down, and sat back in his plastic chair, hands resting just above his belly. He was ready to hold forth. The old professor was enjoying himself.

"Starting in 1977 and up into the early 90s, I was doing a lot of work focused on religious cults. A colleague and myself actually infiltrated several. Lived with them for a few weeks, gathering information. Organization, recruitment methods, patterns of belief. I was particularly interested in the sociological implications of membership. Why people joined. Why they stayed. Why they left. It was fascinating work."

"Well, it was the winter of 1979, and I had infiltrated a local group, right here in the valley, run by a fellow named Jacob Speck. He's still around, with a few disciples. Real quiet. Speck was a psychiatrist before he lost his license. Needless to say, his practices are... different."

"But the late 70s was Speck's heyday. He had quite a following, up Rattlesnake Creek, out on his family's ranch. So we joined up, my partner and I. It was pretty standard stuff. Very communal. A lot of pseudoscience dressed up in New Age nonsense. Vows of absolute chastity, which meant everyone was sleeping with everyone else. Lots of drama."

Avery gave a little chuckle.

"At its root, Speck was all about communing with the dead. Not seances, per se, though there was plenty of Madame Blavatsky running through it all. Real nineteenth century stuff. No, Speck had a whole cosmology. The dead weren't gone. Just existing on another frequency, a few ticks over on the dial. Speck claimed that he could tune in to that frequency to talk with the other side. So, you can imagine who flocked to him. The grieving and broken.

"About two weeks into my field research, Arthur Boorman shows up. We didn't know each other. Our departments didn't mingle. But I knew of him. He was a minor celebrity, what with the prize. So he starts coming out to the Ranch almost every day. He's not *in*-in. He hasn't given away his possessions and renounced the fallen world like some of Speck's other converts, but he's wading in. Testing the waters. He's real interested in Speck, and Speck seemed pretty interested in him, too."

"Like *interested*?" Avery said, raising her eyebrows.

Karl considered that for a moment and then shook his head.

"No, Speck, while maintaining a strict vow of celibacy, fathered about a dozen children with various women over the years. Not to say that precludes anything, but I don't think sex is what the interest was about. Speck was interested in Boorman because he had money and a name, a certain cachet. Boorman was interested in Speck because he was working on a new book. He wanted to incorporate Speck's ideas. Two peas in a pod for a while there."

"But he never wrote anything after *Incantations*," Jack said.

"Nope." Karl gave another of his grins. "He made a movie instead."

"*House on Blood Street* is tied to the Speck cult?"

Karl leaned in, relishing his own story. "Jacob Speck directed *Blood Street*. Everybody in that movie was a member of the cult. It was filmed right up the road, out Rattlesnake Creek."

Jakob Spezialle. Jacob Speck. Jack was giddy.

"What did Speck get out of it?" Jack said.

"Not sure. I was long gone by the time they were making the movie. Arthur broke with the cult right after. Production was something less than a pleasure, I guess. Of course it lost all of the money they put into it."

"Crazytown," Avery whispered.

Jack sat forward, too. "What does the word 'Shurpu' mean to you?"

Karl blinked, and Avery looked confused.

"It's repeated throughout *Blood Street*."

"Rings no bells."

"But it's not just the movie," Jack said, turning his phone around and sliding it across the table.

Karl picked it up and studied the photo of the fuse box label, enlarged it. Avery peered over his shoulder, her face darkening.

"Wow," he said finally. "All this time, I thought he was just a grifter, milking Speck and the rest of them for his little project. Maybe he was a true believer after all."

He smiled and handed the phone back.

"But the word," Jack said.

"Mumbo-jumbo, like I said. There were a lot of rumors that things out on the Ranch got pretty dark.

Genital mutilation. Female circumcision. Some kind of purity fetish."

"Jesus," Avery said. "How is he still walking around?"

"I never witnessed anything like that. It might all be smoke. But, if it's true, it would also be voluntary."

"Super gross."

Karl nodded. "Also probably bullshit."

Avery stares at the photo, forehead wrinkled in concentration. "Okay, but why is this in our house? Nuh-uh. Do not like."

Karl looked around the yard, then into his empty coffee cup.

"Well, I should let you two get back to it. Just return the dish whenever."

They all stood, and Jack shook Karl's hand, and led him through the house, and then he and Avery were standing in the living room, staring at each other with wide eyes.

"What the actual fuck?" Avery said.

Jack just shrugged. He had nothing to say. He was busy tumbling down a rabbit hole that kept opening into new and ever-stranger passages, and somehow all of them led to the same place. Jack and Avery stood just above it.

22.

Sleeping in their own bed was nice, especially after a change of sheets, and they didn't really notice the smoke smell upstairs. It was only after being outside and coming back in that Jack's senses caught it, a campfire smell that tickled the back of his nose. They'd eaten Karl's casserole and watched an episode of some semi-supernatural detective show that was badly dubbed from German.

Jack barely followed it. He was flipping between Wikipedia, IMDB, and Letterboxd, looking for any information on Jakob Spezialle. There was nothing. *Blood Street* might have a cult following, but not enough of one to lead anyone to attempt to track these people down. Just a long line of blank headshots for the cast and crew. *Cult following*, he thought, and laughed to himself.

Now, the house was tied up in all of this weirdness. It was interesting in a dinner-party-conversation kind of way, but Jack felt a genuine kind of urgency to understand it that he couldn't explain. He had a half-formed feeling that it was all connected. Those words written on the fuse box lid, the fire, the collage, the sense of general unease he sometimes felt late at night. A flash of some skittering thing running past his foot and up the wall. The answers were here somewhere, but he couldn't seem to grasp them. The internet offered endless paths, but each one came to a rather dramatic dead end.

Maybe the answers were in the movie itself? He shook his head at himself, thinking of the ridiculous documentary they'd watched about *The Shining*, and the fans who had devoted themselves to picking the film apart and applying occult significances to every detail, from room numbers to hallway turnings. It was conspiracy theory-thinking, a circuitous not-logic that presupposed meaning and then miraculously discovered it.

On the other hand, there was a direct connection within the film to Jacob Speck and his freaky cult. Was *Shurpu* a word that had significance to Speck and his followers? Couldn't the film illuminate its meaning, or at least give context? And might that not point to some answer to why Arthur Boorman had written those words inside the door to the fuse box?

Jack kept scrolling, looking for another way into the puzzle. There was shockingly little online about Speck. Links to academic articles locked up behind a paywall. But YouTube was another story. Speck actually had a whole channel, and Jack clicked through a couple of videos with the sound off. They had self-help-flavored titles like "Breaking the Circle of

Grief," and "Touching the Spirit World." The videos themselves were well made, although Speck wasn't in them. The hosts were young women, beautiful and smiling.

The episode ended, and Avery kissed him and rolled over to sleep. Jack turned off his lamp and put his phone away. He knew the whole thing was ridiculous. Meaningless. He was searching for meaning in late night B-movies, and that was what they called crazy. Even still, another viewing of *Blood Street*, paying closer attention, couldn't hurt.

He lowered himself into bed, feeling the singular pleasure of clean cotton sheets on a summer night, and he pressed himself against the curve of Avery's body. She was too warm for the hot night, but he snuggled closer anyway, happy to be there in their bed, in their bedroom, in their house, in their friendly little neighborhood full of kind old people who brought casseroles. He didn't so much drift as plunge into sleep, as if he had fallen through the bed, down into the dark, smoke-scented place beneath them, where something waited and watched with silent, unblinking patience.

Hours later, he gasped awake, shaken out of a dream already fled.

Avery was not in bed. He sat up, looking toward the darkened bathroom, its door standing open. He listened, heard no movement.

Slipping out of bed, he crept into the living room, but Avery was nowhere to be seen. The floorboards uttered their soft, creaking cries beneath his bare feet. Avery wasn't in the kitchen, either. He thought of going up the stairs to see if she was in Dylan's room. He knew she missed her son, could be overcome by it sometimes. But he knew better. He knew where she was. There was only one place.

He opened the basement door and was hit immediately by the campfire smell. The light at the base of the stairs was off, but he could see an electric glow further in. He knew she was there, standing before the collage. At the hole. He felt a sudden, inexplicable fear.

He didn't want to see. He didn't want to know.

But he inched slowly down the steps anyway. The room revealed itself to Jack in slivers with each downward step. Barred shadows and the soapy glow of the plastic sheeting. The light at the other end of the basement drew him forward.

Avery was sitting on the floor directly beneath the last bulb, haloed by the pale circle of magazine clippings. Her back was to him. She was shaking slightly, as if crying.

He moved slowly through the weird twisting path laid out by the framed and empty walls. As he approached, he saw that she was holding a bundle in her arms. There was a trail of clear, blood-tinged fluid running from where she sat, leading across the floor, up the wall, and into the hole. Jack began to breathe too quickly, and he felt lightheaded, just as he had when he'd been wearing the oxygen mask. He said Avery's name, but no sound emerged.

At first he thought she was holding a dog, but that was wrong, its legs too long, too spindly. Its ears were too large for its head, pointed at the tips, and he recognized it as a fawn, newly born, cradled in her lap. The deer's black mouth rested against Avery's chest, but the animal made no movement or sound. It was dead.

Avery looked up at him, tears on her cheeks, nose running.

"I couldn't save it," she said, her voice wet and crackling. "It couldn't even stand up."

Jack fell to his knees beside her. The deer was so delicate. Too small. A stillbirth. His eyes traced the trail of amniotic fluid up to its source in the wall. The black space gazed back, weeping its blood-tinged tears.

"Avery," he said, but choked it back. He didn't know how to even ask a question.

"I heard it crying," she said, bowing her head over the corpse again. "Down here in the dark."

Jack sat there on the cold pavement beside her as she clutched the fawn to her breast, under the house's watchful eye.

23.

They buried the fawn in the backyard, beneath the big tree. Wrapped in an old black T-shirt, it was terribly small, just a bundle of sticks down in the hole. Avery placed several large stones atop the grave, afraid that other animals might dig it up. She couldn't handle that. Not a second lifeless birth. They'd worked in the light from the back porch, and Jack felt a vague guilt, as if they were doing something criminal.

Mostly, he concentrated on the task at hand, trying not to think about the thing in the house, how it had apparently birthed an undersized deer. He told himself there was some reasonable explanation for it all, but his brain short circuited as soon as he tried to make sense of his experience. Even a lifetime of haunted house movies did little to help. *Amityville* didn't prepare him for any of this: Avery's arms and legs were covered in the dried afterbirth that had come out of that hole, blood and amniotic fluid caked with dark earth. The front of her night shirt was stiff with it.

Inside, he pulled the shirt over her head, and she let him, her arms heavy and loose, staring just beyond his left ear, eyes still filled with tears. He ran a shower and guided her into it. While she cleaned herself off under the steaming water, Jack collected their grave-smeared clothes and placed them in the hamper. He started coffee, because that's what people do. He leaned against the kitchen island, staring out at the dark yard, thinking of nothing until he heard the shower stop.

While Avery dressed, Jack cleaned himself up.

They drank coffee in the yard as the sun came up. The morning should have been beautiful. God-damned magical, especially with the way the layers of smoke in the air colored the sky in dramatic colors. Instead, they sat in perfect silence, sipping their coffee and feeling their gazes pulled always toward the base of the tree.

Finally, they went inside, and Avery prepared for work while Jack cleaned up the kitchen.

That day, Jack did no work on the house. He had planned to begin on the bathroom. They'd picked new faucets, and Jack had psyched himself up to change those out, expecting it to turn into a protracted and expensive project, because that's how these things worked. They were still going back and forth about replacing the toilet, which was oddly small and had trouble flushing anything down.

Instead, he sat in the living room with the blinds shut against the sun and watched *House on Blood Street* on his laptop. Much like the early morning burial, he felt inexplicably guilty as he cued up the movie. Watching it in the daylight, with the fresh hours of summer vacation raging away just outside, sent him back to adolescence, when watching inappropriately gory or racy movies was a clandestine thing, done at sleepovers in the small hours or in someone's living room while their parents were at work.

Plus, he paid $7.99 to buy it after the rental expired.

He sat with his notebook on his knee, pen poised. He was looking for answers. But by the time that the woman sat with a fawn in her lap, forming some pagan Pieta, Jack was feeling disoriented. The shot of the exterior of the house. The woman coming out of it in slow motion. Jack's mind flickered to the night of the fire, seeing in the *Blood Street* footage the picture of smoke rising from his own front door. He remembered the sensation of his over-oxygenated brain swimming through smoke and time, and he wanted to turn off the movie, to run out of his house. Go do anything else.

Watching *Blood Street* a second time—during daylight, no less—did not clear up Jack's confusion. Outside of its recurring imagery, and a few recycled set pieces, the film didn't subscribe to any discernible logic. The deer had nothing to do with anything else in the plot. Were they symbolic of the original murder of the woman in the black negligee? Was it sacrifice that opened the doorway in the wall? The movie refused to tell, and it bothered Jack that he wanted it to make sense, that understanding it felt so important.

He closed the laptop and wandered aimlessly around the house in his bare feet for a few minutes. He was full of nervous energy that needed an outlet, but he couldn't focus enough to think about home repairs.

He ate a bowl of cereal and drank another cup of coffee, then put on his shoes and decided to get away from the house, just for a little while. Take a walk.

Out on the sidewalk, he met Mel, taking groceries out of her car, and he jogged up to help.

"Settled back in?" she said.

"I think so, yeah."

They climbed Mel's porch.

"Scary stuff," she said, unlocking the front door and leading him into the house.

Jack set the bags on the kitchen counter.

"Well, I'm having you two over for dinner soon," Mel said, putting milk into the refrigerator.

"That would be lovely," Jack said. He had to fight back the sudden urge to cry. He didn't know where it came from. It wasn't a reaction to Mel or her invitation. Just a sudden wave of sadness.

"Everything's okay?" Mel said, cocking her head at him.

"This week has been, I don't know. A lot."

"Okay. Well, talk to that wife of yours. Pick a day. I'm cooking."

"Will do. Thanks."

She watched him from her doorway as he strode up the walk, away from the house, and he raised a hand in a parting wave, then fell into the hypnotic rhythm of his stride.

Jack liked to walk. He liked the solitude of his own thoughts, the freedom. He crossed Brooks Street, officially leaving their cockeyed little neighborhood, set at a forty-five degree angle to the rest of the town's grid, and headed north.

He stopped in the record store and looked around, not really shopping for anything. He was on autopilot. He left after a cursory circuit, and headed toward downtown.

The summer traffic was in full effect down here, and Jack was glad to be on foot. He walked past the local shops: secondhand and vintage clothing, a used bookstore, and a head shop.

He stopped in front of Avery's salon, cupping his hand against the window to see inside. Avery was busy with a client, combing long bunches of the woman's dampened hair out between her fingers. She chattered, snipping almost automatically. He could see his wife's mouth move as she laughed at something the client said. He felt glad to see it. It was a little gift, this view inside, with himself unnoticed. To see her laughing.

He moved on without catching her attention, and at the bridge, he went off the road, following the walking path down to the river. The Clark Fork cut straight through town, and there was hardly a piece of it not in use by somebody in these summer months. A pair of kayakers slipped by, and there were college-aged kids sitting in the grass along the bank, fat inner tubes laying up under the spindly trees.

Jack walked down to where the bank crumbled into the water. He loved the river. The first day he'd come to town, he'd walked straight into it. The water was perpetually freezing, even at the height of summer, and his hands had turned blue, but it felt good, just knowing it was there, like an artery snaking through the body of the town. Like something wild.

He thought of the fawn then. Saw Avery placing the stones at the base of the tree. The river was a wild thing within the boundary of the town, proof against the insistence of concrete and chain stores and the interstate that ran parallel to it like a dark shadow. But the fawn's very existence was surreal. The town had been built around the river, but their house was its own thing. The basement was a long chamber of cement, and it denied all but the spiders; Jack hadn't seen any sign of rodents at all.

He felt himself thinking his way around the hole—the real heart of it all. That hole in the wall. Its dilated pupil must have stretched and opened like a cervix, pushing the unfinished deer out. How? No, he couldn't even get to how, because to ask how meant to first accept that it had occurred, and he couldn't quite do that, despite what his own senses told him, despite the fact that he had helped place the thing's body in the hole he had dug.

A vision of Avery filled his mind: he saw her cradling the fawn, nursing it even as it died in her lap. By the film's logic, his wife was both witch-mother and sacrifice. That idea sent a wave of panic through him, and he turned away from the river, marching up the slope to the road, away from what was wild and disordered, to lose himself once again in the logic of the city's oddly chartered streets.

24.

Avery awoke in the night, certain she was back in the dream, a loop, an endless repetition of the previous night's horrors. She could hear crying. It drifted up through the floorboards and the bedroom's ratty brown carpet, piercing the film of sleep that still covered her. She lay there and listened, telling herself the sound wasn't real.

A high pitched cry, short, almost a squeak, but unmistakable. Familiar. It was in the basement.

She slipped from under the sheet and made her way quickly downstairs. No hesitation this time. If she could reach the baby sooner, maybe she could save it. The basement was dark, and she hit the switch at the top of the stairs. Another cry. She almost flew down the stairs.

The fawn stood below the light at the far end of the basement, fur still slick and spiked with fluid, wobbling on its matchstick legs. Avery ran to it.

This deer was bigger than the one from the night before, but still so small. Was this how small they were in nature? She almost dropped down beside it to take it in her arms, but stopped herself, hurrying back to the laundry area and taking the dirty sheets out of the plastic bin beside the washer. When she returned, the fawn's front legs had already folded beneath it, and it was pushing itself ineffectually across the smooth concrete floor, mouth gaping in silent cries.

Avery wrapped the infant in the sheet, lifting it as she did. She rubbed its fur through the sheet, bouncing a little on the balls of her feet. She was shushing it the same way she would have soothed Dylan when he was just a baby, and patting it dry just as she would have dried Dylan after his bath.

"You're hungry, aren't you," she whispered. Its tiny face looked up at her with shiny black eyes. Its dark muzzle seemed to move, as if it were trying to speak. The tiny, frail bundle was almost weightless, calm in her embrace. And it was her job to protect it. She wouldn't let this one go like the last one. This baby was bigger. Stronger. She'd save it.

She brought it upstairs and found it almost impossible to do anything with the bundle in her arms. The fawn's eyes were shutting, and she felt panic flutter in her chest.

"Jack!" she called, trying to keep the panic out of her voice and failing. "Jack. Can you help me?"

Jack almost flew out into the living room, wearing only a pair of cotton shorts, and he looked as frail and spindly-legged as the deer had, but his eyes were wild. Too many nights being awoken to horror.

"What—" he stopped at the entrance to the kitchen, seeing the bundle in her arms.

"We have to save it," she said, and only hearing her ragged voice told her she was crying.

"Jesus." He stared at the fawn's narrow, delicate face, and he blinked several times.

"Can they have cow's milk?" she said. He looked up at her, his face a blank question.

"Milk," she repeated. "It's hungry."

"I have no idea," he sputtered. "Why would I know this?"

"We have to try," she said, bouncing the fawn gently. "Warm up a little milk. Just wrist temperature."

He wasn't fully present, she knew, but he began to move, pulling the milk from the fridge and grabbing a mug from the cupboard. He placed it in the microwave and stared at the descending numbers on the display.

"We need a bottle," she said.

"We don't have any," Jack said, not looking up.

"What about soaking a rag. That's a thing, yeah?"

Jack pulled open the drawer, taking out one of the kitchen cloths. The microwave beeped and Jack took out the mug, testing it with his finger, nodding to himself.

"How do we do this?" he said.

She snatched the rag from his hand and dipped it in the milk. Holding the wet corner of the rag up to the fawn's mouth, she whispered and cooed to it, trying to coax it into opening its rubbery lips. It did nothing. She pushed its mouth open with her finger, saw the flat pink tongue inside. Its eyes were dark and glassy.

"No, no, no," she chanted, squeezing the rag, letting the milk drip into the open mouth. A drop of milk ran in a line from the muzzle back into the fine fur.

"No. Please," she sang, bouncing it lightly. She thought of Dylan, in Ohio, so far away. She wanted to see her son, clutch him to her, and feel his heat and his breath, his bones beneath his skin—to know he was whole and well.

Jack wrapped his arms around her, the dead fawn in its little bundle between them, and she wept onto his naked chest while he rubbed her back, ran his fingers through her hair, right at the base of her skull. He was whispering now, too, cooing out a message of contentment to her, just as she'd done for the fawn.

Finally, she nodded, pulling away, wiping her nose with the back of her arm.

"I'm sorry. But this is deeply fucked up," he said, running the palm of his hand over his face, like a mime wiping away his smile and replacing it with a frown.

"It was trying so hard," she said, looking at the deer's tiny features. "We almost got it right."

Jack went to stand by the back door. They both knew what came next: digging graves in the wee hours. He flipped on the porch light.

"What the hell?" he said.

She came up beside him, looking out through the glass. The light from the porch cast a yellow circle on the pavement and a wedge of grass. Everything else was just shadow edged with a yellow glow, but she had no trouble sensing the watchers. They were in the yard, under the trees. She raised her hand to the line of switches and flipped off the kitchen light, leaving the two of them in darkness. The figures on the grass resolved before them.

Deer, four—no, five—watched from the yard. A buck with wide antlers sniffed the ground around the base of the tree with several does, nuzzling around the grave dug the night before. The others just stood, eyes pinned on the house. They didn't startle. They didn't run. They just watched.

Avery clutched the dead fawn tighter, protecting it. From what? Jack pushed open the screen door, rattling it against the railing, and the group of deer flew off into the night in dramatic bounding leaps. Jack watched them go, and then he went out to dig the hole.

25.

They spent the morning pretending things were normal: puttering around the house, drinking coffee. Jack spun records in the living room. Billie Holiday and then The Clash and then Neil Young. They didn't speak about the deer, or about the basement, or about the way that reality seemed to be gently unspooling in their hands.

In the early afternoon, there was a knock on the door. It was Mel.

"How do you two feel about dinner at mine tonight?" she said.

Avery glanced at Jack who nodded.

"Sounds great. Yeah," Avery said.

"Six?" Mel said.

"We'll be there. Can we bring anything?" Jack said.

"Stop it," Mel said, turning away from the door, waving over her shoulder.

Dinner was eggplant parmesan, with a massive green salad and a bottle of wine that tasted to Avery like ambrosia. They sat in Mel's kitchen at the little table pressed up against the back window. Avery felt herself filling back up. Reconstituted. As if the scene with the deer had hollowed her out, left her only half-there, but the food, Mel's gruff friendliness, and the snug little house that was so much like their own, were healing. Like she was finally awakening from a deep sleep, from a terrible dream.

But she could still hear the fawn's cries.

"My son was supposed to come see me next week, and he just called and canceled on me," Mel said, her chair pushed back from the table, wineglass in her hand.

"Where is he?" Jack said.

"California. San Francisco. Sometimes New York. He shares apartments with some other guys in the firm. Wherever the company needs him. That's where he goes."

"Sounds impressive."

Mel crinkled her nose in disgust. "He's a Harvard MBA, working for this asshole venture capitalist. Swimming in money. Very successful."

"I'm so sorry," Jack laughed.

"It's gross. I have no idea what he does. I don't know if he knows. I don't know that he *does* anything. Takes meetings. Builds his client list. A pyramid scheme, I'm thinking. I really did my best, I swear, but you can't control kids. You've got to cut the cord at some point."

Jack looked at Avery, saw her wince.

"Dylan is twelve," he said. "Our boy."

Avery liked it that Jack thought of Dylan as his and didn't slap qualifiers on it. He was a good dad to Dylan. Better than she had ever been.

"My sympathies," Mel said. "They get real cagey around that age. Secretive. Mean, sometimes."

"Oh, we know," Avery said, taking the last swallow of wine from her glass.

"When will he come back?"

"Mid-August," Jack said. "I had planned to have the work on the house finished by then. Not looking good."

"Oh, relax. It's like parenting, having a house. You're never finished. It goes on and on. A lifetime project."

"I guess I'm a house half-finished, then," Avery said, the plain bitterness surprising even to herself. "My folks called that job done a long time ago."

Mel's mouth formed into a tight frown that was somehow also a smile.

"I'm sorry. I know it's different for everyone. I was just speaking for myself. Dave is forty-two years old, and I still worry. Every day." She sat forward, elbows on her knees, glass suspended between her fingertips. "I had a similar experience with my parents. Left early. Didn't look back. Half-finished, like you said. Just a frame and a roof. But you know what?" Mel's gaze was intense, locked on Avery's face.

Avery raised an eyebrow.

"Frame and a roof. That's shelter. And you build the rest as you go."

Avery gave a little nod, felt tears sting the backs of her eyes.

"You build as you go, and you find people who give you the things you needed that your parents didn't. That's how we do it. Like this one here." Mel tilted her head toward Jack. "This one better be a foundation for you."

"I'm more of a detached garage," Jack said, joking, but his face was serious. "Mother-in-law unit, maybe."

"A smart ass, too. That helps."

"It does," Avery said. She didn't trust her voice. Part of it was Mel and her unexpected motherly care, but it was more than that. She kept thinking of the deer gone still in her arms, and she wanted to weep.

Mel leaned back in her chair, set her glass down beside her plate, and took a deep breath. She nodded at Jack and Avery.

"I'm awfully glad you all moved in here," Mel said finally.

"So are we," Jack said, extending his hand across the table, palm up. Avery placed her hand in his, but inside she thought of the family of deer standing in the yard, searching for the lost fawn. She thought of the cries rising up from the basement, sharp and small, like needles. She thought of Dylan, so far away, an unfinished building, a half-formed thing. She couldn't help but imagine him crying out in the night from down in the dark, waiting for someone to save him.

26.

This deer had two heads and six legs, and it was already dead when they found it on the basement floor. There was the usual trail of slick dribbling from the hole in the wall. The deer was splayed right below it. Born dead. It had not even tried to rise up on its many legs or tried to raise its several eyes to take in the bare surroundings. Freakish and small and impossible.

And they'd buried it in the yard, just like the rest. What else was there to do? Jack had mentioned calling Animal Control. The conversation never went further than Jack's mentioning it. What could they even say?

That Sunday, they were both tired and lazy, drinking coffee in the yard, scrolling through their phones, listening to the little birds screech and tumble through the branches. The heat was already oppressive, the air quality getting worse by the day.

Avery sent a text to Dylan, just a quick hello. There was no reply, and she wondered if Janie had become the Sunday morning church-going type? Would Dylan say anything if she had? What kind of poison might the pastor be pouring into his ears?

Avery had been dragged to church every week through her entire childhood. It was a boring, liberal-leaning church, big on social justice. Even as a teenager she had sensed the unthreatening emptiness of it all. The congregation's self-satisfaction and lack of any real program. It felt more like a middle class country club. Everyone was white and old, and Avery knew enough to sense the boundaries of the congregation's "open and affirming" policies. They didn't want her. Not the real her. She could feel it in their polite distance, see it in their forced smiles. Just like her parents.

She missed her kid. Sure, it was nice having time with just her and Jack. They'd never had that part of a relationship, in the beginning. Dylan was always already there, but it still felt wrong. And they'd moved houses while the boy was away, which was extra-weird—the house on Calliope Street would be weird for him, she had to remember. The change in his absence added to the distance between them.

She scrolled Instagram, barely looking, mostly thinking about what Mel had said the night before. Parenthood was like building and maintaining a house. Avery liked that, but also, at the back of her mind, she couldn't help thinking about their *real* house, the one that birthed deformed corpses. The site of a murder, its floor still stained where a young woman had died an ugly death.

But wasn't that parenthood, too? Handing off a world you knew was poisoned and doomed, hoping that your children might be able to do better than you had, though you knew that—despite your loud complaints—you hadn't really tried that hard.

She was spiraling herself right into a deep depression, and she needed to stop it.

"Wanna go for a swim?" she said.

They drove to the park at the edge of town where the river branched into many little streams and filled deep pools with cold water and the trees shadowed the water like protective hands. Avery, in trunks and a loose-fitting tee, lowered herself into the pool, up to her chin. The water was icy, and her skin prickled with gooseflesh. Jack sat on a big rock with his legs in the water, reading Boorman's book. His face was shadowed by the brim of his cap. Avery wished she could paint him, just the way he was, right there. A big, Pre-Raphaelite oil painting, with Jack draped in flowing robes and fat cherubs floating around his head.

Her phone was on the shore, under her shirt, and she wondered idly if Dylan had responded. But that could wait. She was happy in the water, body vague with cold, watching the sunlight reflect off the water and dance across Jack's upheld book. *This* was the house they would build, made of the already-existing ingredients of the world. Soon, Dylan would come home, and they would have made a place for him. There was all the space in the world. Infinite, or near enough. She closed her eyes and leaned back, letting the cold water fill her ears and make everything go muffled and soft. She and Jack were building the house right now—she chose to believe it was strong and safe.

27.

It was late, and Avery filled a glass of water at the sink. Her chest and shoulders stung from too much sun, would probably be peeling by morning. She filled her glass at the faucet, drank it down, filled it again. Carrying it to the back door, she looked through the glass, out into the yard. She sucked in a breath at the sight of the eyes peering back at her from the grass. Three pairs, then four, then five. They caught the light and reflected it back, yellow and eerie. A whole family of deer. A herd? They stood and lay all around the yard, ears twitching, eyes on the house.

The low chain link was the easiest thing for them to jump over. She was feeling the concentrated gaze of all those eyes, as if they were trained directly on her. They might be.

Her phone buzzed. It was Dylan.

Miss you too.

Radio silence all day, and now, in the small hours, a single text. She blinked, bleary-eyed, and responded.

Everything ok?

As the three dots did their little march, Avery stared back out into the dark, into those reflective eyes. She felt a strange kinship with these animals, half-wild and grieving.

Yeah. All the cousins are here.

Avery smiled, remembering those summers with her own cousins. The house suddenly over-full with children. Sleeping on the fold-out couch in the living room. Going most of the day without ever talking to an adult.

Having fun?

She wanted to turn on the porch light, see if the deer would startle. But they might simply stay there, stock still, eyes reflecting the light, unafraid, and she didn't know what she would do then. Didn't know how that would make her feel. Perhaps they were waiting for her to join them.

She heard something from the basement. Not a cry this time, thankfully, but a shifting sound. As if the house were settling. She didn't want to see what might be down there. She'd seen enough, and it kept getting worse.

Her face lit by her phone's screen, she took one step toward the door, heard the creaking sound again, and stopped. She still had a full glass of water in her hand. She drank some of it and set the glass on the island.

There was the sound again. A light rustling. *No. Just ignore it.* She had a flash of that recurring dream from that stupid movie. The woman opening the hall closet, the monster waiting inside to chase her in goofy loops through the darkened streets. If Avery opened the door, would a half-formed deer with a human face stare up at her from the top of the stairs, gurgling and gasping with its last breaths, trying to form human speech? How many limbs this time? And whose face?

No. Not tonight.

She refused to accept that *this* was the kind of house they were maintaining. Why had they still done nothing about that hole in the wall with its creepy shrine? She knew about Jack's top-down theory of repairs, but it needed to go. She'd tell him again in the morning. She was familiar with Jack's pattern of manic energy, how his enthusiasm always trailed off into boredom. No reason to think this particular project would be different. She just needed to keep him motivated. Rip out that thing on the wall. Patch up the hole. Maybe then things would settle down.

Another creak from below. She imagined a foot on the stairs, the wood groaning beneath the monster's weight.

Goddammit.

She went to the knife block, pulled a chef's knife out, held it clutched in her fist, and turned her phone's flashlight on, holding it up in her other hand. This was her house. Jack's house. And soon Dylan would come home, and it was his home. She wouldn't allow this chaos to keep happening.

Knife in hand, she turned the knob, gave a little pull. The door swung open, a cluster of jackets hung on the pegs inside. Once again, the light at the base of the stairs was off, but the other light—*that* light—burned deep within the basement. She shined the flashlight down the steps and descended.

28.

The sound seemed to be coming from the hole itself, as if there was movement back there, and as she approached, she thought she could see some slight movement behind the staring faces. Just a ripple. A shifting shadow. She heard the click and creak, like the house was manufacturing something in its hidden rooms.

She stopped before the shrine, watching the hole, trying to see that movement again, to confirm she'd seen it. The hole stared back, blank. But then she saw movement within. Dark within darkness, some shifting shape.

She kneeled down, keeping her distance, putting her eyes at the level of the hole. She needed to see.

She heard the cry from deep within the wall.

She stepped back, holding out the knife.

She wanted to get Jack, but she didn't want to abandon whatever was in there. Some difficult birth.

Then the cry resolved into a voice. Dylan's voice.

She recognized it at once. She looked at the phone in her hand, its useless flashlight still picking out a blue circle on the floor. Its screen was blank, and when she swiped it open, there was no call.

Mom?

The voice was a little boy's, high and reedy. The sound of Dylan talking to her from her doorway in the middle of the night, scared and wanting to sleep in her bed.

Mom? Please.

Her throat clenched, and she turned back toward the sound, toward the hole birthed the dead. It was a bad place. A wrong place.

Mom?

The voice was unmistakably coming from inside the wall, back behind the collage, the dark hole that spat out its tiny aborted things.

Please.

She got down on her bare knees, the grit digging into her bare knees. Dylan was in there. She put her eye up close to the hole, tried to see inside. She could just make out her son's face, side-lit by red light, but it was him. He was right there.

Mom.

Her little boy. She had to get him away from whatever the house did to the things it found or made or dreamed. She wouldn't allow the same thing to happen to Dylan as had happened to the fawn.

She set down the phone and the knife, and pushed her fingers into the hole. She expected its edges to be dry and crumbling. She would rip the brittle paper and concrete away until she could get him out. But the edges of the hole were soft and pliant, and when she pulled, the opening stretched. She thought of the deer staining through, and she eased both arms in, up to her elbows, groping blindly.

"Baby, can you feel my hand?" she said, hoping Dylan could hear her. "Just grab my hand."

Beyond the wall, everything was soft and wet. Warm. How deep did it go? And where did it end? She pushed in further, her cheek pressed right up against the cut-outs of the smiling women. She couldn't feel anything solid. Only warm flesh, which seemed to go on forever.

Mom?

When she couldn't reach any further and her face was pressed hard against the wall, she heard another mew from inside, and that's when she knew what she had to do.

She pulled out a little, her arms still inside up to the elbows, and she tucked her head down, chin against her chest. The hole expanded just enough to let the top of her head push through. It tightened and relaxed, throbbing like a muscle, and then her shoulders were through, and she was guiding herself forward. Her bare feet scraped across the concrete; then her toes were off the ground, and the darkness took her. The air was thick and hot, the light red, the walls of the tunnel warm and slick against her skin.

The room was quiet.

The phone buzzed on the floor, the screen lighting up.

Yeah, having fun, the text read, and then the screen went dark again.

The house creaked and shuddered, and the deer in the yard all looked up at once, then startled and ran, leaping over the low fence and vanishing into the night, white tails flashing in the dark.

Everything was quiet.

29.

A human voice woke Jack. At first, he thought it was something happening out in the street, in a neighbor's yard perhaps. He placed his hand on the mattress where Avery should have been and when he felt the cool sheet, he knew who was calling for him. It was Avery, and she was in trouble.

He raced through the house, slamming open the back door and running barefoot down into the dewy grass. Inky shadows lay beneath the trees in the predawn. He stood still, head cocked, wishing there was some way to strain his ears. He screwed his eyes tight and listened. But there was nothing out here. Only the sound of morning commuters on the road a block over and the short, sharp cries of birds. The sky between the branches was purple-black.

He skipped both steps back up into the house, stopping at the archway between the kitchen and the dining room. The circle chalked onto the floor didn't look quirky or fun anymore. It felt wrong. He knew the oblong stain at the edge of the circle was blood:

Becca Mays's blood. It was proof of murder, a victim killed in her own home, in this home. In this room.

They'd laughed about this.

The sound again. Definitely a voice. Avery's. Calling out, though he could not make the words out, and now he could finally identify the source of the sound. It was coming from the second floor, from Dylan's room. He almost laughed, the relief that he was not—once again—descending into that basement to witness yet another horror. Avery was up in Dylan's room, calling to Jack because something was wrong. Whatever she needed would require his immediate attention, maybe even an early morning trip to the hardware store. But that was okay—anything could be fixed. He liked the big store in the early hours, when it was all contractors loading up for the day, and he'd make his purchase and return home, and things would be fine.

"Avery?" he said, calling up the stairs.

No response.

He climbed the carpeted stairs. The nap was stiff and crinkly beneath his feet. It should go. One more project for the list. He called again, halfway up, got no reply. Jack flipped the switch at the top of the stairs and the recessed lighting sprang on, leaving the long narrow room still half-dark, each light illuminating only its own self-contained circle.

Avery wasn't there. He walked from one end of the room to the other, then back again, his head lowered beneath the sloping ceiling. He looked out of the small, square windows at each end of the loft.

The street was a dark mass of shadowed branches lit from within by streetlight. The back was lightening into the television blue of pre-dawn. There was no sign of Avery.

But then he heard her. Just over his shoulder, two syllables, still indecipherable. He turned, eyes stabbing into the shadowed corner. Again. The same two syllables. He could almost make it out.

He moved toward the sound's source at the front end of the house, where the room did a little jog around the stairwell and opened up about two feet wider. They'd put Dylan's bed there, with the ceiling slanting down at both the head and foot of the bed, the window centered over it.

Jack stood hunched in that space, listening, and when the voice came again, it was once again over his shoulder, but closer. The voice emanated directly from the shadowed space where the ceiling met the wall, opposite the window and the bed. But no, that wasn't quite right; it was still muffled. But the other side of that wall was either the stairway or outside the house.

Avery called out again, and he called her name, and his voice seemed to slip away, not echo back as it should. He dropped down to his knees in that dark corner. The smell of fresh paint was still sweet, and they'd left the windows cracked to let the air move through. He called out and could almost hear his voice drifting out into the distant night, heading someplace far away.

When Avery called again, he finally recognized what she was saying.

"Dylan."

She had to know that he was a thousand miles away, safe with his other mother. Avery must be sleep-walking. She had this unfortunate habit of screaming out in her sleep, thrashing around as if fighting off an invisible attacker, babbling indecipherable words until Jack eased her awake. Sleepwalking was a natural progression from that type of dreaming, wasn't it?

But where had she wandered?

He reached his hand out toward the lower corner of the room, fully prepared for his hand to move right through the wall, out into that other space where Avery wandered blind, calling out for their son.

Instead, his fingers met the textured wall, the cool paint.

"Avery!" he cried, and he heard her again, though she seemed further away now. "Avery! This way. It's me!"

There was no response.

He half-crawled, half-walked around the corner and down the first five steps, running his hands against the other side of the wall where he'd heard her voice. It was solid. Cobwebs hung ragged in the corner.

He descended the stairs, moving swiftly through the dining room. He stopped at the back door, looking out into the yard. The sky had lightened by several degrees. Soon it would be morning, and none of this strangeness would be acceptable in the cold light of reasoning day.

He made a circuit through the whole ground floor and came up empty. She was not there. Finally, he stood at the closed door to the basement. He didn't want to go down there again. He didn't want to search for his wife in those dark corners or behind that concrete wall. He didn't want to see what new thing the basement had birthed.

But he opened the door anyway, and he moved slowly down the steps. His limbs were light and weightless, his throat tight.

He could see something in the circle of the light. As he approached, he recognized it. A phone. Avery's phone, in that terrible Nickelodeon-orange case. And a kitchen knife laying beside it. The chef's knife from the set they'd received as a wedding gift. There was a burn mark on the handle, frightening in its familiarity. He gritted his teeth, moved forward, and put his ear right up to the hole in the wall, straining once again for any sound of Avery's voice. Nothing. He tried to see inside, but there was only dark. He listened again.

This time he heard a small cry, far away and animal. Sharp and short.

"Avery?" he said to the empty room, though he knew full well it was not Avery.

A squelching sound made him step back. Maybe it was her. Maybe she would come sliding out, birthed here like the fawn. Come back to him from her trip beyond the wall.

But when the hole filled and stretched and bulged outward, he knew once again that it was not Avery. Slick hair filled the dilating hole, and soon a head emerged, with a long, narrow snout, big ears pasted back, and then the rest of the body followed quickly, slipping out into the room, falling down to the floor, tumbled sideways. It lay belly up, thin legs curled close to its body.

Another deer, dead, just as everything that came through this portal was dead. He was unable to do anything but stare. It was so finely made. The little black line of its mouth. The gray-white down on its belly. The tiny black hooves, shiny and sharp.

"I'm coming, Avery," he whispered. He knew that she could hear him, because it was that kind of house. Their house.

He hooked his finger inside the hole and pulled. The paper was thick, layer upon layer pasted on top of each other, once again making a hard shell. It cracked and then tore in big strips. He could already see a larger opening behind the collage. Packed earth and white spidery roots, and a black hole about a foot in diameter.

He kept pulling and tearing, the torn scraps of women's bodies falling down so that they covered the now-still body of the deer.

When the hole was broken open, Jack sat back on his heels, still crouching, and stared. The concrete wall had been chipped away in a space about four feet across. Dark earth was visible, with the deeper hole at the center of the tunnel. The entryway.

30.

This is it, he thought. *This is where I am finally brave, where I turn my back on reason and embrace love.*

He pushed his arms inside the hole, half-expecting the gap to dilate and allow him through. It did nothing. His hands fumbled around in the cool damp until he felt something solid. He jerked his hand back as if stung, heard his own breathing in the silent room, and reached in once more. He grasped the object with both hands and drew it out.

It was a brown cardboard case with accordioned sides, wrapped several times around with black string. It was covered in a thick layer of greasy dust but seemed otherwise whole and undamaged. Its ordinariness was startling, frightening in its very banality.

He sat down on the floor, his back against the wall, and slowly untwined the string. If it was money or legal documents, he would burn the house down with himself in it. He couldn't handle that kind of deception. This mystery could not resolve so simply.

He opened the flap and reached inside.

There were two sheaves of paper, each bound with a black metal alligator clip. Using the case as a makeshift desk, he spread them out on his lap. The first bore only a title typed in the center of the page: *House on Blood Street*. Jack riffled the pages, saw that it was a typewritten script, with margin notes and scribbles in blue pen. The next sheaf also bore its title in the center of the page: *Red Witch* by Arthur Boorman. He flipped through it, saw no pen markings. A clean copy of an unproduced script?

He lowered it to his lap, defeated. He had prepared himself for his journey, his quest. He was ready to enter the deepest chambers of the house and accept its laws of illogic, to rescue Avery. And this was what he got.

With the logic of a dream, which was not logic at all but emotion translating ever-shifting events, he understood. This was no end but a beginning. This was key to a door that had not yet been built. He finally knew what he had to do.

31.

He bathed, dressed, and walked across the street to Karl's house.

The wildfire smoke had descended into the bowl of the valley, and it hung thick and pungent in the air. He felt as if he were wading through it.

Karl came to the door smiling. He looked at Jack over his reading glasses.

"Hello. Everything okay?"

"A question for you," Jack said.

"Shoot."

"Speck: you said he's still got a place, up the Rattlesnake?"

Karl's eyes narrowed a bit. "He does."

"And you could tell me where?"

"I could."

"I just have questions. About Boorman. I've been reading *Incantations*, and then there's all of this stuff with the film and Speck's cult. I think there might be a book in it." *Here I am, standing on my neighbor's porch, saying these words*. But he couldn't tell the truth. The truth was impossible. The house on Calliope Street operated by its own incomprehensible rules, and all he could do was try to follow them. Avery was inside the house somewhere, and Jack needed Speck to get her out. And if Jack's plan didn't work? He couldn't think about that.

Karl's eyebrows rose. He still seemed skeptical. Jack didn't blame him. At the same time, he couldn't bring himself to describe what he'd witnessed. His missing wife. The sloppy hole that disgorged dead fawns. The kind of help he needed wouldn't come from his neighbors.

"Well, I can tell you right where it is. Not hard to find. I can't promise what kind of welcome you'll get. Might run you off or they might initiate you on the spot."

"Hopefully neither." Jack managed a smile. He hoped it looked like a normal person's smile. He felt like everything in his life was fake now, that he was playacting his way through life.

"Come on in. I'll draw you a map."

Jack could see that his neighbor was an early riser. Karl had been at the kitchen table, reading the paper, which was scattered into sections. He pulled a blue piece of paper out of the stack: a flyer for a car wash. He turned it over to its blank side and fished around on the table, lifting papers and dropping them, until he found a pencil.

He started drawing big looping lines across the page.

"You're going to go a ways out the Rattlesnake, just keep following the road. Once you cross the creek, there's a church on your right. Keep going, but keep an eye out. Take a right on Tamarack. Easy to miss. Just a little country road. I think there are actually houses built on it now. Follow it up to its end. There's a driveway, looks like a walking trail, heading up and to the right. You can drive up it, but it's tight. That will take you up into the trees and over the top of the rise. Speck's place is up there."

Jack took the paper between his hands and studied it as if it might offer some greater guidance.

"You really think Speck can offer you anything useful about Boorman?" Karl asked. Jack could see that he wanted to say more.

Jack looked up. "I hope so, yeah."

"A few minutes with him might well disabuse you of that idea. He's—" Karl brushed his temple with his fingertips and then fluttered his hand away, like a bird rising off a lake.

"Well, I guess we'll see," Jack said, folding the map in half. "Thanks for this."

"Not a problem. You'll come by and tell me how the visit goes?"

"Absolutely," Jack said. Karl walked him to the door.

Outside, the heat was already rising, and there was that thick layer of smoke. Jack hadn't looked at any news in days, but he was sure the whole Bitterroot Range must be burning.

"Hey," Karl said as Jack reached the sidewalk. "I won't tell you to be careful. They're not dangerous or anything. But just... watch yourself. Speck is goofy, but he kind of sells it. You understand?"

Jack thought he did. "Will do," Jack said, lifting the blue sheet of paper in a salute as he crossed the road home.

He made a sandwich, ate it over the sink, packed his satchel with a pad, pens, and his copy of *Incantations*. No reason to dispose of a perfectly serviceable lie. Mentioning Boorman might at least get him in the door. Then he placed Arthur Boorman's two scripts inside.

He thought briefly of the handgun stored in its lockbox. No. This wasn't that kind of trouble. And he might already be digging himself in too deep.

He stopped at the doorway, suddenly struck with guilt. He wasn't behaving like a man who had lost his wife. Why wasn't he crying, screaming, raging? Why wasn't he taking a sledgehammer to the house's walls, tearing out that thing in the basement? Why hadn't he called anyone? Was he really just inventing puzzles to solve? Now?

Deep down, he knew that there was no one to call. This was a special kind of disaster, and he both wanted to tear the house apart and to protect it. Avery was here. He could feel it.

"I'll be back soon," he called out into the empty house, to Avery, trusting that she was nearby, listening, awaiting his return.

32.

It was already hot by the time Jack followed the road under the interstate and out of town. The sun hammered on the rows of clapboard houses along the two-lane road and the yellow hills rising up beyond. The Replacements were on the radio, but he turned it down a little, the music much too loud in the car with the windows shut tight against the smoke that hung in a dirty haze all through the valley. The road stretched and curved out and away, following the shape of the unseen creek, and the houses spread out further and further as the ground around the road widening out. There was the church on his right, just as Karl had promised. Then, a little school.

When the road crossed the creek, Jack slowed, keeping an eye on the road signs. It was a familiar type of rural neighborhood, with trailers and one-room houses tucked back under the trees, with unfenced fields stretching out behind them. Quiet. He found the turning at the end of Tamarack and took it slow, creeping along. The road ran off for two country blocks and then seemed to dead-end in a thick line of trees that climbed the side of the hill. Only a big black mailbox poking out from beneath the hanging branches gave any indication that there was anything else back here. He spotted a trail running up and to the right, into the trees, barely more than a game trail.

Just as Karl had said.

He nosed the car up the path, half-certain that his Honda would get stuck going up the slope. Branches scraped along the car's hood, the windshield, and the roof, shrieking like metal on metal. And then, as if emerging from some endless car wash, he emerged into blinding sunlight. The road curved along the hillside, climbing at a good pitch, so he took it slow, too. The valley spilled out on his right, yellow and flowing with green veins along the creek's run. The sky was the flat gray of smoke. It all looked false, like a matte painting from an old Technicolor film.

The road began to drop again, and he drove through the shadows of big cottonwoods along the road. A leaning barbed wire fence ran along the side of the road now, and Jack saw an old horse in the distance, head bent to the grass. The road went on, taking him further back into the property. He turned the music off, listening to the wheels crunch along, keeping his eyes ahead.

Then, he popped out of the shadows once again and into the bright glare of the sun. He was in a wide gravel yard. There were a few cars parked along one side, most of them in various states of disrepair. A gray barn slumped to one side, and some small outbuildings lined the left of the lot. Up ahead, through another stand of trees, stood a big white house with a wrap-around porch and high peaked roofs.

No apparent signs of life. Maybe Speck and his cult had cleared out?

He pulled off to the left, a good hundred yards from the house, and killed the engine. A thin cloud of dust, kicked up by his tires, floated up into the trees and vanished. He sat and listened. So much of his life involved listening for unknown sounds, these days.

Pulling the key from the ignition, he grabbed his satchel and climbed out of the car.

He was halfway to the farmhouse when he heard barking. Four dogs shot from beneath the trees, running toward him—none of them big, a mix of some kind of spaniel and some ancient farm dog breed, but they still stopped Jack in his tracks. He clutched his satchel to his chest and hunched his shoulders up to his neck, as if he hoped to just lift himself right up and away. He glanced back to the car, gauging the distance, and then turned once again to the line of yelping dogs.

They reached him in only seconds, and Jack closed his eyes, awaiting sharp teeth sinking into his legs. Instead, paws hit him in his middle, and instead of attacking, all of the dogs were leaping and yipping, tails wagging, tongues lolling. One dog began circling around as if chasing its own tail, seeming to forget Jack in its excitement.

"Okay, okay, yes. Hello," Jack said, scratching behind the ears of the most insistent dog, which had its front feet planted on his stomach. "Hello. Okay."

A sharp whistle cut the air, and the dogs all stopped and sat down in the gravel, ears perked up. The biggest dog was a gray thing with one blue eye and black spots all over its face, and it looked like it was listening to a lecture.

"Come," a voice called from the treeline, and the dogs were gone as quickly as they'd appeared. Jack could see the lower half of a man, his top obscured in shadow, about twenty yards from the house. Faded jeans and work boots.

"Hello. Sorry to intrude," Jack called out, staying where he was.

"Can we do something for you?" A high voice, reedy and clear.

"I just had some questions for a project I'm working on."

"Student or journalist?" Flat and even.

"Neither, actually. I teach in town, but I'm working on something around Arthur Boorman."

"We don't have a lot of time for poetry out here, sir. I'm going to have to ask you to go."

"How about movies? You have time to talk movies?" He might as well shoot his shot. If Speck ran him off, he had nothing.

The man was a pair of legs beneath the shadows of the trees, one knee slightly bent, the toe of his boot pointed out.

Jack pressed his luck. "I know you were all part of Boorman's movie, back in the 80s. I just have some questions and then I'll go. Right away."

"We renounced all that business a couple decades ago, sir. Don't have a thing to say about it."

The dogs crept from behind their hiding place near the house and laid down around the man's feet.

"I was hoping you might be able to clear some things up related to who did what? It wouldn't take much of your time."

The legs didn't move. "I'm sorry you came all the way out here. Have a good day."

"I bought Boorman's house," Jack said.

More silence.

"You familiar with the house?" Jack called out.

"I am."

"I think I might need your help, sir," Jack said.

"Buy a new house. That's about all I can think to tell you." The legs turned, making the dogs leap up, the animals running in circles around their master as he started toward the house.

"It took my wife," Jack called out. It sounded silly even to his own ears, but here he was, talking to the leader of a decades-running cult.

The man stopped.

"When?"

"Last night."

Somehow, only seeing his lower half, Jack could see the man's posture sag.

"I guess you better come inside, then," he said. He started on toward the house, the dogs lined up at his side, and Jack ran to catch up with them.

When he got to the porch steps, Jack could see that Jacob Speck was small and wiry. He wore a cream-colored western shirt with pearl snap buttons. Short sleeves revealed wiry arms covered in fine white hair, and the skin around his face seemed loose, as if he had recently lost a great deal of weight. His gray hair was cut close to his head, curling along the top. His face was long and smooth. He looked like a thousand other old timers from the area, nearly anonymous, but then Jack saw his eyes, which were small, with slanting lids and irises so pale as to seem white.

"I'm not sure what I can do for you. This isn't my thing. Understand?" Speck said.

Jack nodded.

"Okay. Come in and tell me your tale."

33.

Jack followed him into the house, too pleased with this minor success to even consider being frightened. The entryway was small and cramped, with a stairway leading upward and two doors leading further into the house. The one on the left led into a sitting room that Jack could see was almost bare, with just a semicircle of high-backed chairs arranged on the worn wooden floor. Leaded windows stretched around the room, curtainless and narrow, and the sun through the trees outside came in greenish and wobbly, as if the house was underwater.

Speck passed the stairs and went deeper into the house, and after a brief pause, considering for the first time the wisdom of this enterprise, Jack followed. The short hallway had narrow doors shut into ornately carved frames covered in so many layers of white glossy paint that the scrollwork and ornamental molding was rounded and soft. They stepped into an open, airy kitchen. It too was painted white, and the ancient linoleum, which was once white with blue cornflowers, was so stained and scarred and pitted that it looked like a relief map. The cabinets were a dark wood with some transparent yellow substance either coating them or seeping up out of the wood, frozen and hardened in streaks and droplets. It all gave Jack a sense of sepsis, of something in need of lancing.

A bare oval table stood in the center of the room, battered, with spindly wooden legs, and four mismatched kitchen chairs. Speck gestured Jack into a chair with copper tubing legs and a green cracked upholstery on the seat. Jack sat down carefully, holding his bundle to his chest.

Windows lined two walls of the kitchen, and out from under the trees here, the sun glared into the kitchen, almost erasing the view of the hills sloping down behind the house. Jack counted two more crude outbuildings. *What do they do out there?*

Speck sat down across from him, his legs stretched out, arm resting on the table. He looked like he was ready to shoot the shit. Like he should have a cheap beer in his hand.

"Tell me about the girl," he said.

"The woman. Avery. My wife. She's disappeared."

"Girls go missing all the time." Speck seemed to be looking at something on the wall up above the stove's vent hood. He spoke without affect, as casual as talking about the weather or the price of gas.

"She was in our house. Just last night." Jack sat forward, elbows on the table. "She left her things. She didn't run off."

"Didn't say anything about running off. Said girls go missing. She Indian? Lots of Indian girls go missing round here. The interstate ain't nothing but a river, and the girls get sent right down it. Grabbed off the street, out of their cars. Sometimes out of their homes. Get sent all over." He chewed the inside of his cheek.

"No one took her out of our home." Jack had to control his voice, modulate his tone, keep the panic at bay. "She went into the basement."

Speck's eyes focused on Jack's face, then returned to the spot on the wall.

"Lots of ways for a girl to get lost in this world. Takes real work to keep 'em from getting lost, really. Whole world wants to swallow 'em up."

"Can you just tell me what you know about the house? Maybe, Boorman?"

Speck gave a grimace that Jack took for a smile, revealing a set of long yellowed teeth.

"Art talked about a lot of things. Talked and talked. That house of yours brought him out here in the first place, too. Said it was 'haunted.'" Speck held up both hands, wiggling his fingers in mockery.

"And you didn't believe him."

The eyes flicked back to Jack, held him for a moment with their flat, affectless gaze. Then he looked away again.

"Lots of places are haunted. World's haunted. All the devils are here." He suddenly sat up, pulling his legs up under the chair and leaned onto the table. He flattened one hand and ran it across the top of the table.

"All the evil of the world, it leaves scars. Gouges and pock marks." He ran a thick thumbnail along a scratch in the wood. "Eats away at the world. Pretty soon—won't be long at all now—the things men do will eat right through the surface of the world. And then," he paused, looking hard at Jack, "it'll be like someone pulled a plug, and everything will slip right on down the drain."

"That's what you're waiting for out here?" Jack tried to keep his tone level.

"Why wait for winter when you know it's gonna come? No. That's not our business."

"Okay. But what about my house? Avery?"

"Well, some places, the things that are done leave a deep cut, and some of what's underneath seeps up, like bad water. Sometimes it's bad enough that it punches a hole right through on its own, and the whole place goes bad. This has happened many times. We have documentation of it happening in Saudi Arabia; Orange County, California; Lincoln; Salt Lake. Those places aren't just haunted. They're sick. Infected."

Jack waved most of this away with a hand. He wanted to know about the house on Calliope Street.

"And you think my house is one of these places?"

Speck made a sour face. "Didn't say any such thing. That happened in the valley, we'd all be done for. No, that house is something different." Speck pointed one finger down onto the surface of the table. "What happened there, all them years ago, with that girl, it was bad, but not *inordinately* bad. I know that sounds cold, but like I said, the world is hard on our sisters. A dangerous place. So while it's bad, certainly, it's not enough to create some kind of crack in the world. It just took a little divot out of the surface. Most common thing in the world. But then your friend and mine, Arthur Boorman, thinking he was smart, decided to do something about it. He felt the badness there, see. Couldn't take it. Couldn't sleep. Couldn't write. Took to self-medicating."

He mimed tipping a bottle to his lips. He was warmed up now—a man who liked to talk, to be listened to.

"And that's when he came to you?"

"Oh, no, this was a while before that. At first, he tried to heal it up, all on his own. Created little rituals and worked out a whole system of 'magic.'"

Speck leaned in further across the table, holding his left hand out flat, palm up. He pointed into the center of his palm.

"The evil left a mark, a wound. And then Art did his thing, said his words, and he closed it all up." He brought the fingers of his left hand into a fist. "Sealed it up pretty tight. But you know what you get when you don't let the wound breathe and heal? When you seal it up tight like that? It just festers and grows and turns sour, and eventually it either blows out—" he opened his fingers, presenting the invisible infection to Jack. "Or it kills ya."

"He came to you because his magic wasn't working?" Jack said, brows gathered tight between his eyes.

"To lance the boil, son. To cleanse the infection. To undo what he so foolishly had done on his own."

"How does *Blood Street* fit in?"

"Fit in? The movie was the work, son. The spell we spun together."

"Did it work?" Jack said, his voice little more than a whisper.

Speck brought his hands together and gave Jack a look so direct and so unnerving, that it made Jack realize the man's power.

"If it worked, I don't suppose you'd be sitting here with me right now, would you?"

Jack lifted his satchel onto his lap, threw back the flap. Fishing inside for a minute, he finally pulled out the script for *Red Witch* and tossed it onto the table. It slid over the pockmarked wood and came to rest against Speck's arm.

Speck glanced at it, leaned in, turned a couple of pages, face still unreadable.

"And you want me to do what?"

Jack smiled.

"I want you to help me make a movie."

"He came to you because his magic wasn't working?" Jack said, brows gathered tight between his eyes.

"To lure the best [illegible]. To cleanse the Inferno. To undo what he so foolishly had done on his own."

"How does [illegible] fit in?"

"[illegible] The movie was the [illegible]. The [illegible] we spent together."

"Did it work?" Jack said, his voice little more than a whisper.

Speck brought his hands together and gave Jack a [illegible] made Jack [illegible] power.

"If it worked, I don't suppose you'd be sitting here with me at [illegible] now, would you?"

Jack lifted [illegible] flap. [illegible] finally pulled out the script for Red Witch and tossed it onto the table. It slid over the pocked wood and came to rest again [illegible] Speck's [illegible].

Speck glanced at it, leafed through a couple of pages. It was still unreadable.

[illegible]

Speck [illegible].

"I want you to help me make a movie."

Part II

In the Locust Tree

1.

Avery stumbled through the half-dark. Dry, stiff grass scraped her legs and pulled at her shirt. The light was sourceless, gray and insubstantial, only present enough to pick out layers of shadow. She looked back the way she had come and saw the slope of the hillside above disappearing into a fine mist. How far had she walked already, and in which direction? She remembered some rule about being lost in the wilderness: stay still and wait for someone to find you.

But no one was coming for her here.

The slate gray sky loomed, changeless, offering no sense of time or direction, though she sensed somehow that she was high up, that the land dropped down around her. She wore only an oversized black T-shirt; her feet and legs were bare.

The grass seemed to waver like heat, and a deer stepped out of the mist and stood before her, staring with its depthless black eyes. A mother. Avery knew this animal, who had stood sentinel in her yard for a week, following the births of the broken fawns.

The deer twitched. A shiver moved down its haunches, and then it turned and trotted several yards down the slope before stopping and looking back. One ear flicked in a clear sign of impatience, and Avery stepped forward, bare feet crackling on the dead grass. Turning away, the deer cut a narrow, winding trail through the brush, Avery following close behind. Maybe someone had come after all.

They walked together for some time, the deer sometimes trotting ahead in little bursts, but then slowing again, always looking back to be sure Avery was there. Its hooves made no sound on the dry ground.

Some minutes down the slope, Avery could make out the valley spread out below, dark and still, but also familiar, if only in its shape. No buildings or structures of any kind, just the river cutting the valley reflecting back the unseen light like quicksilver.

She had no way of measuring time, but it felt as if some hours had passed by the time they reached the river's steep bank. The water flowed on noiselessly, and the deer picked her way down into the shallows and dipped her head to drink. The bridge leading into downtown should be there, further down, which meant she was closer to Higgins than Orange Street, and Calliope Street was roughly that way.

"Shall we?" she said to the deer, the first words she'd spoken in this dark land. Her voice rang out, too loud, too harsh. The deer's ears twitched as it raised its head to look at her. It stepped out of the water on delicate, spindly legs, climbing the bank with no effort. It paused beside Avery for just a moment, looking at her with black-rimmed eyes, and then trotted out, away from the bank.

"I guess we shall," Avery said to herself.

The whole valley was parched grass, chest-high and pale, absolutely still, unmoved by any breeze. Avery thought how unnatural that was. The town she knew was canopied by thousands of trees; even the valley before westward expansion, before the gold booms and lumber camps, would have been nothing like this arid plane. No, this was a *made* place, deliberately emptied.

The deer cut a path and Avery trailed close behind.

When the deer froze in place, the silence seemed to deepen. Avery's own senses, also on high alert, scanned the surrounding area. Only dead meadows and fog. But the short hairs on the back of her neck bristled, and she felt her chest flush. Something was nearby.

A rustling sound made her spin, and the deer jerked its head around. Something low to the ground, maybe a mountain lion?

"Let's go," she said, and now she was the one leading the doe onward. She walked swiftly, though her legs were itchy and red, her feet sore, and her pulse beating hard in her neck. The deer trotted beside her, its ears constantly turning and twitching.

With no landmarks, it was difficult to gauge just where she was, but she sensed their destination: the house on Calliope Street.

Finally, off to her left, Avery saw a break in the endless grass: an irregular shadow in the center of the field. They changed their course and moved toward it. It took a while to realize the size of the thing, shrunken by distance as it was, but soon she could make out the boxy shape, the slant of a roof, the crown of a large tree.

It was Avery's house. Of course it was, but standing beside it, the large tree, unlike any tree in their yard—in that other yard, the one in the brightly colored, living reality Avery had left behind. The tree's crown reached high above the house's rooftop and was the only sign of color in the whole world, as far as Avery could see. A full tree with big clusters of fern-like leaves. Beautiful.

The house was unchanged. It was their house, though Calliope Street was no more. The weeds grew right up against the house, half-hiding the concrete steps leading to the kitchen. For a moment, Avery was overcome by the certainty that the door would open and Jack would be standing in the doorway, welcoming her home, shaking her gently in their bed, telling her she was crying out in her sleep.

No. The door stayed stubbornly closed.

Avery moved through what should be the deep shade of the yard but was only grass, open to the blank sky. It made the house loom larger, creating a kind of vertigo.

The deer turned around twice and then folded its legs underneath it. It settled down beneath the tree, head still raised and ears alert.

She climbed the steps and cupped her hands to the window in the door's upper half, but saw only the gauzy curtain and darkness. To knock or not to knock?

"Mine," she said, turning the knob and pushing the door open.

Inside, the house was quiet and empty. The living room was bare of furniture, and what little half-light seeped through the windows deepened the shadows to the color of a fresh bruise. She brushed her hand along the wall, found the switch where her memory left it, and flipped the plastic tab up.

Nothing.

The kitchen was empty as well, except for a single water glass resting upside down beside the sink.

Beyond the kitchen, where there ought to have been a dining room, a beaded curtain hung over the opening of a double doorway. Avery pushed the beads aside and peeked through their plastic-jeweled strands. Empty. No furniture. Not even the dark stain on the floor.

She looked out the back window, saw the unmoving hills stretch off and away into the immobile sky. If there was anything in this house, it could be in only one place.

She crossed the kitchen, grasped the door handle, and opened the door to the basement. The stairs she knew all too well led downward and turned out of sight, but she thought there was light below, the first light she'd seen yet in this gray, washed out world. Slowly, she crept downward, stopping at the turning.

She paused, looking down, waiting, listening. That faint light dappled the concrete floor, yellow and warm, and a soft humming seemed to come from deeper inside the basement room.

Descending further, she wished for the kitchen knife she'd had the last time she'd made this descent. Was that last night? Days ago? There was no way to know. At her spot halfway down the stairs, she knelt, peering down into the basement. The same framed walls jutted out into the open space, with dusty plastic sheeting blocking her view, but the light at the far end was on. Something was there: a shadowed shape, perhaps guarding the hole in the wall, keeping her from making her escape.

The concrete floor was cold on her bare feet, and for the first time she realized how exposed she was. Tugging at the bottom of her sleep shirt, she moved slowly into the room, following the loose path of the half-formed labyrinth. As still as the air was, the basement seemed to breathe slowly, its respiration gently rattling the plastic sheets, subtly ballooning them in and out. Under it all was a near-imperceptible humming sound, almost like music.

She stood behind one golden-lit panel and then stepped out into the open.

The single bulb illuminated that half of the basement. Sitting almost directly beneath it was a man, his back to her, a small card table before his folding metal chair. His hands lay flat on the table's plastic surface. The top of his head was balding, with thick strands of dark hair combed sideways in a failed attempt to hide the fact of his shiny scalp. Dark wisps curled around his ears. He was big, maybe a little more than Avery's size, though it was hard to tell. Her first thought was to rush him, to restrain him, maybe to beat him until he told her what was going on, but she quickly dismissed that impulse. He might be her only anchor here. Better to learn what she could and try to find a way out.

Beyond him, the wall stood bare of its naked women, with just a dime-sized hole.

She stepped out into the light, standing maybe three feet behind him, and she spoke.

"Hello?" Her voice crackled in the space, and the man's humming ceased.

He turned his head slightly, looking over his shoulder.

"Hello." The man raised a hand and gestured to the other folding chair across the table. She sidled around the table, doing her best to keep out of the man's reach, just in case. She could be polite, if that's what he wanted, but she wasn't stupid.

She pulled the chair out, its metal legs scraping loudly across the concrete, and sat down. The stranger was probably in his seventies, his white mustache stained with nicotine, his eyes sunken and shadowed behind his big blocky glasses. He was heavy, his face puffy and red and seemed to sprout from a full, wild beard that was streaked with white. He wore a white dress shirt with the sleeves rolled to his elbows and the first two buttons open. Avery could see the cigarettes in his breast pocket.

The man smiled, and she wished he hadn't. It wasn't just his curved, brown-tinted teeth, made too long by his shrunken gums. It was the falseness of his expression, as rigid as a mask. He squinted his eyes and pulled his face into a shape approximating pleasure, but Avery could see that it was a puppet show.

"I'm so glad you made it," the man said, letting his face fall slack again.

"Expecting me?" Avery said. Her pulse beat in her neck, a heavy beat that accompanied the machinery sound.

"Oh, yes, for such a long time. I built all of this for you, after all."

It was his calm that triggered the alarm inside her skull, his easy insistence, his offhand familiarity. She clenched her fists beneath the table, imagined flipping it toward him, tackling him at his middle.

"You know me, but I don't know you at all."

He nodded and nodded, too long, as if he'd gotten stuck in a loop, his head rocking back and forth on his neck.

"Yes. Yes. That's true. Yes." He twisted his face back up into that mask of a smile. "I'm Arthur Boorman. And I'm your biggest fan."

2.

Arthur Boorman lifted one hand from the table's surface, leaving the other flat and splay-fingered, and pulled the pack of cigarettes from his pocket. He shook one partway out and clamped it between his teeth, then offered the pack to Avery, who shook her head. Returning the pack to his shirt, he dug in his pants pocket and extracted a silver lighter, flipped it open, and lit his cigarette. He inhaled deeply and held in the smoke as he placed the lighter carefully on the table before him. He looked back at Avery, tilted his face toward the light, and let the smoke out in a long, noxious jet. He kept his head cocked at that angle, chin up, looking at her sideways.

"Do you like the house?" He wasn't smiling. A thin curl of smoke rose from the cigarette between his fingers. This was a test, she knew—every conversation with her father. And here, stranded in this washed out place, it was a test she had to pass. She knew this with the certainty of a dream.

"That's why we bought it." Her hands were shaking under the table.

"I wanted you to help fill it up." He tapped out his ash onto the concrete floor and tucked the cigarette back between his lips, his chin still up, head turned sideways, eyes boring into her.

"That's very sweet of you." She found herself nodding at her own words.

"Arthur."

"What's that?"

"'That's very sweet of you, *Arthur*.'" Smoke rose up around his face like a caul. "Say it."

She was frightened, and she didn't like to be frightened. Angry was better, but she couldn't quite get that spark to ignite.

"My name."

"Arthur?" she said, soft, almost a whisper. Her first failure.

His body broke from its rictus, and his face was transformed by a real smile this time, not a mask. With a childlike expression, he leaned forward, forearms on the table, shoulders up around his ears. What was left of the cigarette poked from the corner of his mouth, smouldered to nothing.

"I've waited so long to hear you say my name," he said in one breath. "A lifetime."

Avery pushed back in her chair to distance herself from Boorman's intensity. He was crazed and terrifying, and it was all directed toward her. Even sensing escape was hopeless, she could keep out of his reach, out of the grasp of those big hands.

As Boorman noticed her reaction, his face changed and fell in on itself. He pulled himself back and up, took one last drag from his cigarette, and ground it out with his shoe, all while keeping his eyes on Avery.

"It's alright," he said, forcing a smile, as if he were trying to convince them both. "I forget that this is all new to you. But you'll understand, too. Soon." He placed his hands on the table again.

"What am I going to understand, Arthur?" She watched his eyes flash at her use of his name again.

"The truth, I guess." He made a sour face. "How this whole world is all for you."

"Arthur." She leaned forward, trying to control her voice. "We don't know each other. There's no reason you should have done anything. Not for me."

She was afraid of provoking him; maybe her attempts to break his fantasy open would lead him to rage, to attack, but he just smiled. The corners of his mouth turned down beneath the untrimmed mustache. He shook his head gently. He looked like a wise father, amused at his child's folly.

"I know you," he said, and he gestured toward the wall at her back.

She turned in her chair, looking behind her. The hole looked back at her with a pinprick pupil. She glanced back at Boorman, who pointed her forward with his chin.

"Go on," he whispered.

Avery rose from her chair, not straightening but moving hunched, keeping her eye level with the hole in the wall. It was only a few feet away. She reached out for the wall, fingers tented against the rough cement, and put her eye up to the hole. As she did it, she realized that she was doing exactly what a victim in a horror movie would do. But she wasn't concerned about a blade being shoved through into her skull. This was something else entirely.

At first it was just ordinary dark, but then her eyes adjusted. She could just make out a red light, somewhere deeper back inside the wall. *I've had this dream.* The red light seemed to spread or get closer—it was impossible to tell which—and the shadows flickered against the walls of a room that Avery recognized.

A woman moved through her kitchen—Avery's kitchen—swaying to unheard music, pulling a big kitchen knife from the block to slice a lime, dropping the wedge into her glass, and then gliding across the kitchen and through the beaded curtain. The perspective shifted as Avery watched, and then it was Avery in the living room, the kitchen a splash of warm light up ahead, two gloved hands stretched out before her.

House on Blood Street. She knew the sequence: she and Jack had made fun of it together.

She pulled her eye away from the hole and looked over her shoulder at Boorman.

"Go on," he giggled with delight, shooing her back to the wall with both hands.

She looked back. The knife was already in one of the killer's gloved hands, and the other was pushing aside the curtain. The woman, one breast hanging out of her silk robe, looked directly into Avery's eye as she screamed a full-throated horror movie scream. Her mouth was so wide that Avery pulled away to keep from being swallowed. She could feel her pulse in her neck, and she concentrated on her breathing before she turned around to face Boorman.

"What the fuck is that?" she said, hands balled into fists.

"It's your story. I made it just for you. All of this."

She stepped forward and grasped the back of her folding chair.

"This has nothing to do with me, *Arthur.*" She spat his name at him. "This is fucked up. Did you think I would be impressed?"

He was still inordinately pleased with himself. He said, "You still don't understand what I've done. You're upset. That's reasonable. It will just take time."

"I don't have time. I need to get back. Now."

His smile went sad. "Oh, Becca, there's no going back. This is all there is now."

Avery leaned in over the chair, not even caring anymore that she was talking through clenched teeth. She could see flecks of her own spittle catching the light of the single bulb.

"Who the fuck is Becca?"

He sank lower into his seat.

"I know it's a lot."

When he stood up Avery finally registered how big he really was, easily six-three and over two hundred pounds. He came around the table, hands out like he was corralling an animal that planned to startle and run. *That's me,* she thought. *That's fair.* Before she could duck around him, he placed one hand on her shoulder. His touch was light, as if to reassure her.

"I'm Arthur Boorman." He touched his breast pocket with his other hand. Then he pointed a thick finger at Avery's chest. "And you're Becca Mays."

3.

He led her back upstairs, his broad back filling up the narrow, twisting stairwell. She forced herself forward, one step at a time, telling herself she had no choice. In the kitchen, the single water glass sat upside down beside the sink. Boorman filled the cup with cold water, and passed it to her. The glass was cold against her palm. She drank all at once, her thirst almost overwhelming.

Handing the glass back to Boorman, she went to the back door, pushed aside the little curtain, and looked out. There was nothing, still. Just that same dry grass stretching out and away into eternity. She thought of the deer who had led her here. Was it still lying in the shadow of the tree? She needed to get out, but where to? Outside was nowhere. And Arthur was too close, his breath stale, his smile a falsely friendly rictus.

No. If she was going to get out of here, it would be by the same way she got in.

"I need to get home, Arthur. Back to my life."

He smiled his sad smile. "It's not there anymore. I'm sorry. A lot has changed. It's just going to—"

"Take time. Yeah, got it."

She darted past him, through the house, to the front door, swinging it open so hard that it crashed against the wall, rattling the window glass. She stepped out onto the little rectangle of porch. Night seemed to have fallen in the time it took her to cross the wooden floor, and now the dark was inky black, as if she might reach out and touch it. Two golden disks reflected back at her. It was the deer's eyes. She was still out there, waiting. This gave Avery comfort, and she wanted to run down the steps and go to it, curl up together beneath the wide branches.

But she was afraid. If she stepped off the steps into the dark, there would be nothing there—she would fall through open space, becoming untethered from even this strange and ghostlike world that was both dream-familiar and completely alien.

Instead, she turned back to the house.

Boorman called to her from the archway between the kitchen and the living room. "Come inside. We can talk this through."

She thought once again of charging at Boorman, tackling him to the ground, and pounding his face into ground beef. He was already dead, right? What could it hurt? At least she'd remove that self-satisfied look.

But this was Arthur Boorman's world, and like it or not, it obeyed Arthur Boorman's rules. She'd play his game, and she'd win. She closed the door gently, hearing the slight click as it latched shut.

4.

"I'll sleep upstairs tonight," she told Arthur, and he looked suddenly worried or confused, but nodded and led her up the stairs. There was no way she was sleeping behind the beaded curtain, in the murder room, in what should have been their dining room. Boorman didn't argue, just of-coursed and right-this-wayed at her, smiling all the while. He seemed as easygoing as could be, just happy that she was there, like he'd been waiting for her arrival his whole life. Maybe he had.

She didn't ask where he was sleeping; she was afraid to broach the subject. The unanswered question was *why* he had done all this. What did he want from her? She thought of the basement shrine, all those shiny faces and exposed breasts radiating out from the hole in the wall. That was the circle he'd built to capture her. Well, not *her*, but Becca Mays, a decades-dead B-movie actress who had snagged on some jagged edge of the poet's mind. Of course it was a sex thing. What else could it be? A desperate, obsessive man had poured himself into this house; his desire transformed it into a giant trap, an oubliette that only Arthur Boorman would ever remember. But how? This dark magic had to be more than the titty shrine and wishing real hard.

Boorman had to hunch under the low ceiling at the top of the stairs. Avery looked from one end of the loft to the other. Still, the blank dark sky outside. The long, low room was empty, but all the same, she gravitated toward the space where they had set up Dylan's bed, back in that other house, in her other life.

"Blankets," Boorman said, like he'd just conjured the answer to a particularly difficult riddle. "Be right back."

He stomped down the twisting stairway, leaving her alone. The area where Dylan's bed ought to have been was darker than the rest of the room, away from the light from the stairwell. She glanced back. Since when was there a light? She hadn't noticed it before. They'd been practically swimming through the strange dusky gloom since she'd arrived alongside the deer.

This light cast angular shadows across the ceiling, walls, and floor; where the wall extended out to make way for the staircase, it made a triangle of absolute dark where the angles of the walls and floor converged. Avery looked into that corner, eyes narrowed, head cocked to one side, and found herself listening, as if it was transmitting some weird frequency.

The sound of Boorman coming up the stairs snapped her back to the moment, and then his frame filled the doorway, blocking out the light below. He smiled above the stack of blankets, a pillow on top, and held them out to her. She took them clumsily, feeling his cold hands brush her forearms as she tried to pull away.

"We'll get you all set up in the morning," he said.

Avery had no idea what that meant, but she nodded. For the first time she wondered if Boorman was her captor here, or if he wasn't another prisoner, like herself. Jailer or prisoner, he had been worn down by this place.

"You're very kind," she said, wanting to offer him something.

"If you need anything, I'll be downstairs." And he was gone.

Downstairs or *down*-downstairs? Did Arthur Boorman live in that basement? Would he still call it his home, now that Avery was here? She was too tired to think about it. Dropping the bedding onto the floor, she peered again out of the little window, which should have looked out onto the street. All she could discern was flat gray gloom and the looming shadow of the tree. She wondered if the deer was still beneath it, and she hoped so. Once, she'd felt frightened by the deer who came to the yard, all those watching eyes, but now the animals seemed the only tie back to her real life. A guardian. She wondered if it knew how hard she had tried to save those babies, those long-legged, tiny, broken things.

She spread out the comforter on the floor, and then the sheet over it. It didn't feel warm or cold in the room, but she climbed under the sheet anyway, feeling for all the world like she was at some child's sleepover. What was Arthur Boorman if not a child? A large, deluded child?

No. He was a man, or the memory of a man, and that made him dangerous. She couldn't let his moony gentleness distract from that fact. What did he want with her, exactly? Whatever it was, Avery would try to be ready, and she'd take his goddamned eyes if he laid hands on her.

The light was still on in the stairwell, and that was a small comfort. She rolled onto her side, wishing that Jack was curled up beside her, one arm flung over her side. As she began to drift into sleep, she kept watching the deep shadows in that odd triangle of dark and listening to the noise from within that darkness, high and pleading. At first she thought it was a baby, but then she recognized it: a cat's plaintive cries.

She rose up on her elbow, straining her sight. The sound grew louder, closer, and she crawled forward, then left the white sheet to put her knees on the rough carpet, moving toward the sound. She stopped before she reached the wall, unsure that it would be there. What might this house birth here, in this gray land? Would she see stunted, stillborn cats, or two-headed kittens with too many legs? Suddenly, she felt sure that the space just beyond the triangle was infinite, a narrow well that she would fall through forever.

The cat walked slowly out of the dark, winding around Avery's arm, butting its head against her. It gave one piercing cry and then started to purr, low and rattly.

Avery sat back on her feet and pulled the cat close. She ran her hands over its sleek fur and scratched behind its ears. It had a bobbed tail, and its left ear was a tattered mess. When she cupped its head in her hand and lifted its face toward her, she saw that it was missing its left eye, a pink mass of scar tissue surrounding the socket.

"Cash?" she whispered. "Oh, Cash."

She buried her face in her lost cat's fur, crying into it. Then, she carried him over to her little nest of blankets, feeling the low vibration of his chest against her own and the fierce warmth of his compact little body.

5.

Morning came, though with no discernable change of the light. Avery woke to find Cash curled up in the hollow made by her bent knees. He was warm and heavy, and something about the solid weight of him made her cry. She reached down and ran her fingers over the cat's back, Cash giving a little chirp and shake but continuing to sleep. Cash was no dream. He had really come back to her. But that meant that the rest of it was real, too—real as it could be in this nightmare world.

She felt around on the floor, remembered she didn't have her phone. Didn't have anything. Her meds. She didn't have her meds.

Clattering came from below. Boorman. More than this place, he was the biggest question mark. What did he want from her? He'd let her be, at least. But here they had all the time in the world.

Crawling out from under the sheet, careful not to disturb Cash, she approached the triangle of shadow that had produced the cat. She ran her fingers along the wall, its texture nubbly and cold. She knocked softly. Solid enough. Too solid.

She stood, careful not to knock her head on the slanting ceiling, and pulled at the bottom of her oversized T-shirt. Here, it was the only item of clothing she owned and barely reached mid-thigh, leaving her feeling exposed. She smelled bacon—how long had it been since she'd last eaten? Her stomach gurgled at the scent.

Tempted by her hunger, she descended into the kitchen. *More light*, she thought, looking at the recessed fixtures in the ceiling and the chrome curve of track lights above the island where Boorman stood, dicing peppers and onion. He looked up, saw her, and she watched his face go from slack into that rictus grin, as if wires had been pulled at the back of his skull.

"Morning," he said. "You sleep okay?"

"Fine," Avery said, standing at the foot of the stairs.

"Well, there are clean towels in the bathroom and some clothes." He lifted the cutting board and turned to the stove, pushing the vegetables into the skillet with a dramatic sizzle. "Breakfast will be ready soon."

Avery barely recognized the bathroom. It was all tile, shockingly clean—not at all like the dingy bathroom they had in her real life. A white towel sat folded on the sink's edge. A dress with tiny white flowers hung on the back of the door. She thought, *here's where things get super creepy. He's picking out my clothes*. But, she had to admit, it was kind of cute. Not exactly her style, but cute. She locked the door, rattled the handle to test it, and ran the shower.

In their house—the real house—the shower had sputtered and dripped, with little pressure. Neither of them wanted to think about plumbing issues, so they'd ignored it and made up for the lack of pressure with extreme heat. But here, the shower head was wide and chrome, sending jets of steaming water against the floor of the tub.

She pulled off her nightshirt and dropped it to the tiles, stepped into the shower, and pulled the curtain shut behind her.

It was heaven. The hot water stung the scrapes on her feet and shins, but even that felt good and necessary. She let the stream pound against the top of her head, eyes closed, thinking only vaguely of Boorman entering, Norman Bates-like, to draw back the curtain and attack.

Stepping out, the tiny room was filled with steam. Her real bathroom fan had gone out the week they moved in, and repairing it was one item on a long list of items. But now, Avery looked up at the aluminum grating in the ceiling. Fixed. The switch produced a soft hum, making the humidity vanish like magic.

She dried and wiped the mirror, looking at herself. Like a drowned rat, her grandmother would have said. She brushed her teeth with her finger, rinsing with hot water, and then turned to the dress. Okay.

She slipped it over her head and looked in the mirror on the back of the door. She turned to the side, seeing just how obvious her bulge was. Not too bad. She'd kill for a pair of goddamned underwear, but the dress came down just below her knees, with loose sleeves and a delightfully modest neckline. It kind of looked like something her sister would have worn to church at about ten years old. Better than what she showed up in by a long shot. She scooped up her T-shirt and went back to face Boorman and their breakfast.

Boorman looked up from the plates he was arranging, and his face transformed. He was a pilgrim before the sacred stone, rapt, mind erased of all care. He looked at her in awe.

"You look…" he began, but then looked down, cut a piece of toast into triangles.

"Thank you for the dress, Arthur." She looked to the back door, saw dull fog pressing against the windows. Or maybe it was just empty space, the world not yet sketched in. She realized she was still saying his name, as if to please him. Inside, she rebelled at the thought. She'd play along right up until she could make a better plan. How long might that be? She pushed the question away.

"I need my things. My real things. I need to go back." She kept her voice level.

Boorman set a plate on her side of the island, went out of the room, and came back at once, carrying a heavy wooden barstool. He set it down, gestured for her to sit, and went around to his own food.

"Where'd this come from?" Avery said, looking at the stool.

Boorman pushed a forkful of hashbrowns into his mouth and chewed hard, looking off to the side. "All kinds of things in here, if you know where to look. I can get you just about anything you like." He swallowed like it pained him.

Avery looked at her own plate, felt her stomach clench and gurgle. She plucked up a piece of bacon and folded it into her mouth. It was glorious. Sitting down on the stool, she picked up her fork and started eating.

Arthur Boorman watched her eat, one corner of his mouth bent up.

Clearly, this was everything he'd ever wanted.

6.

After breakfast, they cleaned up the mess together, working silently. So many contradictions She was a guest (prisoner) and this was her own kitchen. Everything familiar was made strange, and Borman himself was both her adversary and a calm and steady presence. Avery put the carton of eggs into the refrigerator, which was nearly full: fruit, vegetables, at least three different kinds of cheese, milk, juice, and a bottle of white wine. Had the house provided this as well? And how did that work? Could she ask the house for things, too, or was this strictly Boorman's party? She'd like to order up a baseball bat and a pair of hiking boots, please. And some fucking underwear.

Cash rubbed his length against her ankle and wandered through the kitchen, nose up, sniffing the air, undoubtedly trying to locate the bacon. Her cat had always been a scavenger of the worst kind. You couldn't leave anything out, or you'd find bites missing.

She scooped him up, cradling him like a baby; Cash tolerated it, looking up at the ceiling in that way that cats do.

When Boorman noticed the cat, he took an involuntary step backward, one hand out in a gesture that read *keep back*, eyes round and bulging. Avery clutched the cat to her chest.

"What is it?" she said.

"Where did that come from?" he said, getting himself under control by picking up the dish towel and squeezing it with both hands.

"This is Cash," Avery said, rocking the cat back and forth in her arms. "He's kind of a grumpy old man." She smiled at Boorman the way you would at a small child, to show everything was okay.

It didn't work.

Boorman stomped around the kitchen, putting the island between them, then pointed to the back door, as if Cash might carry some horrid disease. "Put it out."

"Arthur, settle down."

"Now!" The roar came from deep down in him, and Avery thought he might break the blood vessels in his eyes, the way his face contorted. The cords in his neck stood out.

It was that masculine rage that sent her moving, and she hated herself for it, the way it pushed those buttons, made her ten years old again.

She passed Boorman, out onto the little stoop.

The dry grass that grew right up to the two concrete steps stretched away from the house, into the distance where it was finally eaten up in a distant fog. There was nothing else to see. She looked up over her shoulder at the full, dark branches of the tree, the only other solid thing here.

"I'm sorry, boy," she said, rubbing her chin against the top of Cash's head. "I don't think it's safe for you here." Which was almost certainly true. And Cash was a wiley one, only ever coming home for short bursts anyway.

She kissed his one mangled ear, trying to accept her own rationalizations, and then let him down onto the porch. He rubbed against her leg once and then went down the steps, disappearing immediately into the high grass. Avery watched the blades rustle and then Cash was gone. Again.

His absence turned her cringing fear into anger, and she let that anger drive her forward, riding it like a wave.

"What the fuck was that?" she said, slamming the door shut.

Boorman was sitting on the stool, dishrag still in his hands, chin against his chest. He seemed suddenly very small. It took some of the wind from Avery's sails, but she held onto her anger. If bullying Arthur Boorman would get her out of here, she was fine with that.

"Look at me," she said, standing before him, using her dad's favorite trick. "Arthur, look at me."

The pale, bald head bobbed, and tears were running down his cheeks, snot bubbling at his nose.

He looked like a child waiting to be punished. Or hurt.

Goddammit, she thought. *I wish I were better at this.*

"I'm sorry," he stuttered through his tears, chest hitching. "It doesn't belong."

He wrapped his arms around his middle, sobbing.

Avery took a step back. She didn't like big emotions, especially not from others. It made her uncomfortable, and she didn't know how to respond. A grown man, crying like his life had been destroyed by the existence of a cat?

But it wasn't his life, was it? She was looking at—what? A ghost? Arthur Boorman's spirit, trapped within his own obsessive thoughts, a world he created? Isn't that what a ghost was supposed to be: the spirit that wouldn't move on? Boorman had built his whole life around the life and death of a woman he might not have even known. For all Avery knew, all of Arthur's days and nights in that basement, obsessing about Becca Mays, had built this place, beam by beam and room by room. A trap he built and then fell inside of.

But now she was here, too. Another ghost, walking through her own house—for what? Forever? No. She refused to accept it. She was real. She was the thing that didn't belong.

She turned her back on Boorman, stepped back onto the porch, and called out for Cash. This, in itself, was foolish. No cat ever answered to its name, but she did it anyway.

Nothing.

She stepped down the steps and into the desolate field, feeling the familiar scratch and tickle against her legs. The grass was high enough to brush the hem of her dress.

"Cash!" she called again, looking out over the endless stretch of field. She pushed on—hard to say how far in that unchanging waste. Looking back, the house seemed very far away, shadowed by that massive tree, like a toy she might pick up in her hands. This was no place to wander. She whistled for Cash all the while. To her surprise, he was watching her from the porch in the inimitable way of cats: sitting up, front paws placed square before him, like a bulldog.

"You asshole," she said, scooping him up in her arms and burying her nose in his fur. "Why are you like this?"

Pushing the door open with her hip, she came into the kitchen. Boorman had almost collected himself, sniffling and hiccuping, eyes red and puffy. He looked back and forth between Cash and Avery's faces, unsure what to say. Things had gotten so far out of his control.

"Arthur, look at me." And there it was again, her father's voice and tone. "We need to talk. I have no idea what this place is, what you've done to it, to me. Maybe I'm dead and this is hell. I honestly don't care. The important thing is that we're here—you and me. And if this is going to work, even in the very short term, we're going to need to get some things straight."

As she watched Boorman try to pull himself into something like an adult shape, she realized she knew nothing about him. Extreme emotions like his were frightening: she never knew which way they'd go. Would he try to hurt her? Would she be able to stop him if she tried?

"Arthur." She lowered her voice, made it softer, and Cash leaped from her arms down to the floor, where he wandered back through the bead curtain.

Boorman wiped his forearm across his mouth.

"Here's what we need to set straight. You made this place, and somehow you brought me here. Fine. But you seem to be misunderstanding a very important detail."

She leaned in, exactly like she was in some stupid TV show, playing bad cop. She hissed into his ear.

"This is *my* house."

7.

After their brief tete-a-tete, they went their separate ways. Boorman spent much of the day down in his basement, leaving Avery alone upstairs. She paced, pushing through the beaded curtain as she went in and out and in and out of the square little room where Becca Mays was killed. That murder had somehow set all of this into motion. In this version of Avery's house, there was no bloodstain, no careful circle chalked into the floor. The omission troubled her. It was one of many small signs that told her that this both was and was not their house on Calliope Street. The lack of Calliope Street as she knew it, was another.

She thought of *House on Blood Street*, and the way the exterior of the house was eerily familiar, but the inside was clearly some other house—bigger. Everyday movie magic turned the house she knew into a nightmare. Arthur Boorman had built a set on the back lot of the great beyond. Or something. Either way, the little incongruencies nagged at her, even the improvements.

She knew full well that half of her and Jack's to-do list would go untouched, probably forever, and that was fine. Their living space was imperfect because *life* was imperfect. And she was fine with that.

But Arthur's version of their life was something else entirely.

She pressed her hands against the oddly warm glass of the window and looked out at the endless field. When she'd come, there had been a river, something to give direction and shape to the valley. She'd seen mountains and sloping hillsides. Now it was just barren flatland, like emo Nebraska or something.

She remembered the deer who'd brought her here and spun on her heel again. Was it still there? Could it lead her back?

She hurried through the house to the front door, which swung open, crashing against the wall. She came down off the porch, the half-light casting shadows beneath the big tree.

Not seeing the deer, she walked around the tree's base, beating down the high grass in a search that lapsed into frustration. Nothing. What did she expect, that it would just stay there forever? Shielding her eyes from the no-real-light, she scanned the distance, looking for any sign of the deer's slender neck above the grass. Where could it go when nowhere else existed?

She turned and looked up into the tree's branches. The lowest branches were well above her head, but not out of reach. She jumped up, grasping a branch, and braced against the side of the trunk with her bare feet. The feel of the bark against her soles sent her back to childhood, when she would climb the pine in front of her family's house, way up until the branches thinned. Why hadn't she climbed a tree in the last decades? What had she been doing with herself?

The branches were close together, so she had to snake her way up and around in order to sit on the lowest branch. But she managed it. She liked it there, sheltered away from the house that wasn't her house. But it wouldn't be easy to climb higher.

She reached up, grasping a thin branch and jerked her hand back. The pain drove her to put the wound straight to her mouth, and she tasted blood. Looking at it, there was a blue puncture in the meat of her palm, deep, with blood welling up. She sucked at her skin and looked into the branches above.

Finger-length thorns jutted from the branches in tight clusters; the more she looked, the more clusters she saw, the whole length up. What kind of tree has thorns, anyway?

But as her eyes adjusted, she saw something else above: a human silhouette tangled in the branches, limbs stretched out, caught up in the thorns.

Her first thought was of Dylan, despite the impossibility of it, and her mother's heart seized up for the briefest moment. No, it was too big to be Dylan, with a tangle of long dark hair. Carefully, she picked her way upward, not grasping the thorns but still feeling them claw at her thighs and upper arms. There was no place to rest, so she continued to climb.

When she got closer, the shape came into focus.

She looked up into her own face, eyes fixed and staring, tongue swollen and pushing out between her teeth. Her own body was set in the crook of two branches, arms and legs pierced with long thorns that immobilized her. Blood turned black bloomed from the fabric of the dress with the little white flowers.

Avery almost fell out of the tree, her breath slipping out of her, her vision evaporating with panic. A drop from here and she'd slice herself all the way down, break her neck at the bottom. Would it matter? She breathed in deeply through her nose to calm her racing pulse. Her own left eye in the bloated face above her seemed to pin her in place. She clutched the branch and forced her gaze away from the uncanny reflection. She had to look down at her own body to see that it was still there. Identical circles of blood bloomed from her dress. Her breath stuttered out of her, ragged and wet. They were mirrors, this corpse and herself, but which was the reflection? She squeezed her eyes shut and tried to steady herself.

Something had made this happen. Maybe Boorman was more dangerous than he seemed.

Or maybe something else was at work in these gray lands.

She picked her way carefully back down, dropping the last several feet into the grass, landing clumsily but getting swiftly on her feet again. She scanned the fields around her. She hadn't even had a chance to look out from up above; too caught up in her double's broken body, its pierced flesh, its staring eye.

But she knew anyway, even without looking, that there was nowhere to go but back to the house.

8.

She would not go straight back—instead, she made a slow circuit around the house and the tree, delaying the inevitable. She had to do *something.* She would not be the passive object of Arthur Boorman's obsession. If she was going to stop this, she would have to undo the making of this world. Erase it all, starting with Becca Mays.

She imagined the house alight, fire blazing out of its windows and then spreading out across the dry grass. The whole world would burn, and where might she find shelter? The river had vanished into the black-and-white landscape, and her four-legged guide was gone. She sensed her own isolation as acutely as the scent of wildfire smoke. Here, the only witnesses were Arthur Boorman, Cash, and her double's corpse, mounted in the high branches like a butterfly in a collector's box.

She needed a real plan.

Inside, she made a sandwich and ate it over the sink. Cash brushed against her leg, and she scooped him up. He placed one paw on her chin, as if holding her back, claws just barely pressing against her skin.

"No kisses, huh?" she said. Cash blinked.

She carried him up the stairs, pausing halfway, where they'd taken a chunk out of the drywall, lugging that stupid dresser up. Jack's attempts at patching it had made it look even worse. Remembering his sad-little-boy look when she'd found him trying to fix it, she smiled to herself. Had he ever patched it correctly? He was always going to do things, and the gap between his intention and action was deep and wide.

There was no damage to the house in this reality. Not yet. She passed her hand over the drywall. Its nubbly texture was cool in the dark stairwell. Cash jumped down from her arm and darted up the stairs.

"My house," she whispered.

Lifting her arm up across her face, she twisted, and then swung back around, driving her elbow into the wall. The pain was in her shoulder, not her elbow, and made her wince. The dent she made was barely noticeable.

Descending the stairs once again, she went to the kitchen and removed the knives from their block one by one, laying them out on the butcher block surface. She paused with the big butcher knife in her hand, thinking of that opening scene in *House on Blood Street*. But inside this gesture, there was also another memory. She had done this before. Once, she'd carried this knife down to the basement, following the sounds of Dylan's cries.

How long ago was that? Yesterday? Impossible to tell.

She laid the big knife down beside the others and picked up the wooden block, then looked at the mark her elbow had left in the plaster. She swung the block. The stairwell was a narrow space, so there wasn't much room to get momentum, but the corner of the block knocked the drywall in with a dry thump. White dust drifted to the carpeted riser as she withdrew the block.

It left a nice, diamond-shaped divot. She poked at it with her fingers, and a piece fell back into the wall. The cotton candy pink insulation was powdered with plaster.

She set the block back in its place and, one by one, slipped the knives back into their homes.

Perfect.

9.

When Boorman finally came back upstairs to make a cup of tea and some dry toast, Avery retreated upstairs to her little galley. She sat cross-legged on her blankets, staring into that strange shadowed corner. Cash was curled on her pillow in a perfect circle.

Avery thought of lightbulbs.

The house had electric lights in the basement and the kitchen, but not up here. There were bulbs in the recessed fixtures in the loft's ceiling, big floods, but they didn't do anything. Avery wondered if light would banish that triangle of darkness or deepen it. What would it take to make that barrier pliable again, as it had been when Cash came through?

In her mind, it was the opening of a long tunnel that led ever-upward. There was that scene toward the end of *Blood Street*, with the detective worming his way into the bowels of the house. She and Jack had been impressed by it. That red-lit tunnel leading downward. In a way, the movie version of the hole in the basement seemed like its truest version. The way

Avery understood it had changed, from even the way she'd seen it that first afternoon with the realtor. It was more an idea now, or the idea had changed.

She placed her head beside Cash's hot, sleeping form. The cat chirped and shifted unhappily but soon settled back into the pillow's warm hollow. Avery smiled and brushed cat hair from her face.

"Grumpy little man," she whispered.

She closed her eyes, vowing that tomorrow she would make her way home. She could confront Boorman, knock down the basement wall, and walk until she hit the river. In her mind's eye, she saw herself accomplishing these things; she was a person unaffected by the deep inertia of the house, the hole that sucked her in and held her in its endless, sticky shaft.

Tomorrow. But hadn't she said that yesterday?

A creak from the stairs made her open her eyes. A shadow stretched across the carpet. Boorman stood just outside the doorway, one or two steps down, just out of her sight. But she knew he was there. She saw the shadow hovering in the darkened doorway, but more than that, she felt him, heard his slow breathing, and sensed his frustration.

After all, this was his show. He made this happen. After half a lifetime of work and planning, he made her a movie.

No, not Avery. Becca Mays: some woman that he'd probably never even met. He did this all for *her*. Of course, it was clearly for himself. This was Arthur Boorman's fantasy come to life, but just what *was* that fantasy? Becca Mays camping out in the attic room, leaving him alone below? Not likely.

Boorman still wasn't moving. She imagined him, that dishtowel twisted tight between his powerful hands. Was he waiting for her to be asleep, or was he just trying to get up the nerve to take the next step? Both options were troubling.

She wished for that butcher knife now. Something sharp. Could she do it, though? Could she push a blade into Arthur Boorman's belly and watch his insides slither out?

Hell yeah, she could. Although, last she heard, he was already dead.

She'd stab a ghost to get home to Jack and Dylan. She'd do anything. She'd hack her way right through this world if that was what it took.

Boorman gave a sniffle from the stairs, and she thought he was crying again. *What are you crying about, Arthur?* Nothing good. She'd seen it in his face when she'd appeared in the dress. The longing. More and more, she was filled with the certainty that this was some significant moment, that Boorman was working himself up to some final action.

She crept slowly from her nest of blankets; Cash gave a low rattle and stood, stretching. Avery shifted herself over into the dark corner. Let him come. She was hidden out of sight, and if he came into the room, she'd tackle him at the ankles, push him down the stairs. She wished again for the knife.

Another hiccuping little sniff. Cash sidled toward the stairs, although Avery shook her head silently at him to stop. It worked as well as any command given to a cat. Cash moved out of her line of sight and she heard soft little sounds, pads on carpet, as he descended the steps.

She shifted her right leg behind her, poised with her toes bent, ready to throw herself forward. There was only one little wall separating her from Boorman. So close.

Avery fought a tickle at the back of her throat. Boorman knew she was there: they were both just waiting for the other to make the first move. What had he come to do? Hurt her, but she couldn't guess what form that violence would take. Would a man build a shadow house in a shadow world to bring back a woman, just to kill her all over again?

No, she knew what he wanted from her. That shrine in the basement told her everything about Arthur Boorman—the hideous, crusted thing she and Jack once laughed at. She knew what that was about. Even in this strange underworld, Arthur Boorman was just a sad, horny old man who had wished for the girl of his dreams. He manifested Avery while he was jerking off in his folding chair: a pathetic magic of impotent desire, but the most amazing thing is that it worked. Kind of.

And now, here she was. She wanted to stand up and kick Boorman down the stairs, beat his face to mush, make a break for the hills beyond the tree. And then what? She feared that even if she escaped she'd still be trapped in this place Arthur built, running on her wheel like a mouse in a cage.

Suddenly, a light breeze caressed her legs, cool and fresh, and she looked back. The darkness where the walls met deepened, velvet and depthless. The slight wind was from the place that Cash had come from. This triangle was the nexus between the two houses, the real and the imagined. Maybe, this–not through Arthur Boorman–was her way home.

She turned, quietly as she could manage, onto her hands and knees and faced the corner. Cash came from there. It couldn't be bad. Right?

Boorman cleared his throat, loud and barking, no longer pretending. An electricity in the air told her that the danger had arrived. He was ready.

Avery pushed through the darkness and fell.

10.

She ran through the dark, feeling rather than seeing the dry grass against her thighs. Boorman was a sensed *thing* behind her. She could hear both of their breathing underneath the pounding of her feet. Otherwise, the night was silent. The world was silent. There was only this field and these two figures. Seen from above, their wide, looping passage would be clear, but from Avery's vantage, there was no direction, only the ground beneath her, Boorman's breathing behind, and fathomless darkness on all sides.

She didn't cry or call out, and soon their footfalls found a rhythm, the whisper of grass underneath.

She had been here before. She knew this scene, had seen it played, always the same. That's how she knew her path was not straight. She had seen it from the air, in that two-fold omniscience of dreams, both inside and out, that floating camera of the mind.

Like a nightmare.

She wanted to stop in the center of that endless field, put her hands on her knees, and laugh as she caught her breath. Smile at Boorman as he approached. At the silliness of it all. Call, "Cut!"

But she couldn't stop. That was how this scene went. It had to be blind terror, the monster just behind. Ragged breaths and hollow footfalls as a soundtrack. That burning brightness in her breast.

And how did the scene end? With a jump cut, of course. No resolution. No explanation.

It just ends.

11.

Avery awoke on a hillside, muted gray light filtering down from somewhere. Tall grass rose up round her, something like being at the bottom of a well, looking up. She'd read that you could see the stars in daylight that way, but there were no stars to see. She sat up, her back aching. The grass stuck to her thighs left their indentations on her skin in long arcs. How long had she run, and how far.

Standing, she stretched, arms above her head, rotating her hips until the small of her back gave a satisfying pop. Down the slope of the hillside, she could just make out the bright streak of the river. Before heading down, she looked behind her, up the slope, and there was the deer, watching her.

Avery startled, putting her hand to her chest.

"Jesus Christ," she laughed. "You again?"

The deer just stared, one ear twitching and turning.

"Shall we?"

The deer stepped forward, starting downward.

Avery followed.

It was as if she had taken this path a thousand times, the way it unspooled before her, leading her right down into the valley, right to the door of the house. Her house.

The deer curled down in the shade beneath the tree, and Avery wanted to warn it about the bleeding shape high up above, transfixed on finger-sized thorns.

But she was beginning to understand. It wouldn't do any good. Things didn't change here. Everything in this world followed its script, like a film on a loop.

Inside, the house was quiet and empty. She moved into the kitchen; the bead curtain hung still and silent, just as it ought to. Nothing strange there. But suddenly she was overcome with a dread that was both palpable and generalized, filling the house like smoke. Something waited beyond that curtain, perhaps even now looking out through the beaded strands, watching. Avery looked to the side without turning her head, glancing at the knife block. No. Not her role. The space beyond the beaded curtain seemed to thrum with a malevolent pulse, and she wanted to run away, to flee out and away from the house.

But she knew now that there was nowhere to go, no place beyond this place, nothing outside of the house. All she could do was choose not to be afraid. It was her house, she reminded herself, and she would not run. Not now. Not again.

She stepped forward. One step. She breathed in. She would almost be glad to find Boorman, just beyond the curtain. Maybe he'd chase her again. Despite her vow, she almost longed for the release of that pursuit, to feel her legs burning, the grass whipping at her. That part of the movie was known, and somehow less terrible. It was the fear of what might be that pressed back against her.

Another step, and she reached toward the curtain, ready for a hand to shoot out and grasp her by the wrist. Not Boorman's hand, but some monstrous, skeletal thing with the flesh torn away from its knuckles and long, yellowed nails. *Breathe.*

She pushed the curtain aside and stepped forward.

The room was now fully furnished, with a full-sized bed, its head against the far wall; a night stand with a small red plastic lamp; and an ornately carved dresser to the left. Atop the dresser was a white lacy runner that hung down off the side, dotted with bottles of perfume, little plastic canisters of creams, a wooden hairbrush. The bed was unmade, covers kicked down toward the foot, and Avery noticed the pattern on the sheets: little yellow birds perched on thin branches. None of it was hers, and it didn't look anything like the room from Blood Street.

All this detail was astonishing, especially because she knew this room had been empty—when? Last night? She realized it was all set dressing. Literally. The focal point of the room was to her right, beneath the window. Her eyes traced the frame and then sank to where a pool of blood stretched out and ran into the shadows beneath the bed. Curls of gore splattered the lower part of the wall. The deepest parts of the stain were already congealing on the hardwood floor. As if on cue, the smell hit her, bright and thick, a coppery slaughterhouse sweetness.

Avery took all of this in with a calm that surprised even herself, and she realized she was still holding the curtain aside with her left hand. Even that hand felt stiff and false, as if it might belong to someone else. She stepped away, letting the curtain fall back, where it swung and rattled with a sound like rain.

So it wasn't just an endless loop: it was repetition with variation. That was the definition of music. They weren't reenacting Boorman's movie, they were dancing. That was okay. She could do these steps.

She moved to the basement door, pulled it open, and went down to meet Arthur Boorman all over again.

12.

Time passed—or what passed for time, anyway. Avery cycled through days and nights in the endless dusk, and though the days went on, one after the other, she knew that time did not pass. She'd been without her meds for how long? Weeks, maybe? Yet there were no discernible hormonal changes in her body. The callouses on the fingers of her left hand, built up from years of playing bass, were still thick and smooth. She didn't even need the toilet. She was pinned in this moment like a moth on a spreading board, unchanging.

Each day she retreated to her nest in the attic room to sleep and came down to find the house transformed a piece at a time. The house added a sofa and a big boxy television that only played silver static, pictures on the walls of people she didn't know, curtains in the windows printed in a gaudy orange and brown stripe. Each item seemed new and unused, but each was also several decades out of date.

Avery ate food despite a lack of hunger and took slow, spiraling walks around the house. Sometimes the house grew small at a hundred paces, and sometimes she could walk for an hour, but she always made sure to keep the tree in sight. She couldn't explain it to herself, but she felt an overwhelming fear at the idea of losing sight of the house. Somehow she knew that beyond was only ash-colored fields and fog, and the idea of wandering blind through that endless waste terrified her.

But if she stayed too long in the house, she would be drawn back to the room where Becca Mays's murder was eternally staged. Sometimes she just found herself in there with no memory of having entered, fingering each of the little furnishings that continued to proliferate, all the detritus of a life that was not her own: wrappers and tissues and a half-dried bottle of nail polish. Sometimes she would open the dresser drawers and lift out the clothes. They were in her size, but things she'd never wear, shiny and plastic, the colors garish. All the same, she'd hold them up to herself and look in the mirror on the back of the door.

She couldn't tell if Becca Mays was a presence here, or if Avery herself was the ghost haunting the room, but the room haunted her. The way the congealed puddle of blood came and went. The way its smell hung in the room, whether it was there or not. The way the room held within it both an obvious menace and sense of simple comfort. Sometimes the bed was neatly made, and Avery longed to pull the coverlet back and slip herself between the sheets. But she knew better. Better to be an observer in this room than part of its shifting landscape.

Avery didn't think that Boorman was controlling these changes, at least not directly. The house was some kind of perpetual motion machine, wound up by the poet's obsession, maybe given life by his death? Avery had seen enough horror movies to accept that, in this nightmare world, the house's logic made plenty of sense. Not that it mattered. Reason wouldn't help her here. In this house, she realized for the dozenth time that she had never even opened the door to her and Jack's room. She had no idea if Boorman used it, if it stood bare, or if it was fully furnished. Maybe its door opened onto a vast and chilly nothingness that would suck her out into the vacuum of space.

She just couldn't open that door, and her mind would not let her consider exactly why.

She opened the thin little drawer at the top of the dresser, pulled out a black, nearly transparent cover-up edged in a thin line of faux feathers. *Tacky as shit*, she thought, even as she smoothed it against her cheek.

She dropped the negligee onto the bed and pulled the flowery dress up over her head. Pushing her arms through the sleeves of the cover up, she felt a little frisson in spite of her fear, or because of it. When she stood before the mirror, her body looked barely smudged behind the chiffon, her penis all but invisible. She smiled at herself, happy with what she saw despite the tears on her face. Whose tears, she wondered? Mine or Becca Mays's? And did it even matter anymore?

She heard the curtain behind her, saw movement in the mirror, closed her eyes, and waited. The film had begun. And Avery prepared for her eternal role as the victim.

13.

Her scene played the same, every time. Avery drew in a sharp breath as the knife's blade entered the flesh of her back, glanced off the ridge of her shoulder blade, and tore downward, making a long, shallow cut down her side. There was no pain, only this violation. The pain would come later. Falling forward onto the bed, she clutched at the wound, or as much of it as she could reach, sure that all of her insides would spill out if she didn't hold on to herself tight. She rolled over, legs pulled up both to protect her middle and to aim a kick at her attacker, but he already had her ankles twisted up in his grip, locked beneath his left arm. In his other gloved hand was the kitchen knife. Her knife. Its blade was perfectly clean as he raised it up above his head. She hadn't screamed yet. She knew her part: she knew she had to wait.

Her attacker's face was only a blur, unreadable beneath the brim of his wide black hat.

She never saw his features, but in her mind she imagined that thing in the closet. Those repeated stalkings in *House on Blood Street*, long after this bloody opening sequence. Black, scaly skin and yellow eyes, peering through the crack in the closet door. She knew it wasn't Boorman because Boorman ran away when it was time, ran to his basement and hid.

Avery and the killer had been through this cycle so many times already. It was impossible to keep count, to say just how many, since time was not really linear there in the gray lands. But she knew that as the killer loomed over her helpless body, Boorman was cowering in his basement, horrified and ashamed at this thing he had made, unable to stop it.

Finally, Avery screamed, right on cue: a big, horror movie scream, because that's what was called for. Her shriek was cut short by the swift descent of the knife. The blade plunged through her chest and punctured her lung, making her hitch and gasp, a wet gurgle starting as her throat filled with blood. The pain arrived, searing and deep.

He pulled out the knife, which brought a fine, pink mist with it. Not movie blood at all. Certainly not the bright red paint of *Blood Street* or all the Giallos that preceded it. No artifice, as a reminder that this was make-believe. This was the real stuff, and as Avery tried to scream again, the vivid surge came bubbling up her throat, almost black, and spilled out, down her breast.

This was the second worst part because her killing was actually happening. The very worst time came just before, when she sensed death nearing and recognized the signs of the great spinning wheel that her life had become. The anticipation was the killer.

This part of the movie hurt like hell, and her adrenaline didn't seem to know when to stop, so her vision was filled with dark circles and she felt as if she might vibrate right off of the bed, float right through the ceiling. The pain and the blood. And the fear.

She resented the fear, as she'd always resented it. Fear had ruled so much of her life. Even after she'd moved away, made friends, found Jack, and decided to live without fear, it was still deep within her. Being loved had changed her life. It was a transformation even larger than her transition, life-altering in even more fundamental ways. But it didn't erase who she was.

Now, Arthur Boorman had taught her once again to fear. Here, in this sound stage he built out of an old movie, some lines of poetry, and decades of his life, he'd built a larger shrine, focused on only one thing. Avery's fear was integral to the place's workings. And sometimes she thought that if she could overcome her fear once again, as she had years ago, she could overcome this place, too. Break it open.

But when the time to die came around again, fear filled her like a solid thing. If she hated Boorman, it was for that. Not stealing her away from her life: for this. Each time the monster killed Avery, it was like Boorman had her by the throat, forcing her to abandon herself completely to the fear.

Now, in that moment, she held out a hand, reaching for her attacker, but her fingertips just brushed the front of his coat. And then the knife came down, and the dark spots in her vision grew, consuming everything, and she was gone. Again.

Cut.

She awoke, as she always did, on the hillside, lying in the high grass, looking up at the blank of the sky. Every time she sat up, the deer was waiting to guide her back. This time, Avery lay there, vision tunneled by the gray stalks rising up all around her. She ran her hands over her body, the cotton dress soft against her palms. She touched all the places the killer's knife had pierced. Her skin was smooth and unbroken, but she thought she could feel the ghosts of her wounds, there, just beneath the skin, trapped between memory and premonition, already braced for the next murder scene.

Finally rising, she held her hand out, palm up, and the deer pushed its muzzle into it, its nose cold, breath hot.

Avery had never mentioned the deer to Boorman; she sensed it was not part of his original construction. Somehow, there had been a glitch in the Matrix, and the doe had slipped through like Cash had, and was now just as much a part of the place as Boorman and the faceless killer—but also somehow separate. Maybe she had brought the deer here. All those nights holding those stillborn fawns in her lap had called the doe to her, and now they were inseparable.

She thought about that for a moment as she ran her hand down the deer's neck, feeling its muscles twitch in response to her touch. That thing in the wall was not a hole, after all. She'd thought of it as an eye, with its dark pupil and amniotic tears, but no. She realized it was actually a tiny aperture that projected the image of the basement. Avery perceived the image of herself in the basement, clutching the dead deer, and how that image was at the same moment projected on a distant wall, even deeper inside the house. Upside down, image reversed, a house that was her house and not. The house on Calliope Street was a camera obscura, like a pinhole box camera, and now she was on the inside, upside down, suspended there, feet planted in the dry field.

What if she jumped? What if she let go of this reality completely? Might she not float up, into the matte gray of the night? Might she not return to some other home, her truer one?

Maybe.

But the deer was already picking its way down the hillside, toward home.

Avery followed.

14.

Avery missed music. She'd never thought of that: the way music strung the various scenes of a day together, like a movie montage, the way it underlaid everything. Here, the quiet oppressed her, weighed her down, so she moved through the house, opening doors, hoping to find something else on the other side, knowing she never would.

It was still early days. Boorman hadn't even set up her room yet. There was just the bead curtain, and if she passed through, there was a square room with two windows, a door leading off to the bathroom, and a dark stain on the hardwood floor. The stain grew deeper and more distinct with each revolution of time.

She wondered if Jack could see it, the way the stain was transformed, or if it was only here, in this still place without music. She had to admit, she had trouble picturing their dining room, the real room, back in her other life. More and more it felt like an image from a dream, slipping away after waking.

So much was slipping away.

But not the music. She remembered the music. The music, Jack, and Dylan. Those were her anchors, the only things that kept her from falling completely into Boorman's sick shadow play. And she feared that if any one of them broke, she'd be lost.

So she sang. She wandered up the stairs, up and down the long, narrow room with its slanted ceilings, Cash at her feet, and she sang songs that she'd written, songs she loved, and sometimes—mostly to entertain Cash—she made up new songs. She sang about what might have happened to his poor bobbed tail, creating epic adventures. She sang of home.

Boorman was still a mystery, though she was discovering, not a very deep one. He'd spent much of his life, and a good part of his afterlife, obsessed with Becca Mays, and now that Avery was there, he was both pleased and confounded. Avery was not Becca Mays, but in the circular drama of Boorman's obsession, she played the part, just as that nameless actress had played Becca in *Blood Street*. It was the idea that mattered, not the girl.

What really scared her about Boorman was how he lived inside his own head, the way he retreated there, only to come out—*really* come out—toward the end, when the unheard music really ramped up, and Avery's dread filled the rooms like a physical thing. He'd come up the stairs, drink a glass of water from the tap, and wait.

In Boorman's mind, the idea of Becca Mays was inextricable from her death. It was, after all, the only thing he really knew about her.

But right now, that death was still a ways off, so she went singing softly, bending down sometimes to scratch Cash behind his ears. And sometimes, in that upstairs room, she would crouch down near the corner where the shadows overlapped; she listened, hoping to hear that other music from that other life. She could feel it there, just beyond the wall.

15.

In the story, it was time to fix herself a drink. She sliced the lime using the largest knife in the block. The knife was dull and pressed into the side of the lime, denting it and smashing it out of shape, until she found the spot down near the heel, where the steel was still sharp, and it slipped through the rind, parting it easily.

Avery danced to unheard music. Just a rhythm, really, something stuck in her head, but she swayed at the kitchen island, slicing citrus into thin rounds. She never wondered where the things came from. The limes, the glasses, the bottle of Beefeater gin, and the tonic in its rounded bottle with a waxy foam label all simply appeared, like the fresh groceries in the fridge. She wondered about so little now, though she did wish that she could remember the words to this song. The lyrics' absence nagged at her, like some forgotten task. She thought that maybe it was her song. A song she'd made herself, or a song about her? She couldn't say.

Her drink mixed, she moved round the island, toward the beaded curtain that separated the kitchen from the bedroom, still dancing to that absent music.

And then she saw him. Boorman stood in the far corner, arms crossed over his chest, silent and watchful. Now she understood. She knew: it was time again. She wasn't afraid of Boorman, but his presence signaled other dangers, or rather, one particular danger. The faceless man and his knife. No, *her* knife. This kitchen knife.

Avery believed that her life might be very different, even improved, if Arthur Boorman had simply made a better movie. A romance, or even a porno, would be preferable to this. This dread.

But this was the world Boorman had built out of celluloid, cheap spells, and his own sickness. She held Boorman's gaze as she pulled her nightgown over her head. He didn't like that. He wanted to be an observer only. But returning his obsessive attention was her only revenge.

She stood at the side of the bed, naked, and sipped her drink. She was playing at nonchalance, but her testicles were drawn up tight and her nipples stood erect. Terror transformed her body and made her inhabit herself fully, in a way she rarely did here. She could already feel the knife striking her shoulder blade and the cold line it made down and around her side. Cold turning to fire. She knew every beat.

But Boorman was watching, and intentionally or not, he had made this place so that he could do just that. Becca Mays had lodged in his mind like a splinter, and this house was the infection that built up around it. Usually he turned away at this part, fled down into his basement to wait for the world to roll over and reset back into its blank domesticity. Avery wondered if it was guilt. Boorman knew shame, but she wasn't sure he understood guilt, and there was such a gap between the two. She could work with guilt, but Boorman's shame turned itself ever inward and festered.

But this time he wasn't fleeing. He stood in the corner, watching.

She heard the curtains open behind her, and she did not turn. She held Boorman's eyes as she inhaled, waiting for the knife to strike.

16.

Night. The gray hillside. The deer emerging out of the fog. The descent down into the long round, the short cycle of days, her growing dread.

17.

Avery drew the knife from the block: the biggest, of course, even though the paring knife was right there. The lime fell into two perfect halves on either side of the blade. She saw herself as if from outside her body, enacting these choreographed motions, walking through each alien action. She was beautiful in the yellow light of the kitchen, squeezing half a lime into her glass and running the pulped flesh along the rim.

She was larger than life. She felt herself glowing, as if the rest of the world were a darkened room; everyone was watching her, illumined and illuminating, as she sipped from her glass and danced in swaying movements, glass held up above her head. Light and music and bitter gin and the eyes of strangers watching from the dark. She smiled, and the smile was for herself, but it broadcast out like smoke whipped away by a breeze.

She pushed through the curtain into her room, riding the rhythm of the music and her own newfound grace, waiting for the next cut. She turned at the sound of the beads; saw dark hands, the knife; felt the rhythm of the music jump in time with her pulse; turned to flee.

Boorman stood in the far corner. His massive hands were at his side. His lips looked too red in his pale face, showing the grimace of his yellow teeth.

She reached out a hand toward him just as the killer's first blow glanced off her back and sliced downward along her side.

Had she screamed yet? She couldn't remember now.

Time slowed, and she floated there in the space between blows, her hands clutched tightly to her side, trying to hold herself together, and then Boorman spoke.

"It started with a two-minute segment on the local news. A few lines from the newscaster. I don't even remember them now, though I'm sure I could recreate them with little strain on my imagination. It's always the same speech. A community reeling with shock. Vicious and brutal violence. Found by her roommate. I wasn't really listening. I was looking at you. The black and white photo in the corner of the screen."

The next blow slipped between her ribs, and though she was watching Boorman and not the drama that was her body, she felt the wound's mouth well with a cascade of dark blood.

She didn't have to look. The image was ingrained in her mind—in Boorman's mind.

Boorman lit a cigarette, breathed out smoke into the room. All of this somehow, between blows.

Boorman's eyes locked on hers, meeting her glazed stare in that room where the air had gone sharp with blood, time gone sludgy and thick. "It's not so much different than seeing you across a room, is it? Sometimes we see a face and we know. You were so beautiful. Everyone saw that. They put you on the front page for a week. 'Movie star looks,' one article said. And they were right. That struck me, how right they were. But there was something else in that photo. A sadness, I guess. Hard to put into words. It called to me."

Avery reached for Boorman, even as she felt the knife pierce her again. Blood ran from her lower lip in sticky, looping strings. He did not move, did not draw away. He simply watched, as unfeeling and all-seeing as the camera.

"I bought every paper. Followed the story everywhere, but it was the photo. Always the photo. Those eyes. I put them up to study them. Just stared and stared, waiting for them to tell me your secret. To finally confess. I wanted to be your confessor. I'll admit it. I was sure that no one else saw it, this dark and shining thing behind the photograph."

Finally falling onto the bed, she felt knees pressing down on either side of her, the mattress dipping low, and then the incredible pressure of the blade being pressed down through her back, with her murderer's full weight upon it.

She tried to speak, to call out to Boorman. Not for help. She knew better than to tell him to stop talking, even as the blade was scraping against bone. This monologue was worse than the pain. This writing of himself into the story. It was ghoulish and wrong. He was right there. He could stop this thing. He had started it spinning, after all.

"I stared and stared," he said, and his mouth almost smiled, twitching at the corners beneath his big mustache. "And then it spoke to me. The darkness. It was a pinprick at first. One dot in the newsprint. Like, if you blew the picture up to the size of the world, there would be that one dot, and that was it. That was the darkness inside you, that thing I'd recognized. And that spot was a hole in the world, looking back at me. And it recognized me. Because it was in me, too." And he did smile then. His whole face transforming, his beatific gaze directed always on her, even as she gurgled and spat before him.

She wanted to tell him how he was wrong: the black spot had always been his own. It was a blind spot in his own eye that blacked out the world. It had blocked out Becca Mays, even as he remade her. But she couldn't speak because her punctured lung was filling up, and her throat only sputtered and choked on the wave of thick arterial blood.

But more than that, she couldn't speak because she had never spoken.

He never wrote Becca Mays a single line of dialogue.

"Soon, I saw that darkness everywhere. In all their eyes. All the beautiful women. They looked at me and smiled or sneered or looked away, but I saw it. My eye had found the hook now. I was like a magnet for that dark little hole in the world. And I wanted nothing more than to climb through."

Avery kept her eyes locked on Boorman's, even as her murderer took her by the ankles and pulled her down the bed, away from him. She never heard the last of his speech. She was dead before she hit the floor.

18.

Avery sat on the hillside, the sky the color of television static. The deer stood just down the hill, looking back, waiting. It was disorienting, the featurelessness of it, that endless sky. All she knew was that she wanted to wait, stall to test some boundary. How long could she put it off this time? Maybe if she stayed out here, the killer would eventually come for her.

She didn't think so. She'd never seen him outside of the confines of the house. In a way, she thought he *was* the house. They were bound up together.

She closed her eyes and tried to sleep. She wished for the feel of sun on her skin—thought of those summer days, out in the yard, just her and Jack. The tang of smoke in the air. The sun on the top of her head. A cold glass of water sweating in her hand. Jack, reading a book, his feet up on the table.

It all seemed so far away.

And Dylan. Each night she lay in that upstairs room in her pool of blankets, looking up at that slanted ceiling, Cash curled up between her feet, and she thought how it was meant to be her son's room. They'd worked so hard on it, she and Jack. Maybe he was lying in that other house at this very moment. She hoped so.

When Avery sat up, she was not quite able to look over the top of the dry grass. She saw the deer waiting there, watching.

"Alright, I'm coming," she said, as she climbed to her feet.

The deer took a few careful steps downhill.

"Yeah, I know." She dusted off the back of her dress and started down the hill.

The deer picked its way downward. The river flashed in the unseen light. Avery returned to the house on Calliope Street.

19.

Avery lay in her nest, listening to Boorman's breathing from the stairs. She knew this wasn't the first time, but she couldn't have guessed how many times they'd been through this silent drama. She knew what he wanted from her, and the only thing keeping him from stepping up into the room was the fact that he couldn't admit it to himself.

All those years sitting before his little shrine of naked women and he still had himself convinced that he was up to something noble, that he was saving her. Well, not *her*. Becca Mays.

His rambling monologue about the dark spot in the photo ran through her mind like the fragment of a song she could not shake. All those eyes around that central eye, and Arthur Boorman saw only darkness.

Arthur Boorman, she thought, had a very limited imagination. He was using everything at his disposal, his movie magic, and half a lifetime's worth of obsessive attention, but had created nothing but a giant echo chamber where the past reverberated inside this house which was his head, never changing. No rescue. Becca Mays became synonymous with her bloody end, and the actual woman made so anonymous in her suffering that she was reduced to little more than an idea.

Except for nights like this. Avery didn't know if it was progress or not, the way that Boorman came so close to acknowledging his desire. If this were therapy, he might well be on his way to a real breakthrough.

But this wasn't therapy.

Arthur Boorman stood at the top of the stairs, just out of sight, and his rattling breathing gave him away, and Avery imagined the arguments roiling inside his broken brain. The childishness of it. She wanted to call out to him and break this stalemate, maybe even break this endless cycle that was their lives.

But she was frightened—after all of it, she was still frightened of Arthur Boorman. Maybe the role of Becca Mays was changing her? Maybe she was coming to accept that role? It was a frightening thought.

She tried to calm her own breathing so that she could better hear his. She couldn't even be sure that she heard him anymore, that it wasn't her own breathing, her own blood in her ears. Maybe Boorman himself was just an embodiment of her own fear.

Maybe this was hell.

It wasn't the first time she'd had the thought, but every time she discarded it. Hell just wasn't a very interesting idea; besides, if this was hell, it was Boorman's hell, not her own.

He breathed, and she felt more than heard his presence. Definitely there. Waiting. For what? For something to change in a world built specifically to never change.

That was it. She finally understood the nature of Boorman's sickness, the nature of his torment. It was static. Unchanging. A whole universe, an earworm. That tiny snippet of song looping endlessly until it threatens to drive you mad.

And the way you cure the earworm is through completion. Listen to the song from start to finish, allow your brain to complete the circuit, and you're no longer trapped in a feedback loop.

Boorman had been trapped in one imagined moment for forty years, and it had broken his mind. But once upon a time, he'd had the imagination to dream of what came after that moment. He'd made a whole fucking movie about it.

Avery stood up from her makeshift bed, not quite straightening because of the slanting ceiling. She took a step forward. The floor creaked beneath her step, but she didn't care. She was done hiding and cowering. She was done allowing Arthur Boorman to frighten her.

She would face him, finally. She would claw out his eyes, leaving only dark holes in his face. Little portals into his skull.

But as she approached the top of the doorway, she heard his weight shift and sensed his movement up into the room, mirroring her own. Her resolve vanished like mist.

She course-corrected, cut to the left, dropped down to her hands and knees, and crawled forward toward the triangle of darkness where the walls met.

Every time, she forgot, and every time it was the same. She fled, and he followed, and that was as close as they came to the truth.

She fell forward into nothingness.

20.

Avery ran a wide directionless track through the darkness, only hearing her pursuer, never seeing him. It might not be Boorman at all. Maybe it was the faceless killer or the closet monster. It made little difference. She was a deer, startled from cover, knowing only one impulse: to run.

She ran.

21.

Avery sliced the lime. A good, bright smell. A smell of summer evenings—the juniper pinch of gin, and cloying heat—of cleanliness, her mother cleaning the kitchen floor on Saturday mornings and then running the vacuum while Avery tried to watch TV. It was also a smell that announced a rising dread, a tightness in her throat and chest. Her hand trembled around the knife as it never had before. She placed the knife on the cutting board and looked down at it, next to the lime's two halves, where two pale seeds spilled out in a little half-circle of cloudy juice. The knife gleamed beneath the lights, and she saw the smear of juice across the end nearest the handle. The heel. That's where the blade was sharpest.

She found herself struggling to breathe. The light was on beyond the curtain, and she looked up from the knife to see the way the plastic beads transformed into a hundred multicolored fragments. Just beyond that curtain, her death awaited. She knew this as she'd always known it, but now she felt the ghost of wounds that had yet to be. Her back tingled and crawled, and she thought once again of running, fleeing through the door, out into the half-night, out into the endless sprawl of the dry grass. Anywhere but here.

Still thinking of this, she squeezed half the lime into her glass and poured in the tonic water, hearing the frantic bubbles. That was the sound of her mind, the same as a radio caught between stations, and she gave all of her attention to it, sinking herself down inside it.

She pushed through the curtain, and its clacking added to the radio hiss, and now it was the sound of the ocean. Forward, out into the waves. *I'll never see the ocean again*. This thought troubled her, and she scrunched up her brows as she sipped from her drink.

Boorman stood like a shadow in the corner, watching.

She closed her eyes and listened to the waves.

22.

Avery stood at the top of the basement stairs, listening. The house was silent, but she knew that Boorman was down there. He was almost always down there, doing God-knew-what. All she did know was that something had to change, there in that place where nothing changed. Nothing Boorman could do was worse than this endless circle in which her body was torn from her over and over again. She didn't care if her spirit or her soul or whatever you wanted to call it lived on, haunting this place. Her body was her own. *Hers.* Inseparable from herself. Losing it cost her something intangible every time.

She descended into the basement. The house was all but empty again, yet to fill up with the detritus of Becca Mays's life and that chronic, pulsating dread.

Boorman was sitting at his table, his back to her, hunched over. He was writing, she realized, pen scratching away at loose sheets of paper.

I could stab him right through his back.

It was a quick thought, evaporating almost immediately. How many times had it risen up in her mind? How many times had she discarded it? Somehow she knew that what held her here had little to do with Boorman himself. This house was an idea now, a universe spinning out around the newsprint image of Becca Mays. Boorman was almost an afterthought.

She stepped closer, looking over his shoulder. He glanced back and pulled the papers close, shielding them with his hands. Avery wanted to laugh. What could he want to hide from her? His poems? Hadn't she already seen into the darkest corners of his heart? Didn't she live there, in those shadows?

Suddenly, the idea that this was not the darkest place made her shiver. What else clawed at Boorman's insides, scuttling to get out? What horrors?

She moved past him, around the table, her shadow rising up the wall as she approached.

The wall itself was white plaster over the concrete foundation wall. Long cracks ran through it at odd angles, with the odd triangle of plaster missing where they crossed one another. Thick masses of ancient cobweb hung from the beams at the wall's upper edge. The hole was irregular, angular; a small pile of silt lay at the base of the wall below it, and Avery's shadow lay dark against the white wall. *Like a screen.*

"Tell me about this," Avery said, nodding toward the wall. The hole looked back, black and blind.

Boorman drew in a long breath, filling himself up, seeming to grow larger in that low space.

"I found it like that," he said, his voice resonant, low and rasping.

"What's back there?" she said, and reached a hand toward the hole, ready to hook her finger behind the thin scrim of plaster, pull it out, and widen the hole.

"No!" Boorman said, his voice filling the basement, causing Avery to snatch her hand to her chest as if recoiling from a snake.

Avery looked at the little black hole in the wall, felt its staring eye, and she thought maybe she understood, as much as one could understand. Boorman didn't know any more than she did. He'd been entranced by the hole's gaze, had fallen into it, just like he fell into the story of Becca Mays's murder. Eventually, maybe the two came to overlap?

She shook her head. Wasted time, searching for reasons. That's why a horror movie wasn't a mystery, because the reasons don't matter. What matters is the feeling, visceral and true. Hadn't she spent half her life chasing that feeling, at best finding a kind of mounting dread?

Until now.

But–intentional or not–Arthur Boorman had built a real horror film here in his haunted house, one that built up mounting dread and released it in bloody, visceral terror. And like all good horror movies, its replay value was endless because the fear response never lessened. There was no comfort of familiarity here. And wasn't that also the pleasure of the movies she and Jack loved? The horrors were tamed, expected, part of a rhythm felt in the bones.

But *House on Blood Street* had never been much of a horror movie, had it? A slasher opening by way of Giallo crime films, followed by a surreal plot that was part detective story and part Greek myth.

This was why poets shouldn't write horror. He didn't understand it even as much as the fifteen-year-old kid sitting in the dark. For Boorman, it was about Becca Mays; but Becca Mays was a sacrificial offering, not even a character. If he'd known what he was doing, he would have focused on the sister. What was her name? Avery couldn't remember. It didn't matter.

Cash brushed against her ankle, warm and soft, and Avery scooped him up, rubbing her chin against the top of the cat's head.

"We need to get out of here," she said, only half addressing Boorman.

He looked at her, taken aback.

"And go where?" he said.

"Home." She dropped Cash back down to the floor and leaned down before the hole in the wall. She put her eye right up to it, squinting into the darkness.

It took a moment for her eye to adjust, but she thought there was depth to that darkness, breadth. And maybe movement. Was Jack back there? Dylan?

She felt Boorman looming behind her—on his feet now, nervous—but she didn't care. What could he do to her? She didn't want to think about the answer to that question, so instead, she just raised her hands to the hole.

She hooked her finger in and pulled. It was some kind of plaster mixed with cement, only a quarter inch thick, and it crumbled and flaked, falling away easily. She had a brief flash of a scene very near the end of *Blood Street*: that wide cutaway shot of the tunnel leading downward and the figure crawling through, tiny in the frame.

She pulled at the wall, using both hands now. There was nothing behind the thin plaster but a gray-black blank, like a dead television screen.

Looking over her shoulder at Boorman, she saw him staring dumbly.

"You could come, too?' she said, not sure if she meant it. "There's nothing here."

One side of his face twitched, but he didn't speak.

"Okay, then," she said. She pushed her head inside the cool, velvet darkness within the wall. Cash gave a high chirrup, pressing against her arm.

"Okay," she said again, not sure if she was talking to the cat or herself.

She moved forward, deeper into the dark, bare knees on cool earth, the smell of freshly turned soil. A garden or a grave? Tangles of fine roots hung from the roof of the tunnel, catching in her hair. She pushed on, and she thought that maybe, just maybe, the path seemed to rise.

23.

She awoke on the hillside, the sky staticky above, the dry grass moving soundlessly around her, and she pulled her knees up and rolled onto her side, weeping silently.

But soon she was all cried out. Pointless. Self-defeating. She stood up and saw the deer just up the slope, waiting and watching. She laughed bitterly to herself. Fight or give in, the result is always the same.

"Come on, then," she said, and the deer loped off down the hillside, down toward the silver curve of the river, down into the valley, back toward the house and the ghost of Calliope Street.

She followed.

Part III
Camera Obscura

One Year Later

1.

Jack checked his phone, hoping for something from Dylan: a text or an email. Nothing. It had been three weeks since Dylan's last sad, desperate missive, and he knew Janie was doing her best to shut down communications between the two of them. Janie thought he was dangerous. She wasn't alone in that opinion. Jack pocketed his phone and stepped down off the porch, into the golden glare of a summer morning.

Speck's house sat atop the rise, the land sloping down and away, the whole Bitterroot Valley spread out below. The Rockies, which should have risen like sentinels in the distance, were hidden beneath a thick cloud of smoke. Even still, it was beautiful.

The fires were even worse than last year, burning right up to the highway east of town. Flames took out a little mill town in a flash and displaced some hundred people. The smoke was omnipresent: sweet and thick, scratching at the back of Jack's throat. He hoped the firefighters would keep the fires from entering the valley, where all of the hillsides had been brown since mid-July.

There was the squeak and slam of the screen door, and then Jacob Speck was standing beside him. He came up to Jack's shoulder and pulled a pack of cigarettes from his breast pocket, tucking one into his mouth. Flipping open his metal lighter, he drew in a lungful of smoke and held it, still staring out at the vista below, tucking the lighter back into his pocket. He released the smoke with his words.

"Tanya's ready."

Jack looked sideways at him, nodded, and went back up into the house.

The big farmhouse was quiet, at least down here on the ground floor. The big open kitchen appeared as a square of light down the hall. Jack took the stairs, passing the doors that stood open along the hallway. Six rooms with one bathroom. Open doors. That was one of the rules on the ranch; Jack could see a few of Speck's crew laying on their beds or reading. At the end of the hall, Greg was hauling a metal case up the ladder that led to the attic, and Jack hurried to help.

"What's all this?"

"Just need to tweak the lighting," Greg said, looking down from the square door in the ceiling.

"I thought we were set," Jack said, handing up the last case.

Greg, a Black kid of about twenty, smiled. He looked even younger when he did.

"Just a little tweak."

Jack came up the ladder.

"Can we at least get started?" he asked.

"Oh, yeah. I won't be in your way or anything," Greg said.

Jack straightened and turned. Their actress Tanya was waiting on a metal stool. Her dark hair was teased into a tangled mess, eye makeup smeared and running. She flashed white teeth at him, her smile incongruous with her harried appearance and bloodstained nightgown. Beyond her, the long, low attic space had been transformed into what looked like a cross between a cave and the digestive tract of a massive beast. It was all chicken wire, covered over with a plaster epoxy Greg had blown in and let harden into rough, temporary walls. At the very far end was a circle of green so they could add in whatever effects they needed later. Down that tunnel, through that doorway, was the realm of the Red Witch.

"You good to go?" he said, and Tanya stood up from her seat.

"So good."

Dell and Tracy came up the ladder, and it suddenly felt very snug inside the slanting space. Jack thought briefly of Dylan's attic room, sitting empty, but he shook it away. Time to focus on the work at hand.

Dell was getting the camera ready. It was a little digital thing on a handheld metal rack, but the video quality was great. Tracy walked Tanya over to the back corner where a plastic sheet was tacked down and started squeezing fake blood over her head from a plastic squeeze bottle. The dyed glucose ran almost black down Tanya's face and down her chest. Jack saw Avery's face superimposed over Tanya's, screaming silently, sheeted in blood. He took a step back, hands to his face, stomach tight. Squeezing his eyes shut and concentrating on his breathing, he counted to ten and then counted to ten again. When he finally straightened up and opened his eyes again, he saw only Tanya's face, laughing at something Tracy had said. He straightened his back, rolled his shoulders, and moved on.

It was a fairly regular occurrence, these ghostly visitations, and he both dreaded and longed for the passing sick spells, for any sign of her. He had to see her, even though she was always screaming in his vision, terrified and terrifying.

He moved back to the far end of the attic, checked his phone again.

Nothing.

Maybe Dylan had finally come to his senses and decided to cut ties, too. Almost everyone else had. What did it mean when the only people who believed you were a thirteen-year-old boy and the last dregs of a hippie cult?

Speck came up the ladder, hands on his bony hips, taking in the scene. He spotted Jack and came over. It was day six of filming on what was supposed to be an eight-day shoot. Both Speck and Jack knew they would never be done in eight days, but both of them refused to say it out loud. What money they had was all but gone, but they both knew this was bigger than the money. It was bigger than the movie itself.

"We good?" Speck said.

"Yup. Ready." Jack gave Speck a little nod. The older man stepped forward, shouting out to everyone. "Places!" Jack appreciated Speck's authority. It masked his own sense of being a fraud.

Greg switched on the grip lights, and the tapering tunnel was transformed into something red and glistening. It looked pretty damned good, though Jack's yardstick was always that shot in *Blood Street* where the detective crawled downward into a massive cutaway of the earth. Speck had described how they'd done the shot, down to the lighting and camera movement, but Jack couldn't reconcile it with the image in the finished film. It was too real and too strange at once. It would probably be easy to recreate now, with the benefit of digital effects and all that, but he was determined to make this movie his own. He was casting his own spell now.

Tanya got down on her hands and knees at the opening of the tunnel, and Dell crouched down behind her, just a little to her right. Stacy held the boom across her shoulders, the microphone at its end looking like a dead spider suspended above Tanya's head, just out of frame.

"Action," Speck said, and Tanya began pulling herself forward with blood-covered hands, crying and gasping. Dell kept right beside her all the way down the tunnel, camera trained on her, until she had nearly reached the blank disc of green at the set's end.

"Good. Let's do it one more time," Jack said.

Speck nodded.

They'd do it over and over. Three takes with Dell crab-walking backward in front of Tanya. Two more with the camera fixed at the far end and Tanya dragging herself toward its digital eye.

You couldn't have too many takes, Jack had learned. Filmmaking was all about endless repetition. Do it again. And again. A slow chant. A spell.

2.

He got back to the house on Calliope Street at about nine o'clock, parking on the street beneath the big overhanging branches. The moon was blood red through the smoke. The house seemed abandoned, not by any particular sign—the house looked as it always had, like it had the day they moved in. Of course it did. That had been the self-fulfilling prophecy he'd once spoken to himself, that he would never actually get to half the repairs, that the house would remain a half-finished thing.

It was more of a feeling, anyway. White curtains hung limp in the windows. When he got to his front door, there was a yellow flyer rolled up and tucked between the handle and the jamb. He had a moment of anxiety, sure it was another death threat or that it would bear Avery's photograph, but it was just a flyer for a local pizza place.

He'd come to both fear and hate the house, but he couldn't leave. Avery was in there somewhere. He knew it. The house had swallowed her up, and he was going to get her back. That's what making *Red Witch* was all about, of course. He had to remind himself often. It was so easy to forget, amidst the day to day work of the thing, why he was doing it in the first place. But the house on Calliope Street always reminded him.

He hurried up the steps, not wanting to catch one of Mel's lethal glares. His neighbor thought he was a murderer. Almost everyone thought so. Even after the media storm blew by, the town remembered. Jack was the man whose wife had vanished. And it was always the husband. There'd been one very ugly, and very public, interaction in front of the salon with Avery's business partner Claire, where she'd said so. She'd called him a killer. That scene had none of the romance of a slasher film. It was an altercation, shaming Jack. Just thinking of it felt dirty.

Jack resigned his teaching position and instead, took on two full-time positions teaching online classes: one to college students all over the country, and another to Japanese teenagers. He slept little, by design. When he slept, the house did things: made sounds, thrummed with some energy he couldn't name. He'd lost fifteen pounds he couldn't afford to give up, and he didn't get nearly enough sun. Avery would have said, *Eat a cheeseburger, you pale, scrawny bastard.*

But it didn't matter. Between the insurance money from the fire and his two incomes, he'd made enough to keep the lights on, pay the mortgage, and help finance his project up at Speck's ranch. That film was what mattered. That was the work. That was how he'd bring her back.

Placing his bag on the couch, he fished inside it, pulled out his working script, shoved it under his other arm. He filled a glass with cold water, then he swung the basement door open with his foot.

He moved carefully down the twisting stairs, eyes on the water glass. Getting around was easier once he got down in the labyrinth, moving through the panels of torn plastic. The cops had loved the basement. They thought they'd found the lair of a serial killer, for sure. Or maybe a Poe villain, what with the hole in the wall. They didn't want to believe the room had been like this when Jack and Avery bought it. They wouldn't believe it had been even creepier before they moved in.

Jack set the glass of water on the folding table, dropped the script, and sat in the kitchen chair he'd brought down. This was his office now: a folding table beneath the one bare bulb, facing the ragged hole in the wall, dark earth beyond, slowly sifting down onto the basement floor.

He opened the script to the film's last act, picked up one of several pencils scattered across the table, and got to work.

The crew hated him for showing up every day with rewrites, and he knew it wasn't fair to them, but he had to get this right. To his left was a small stack of books and papers, and he picked up Boorman's *Incantations* from the top. The book was battered, the spine cracked so that it lay open on the table to the fourteenth incantation.

"Incantation XIV" was an Ann-Jane poem, the speaker watching her from his usual perch in the locust tree. Ann-Jane, who was, as far as Jack could tell, homeless, dirty, and insane, talked to herself as she shuffled along through the shade under the tree. Her speech was transcribed by the speaker of the poem. Bits and pieces of it became recurring motifs, little talismans.

All the same the night-fog field to Ann-Jane
Brittle stars say nothing—hear them call
Once was a girl in a dark place trembled
Fawn-legs and clatter—her landlocked heart.

Jack could see it in his mind's eye, that night-fog field, and while Boorman's script called for a firelit cavern where a coven of witches gathered–nude, of course–to spit curses on the world, Jack thought this was the true destination. Through the tunnel, out into a night of silent-screaming stars and fog.

Filming it would be a bitch, though. Nighttime shoots were near-impossible to light, and to fulfill the promise of Jack's imagined shot, they'd need a metric ton of mist. That billowing fog machine stuff wouldn't cut it. He'd talk to Speck and Dell about it in the morning. They'd make it happen.

He ran a big *X* through the next three pages of the script, opened his laptop, and began to write.

As he led the woman down through the field, her face shifted in his mind. She was Tanya, and she was Avery, and she was Becca Mays. A whole lineage of women making the same descent, and he felt hot tears rising in his eyes. He wanted to rescue them all. Instead, he was making the latest representation of their suffering, capturing it all on film.

Not for the first time, he wondered just how different he and Boorman were. Was the poet's face shifting back behind his own? Were they all just playing predetermined parts in a sloppy, low-budget drama?

Probably.

All he knew for sure was that Avery was lost out there in the wide, silent field that was so like a calm sea. He wanted nothing more than to reach out, to guide her home.

Looking up from the screen, he stared at the ragged hole in the wall. He had two thoughts at once. One was the knife and the phone he'd found lying on the concrete slab floor the night Avery disappeared. He'd given the phone to the police, unlocked it for them. He already knew there was nothing incriminating to be found there. The second thing was the memory of all those nights he and Avery had come downstairs to find what the house had produced for them. What new thing, what horror? He could still see each tiny, broken deer. The way Avery had cradled them in her lap, weeping. Boorman didn't put anything about that in his goofy fucking poems.

That led to a new thought: the doe in the backyard, who was gone now—it was all gone now—and how she appeared with her family, waiting and watching every night. A grieving mother.

He woke up the laptop screen again and returned to the scene. This time, there would be a guide through that endless field. A guardian.

3.

The next morning, Jack ate toast with butter, filled his travel mug, and went out. The smoke had descended into the valley overnight, hanging like dirty fog as Jack crossed Calliope Street and climbed Karl's front steps.

Karl was about the only one who seemed to believe him. Well, if not *believe* him, at least not think he was a killer. Mel had all but said she wanted to string him up, and the thing was, Jack couldn't blame her. He knew how it looked. He'd think the same thing, if their positions were reversed. In fact, Karl's continued friendship almost felt like a red flag. Shouldn't *he* be more concerned about hanging out with a possible murderer? This was Jack's life now, this double-sidedness to everything, to each interaction, to each thought. Jack was innocent, but that did nothing to lessen his shame. He needed to get away from here.

He rapped on the door.

Karl, toothbrush in his mouth, waved him in. Jack followed him through to the kitchen, sat down at the little formica-topped table, and flipped aimlessly through the newspaper while Karl finished in the bathroom.

Jack had kind of dropped out of the real world, not reading the news or following politics. He knew what he needed to know anyway: *we're all fucked*. He felt a mild twinge of guilt at his own callousness and lack of concern for anything outside his own life, but finally folded the paper and tossed it back on the table.

He had more important things to do.

"They got you converted yet?" Karl said, coming into the kitchen.

"Haven't even tried. Should I be insulted?"

"Probably."

"From what I see and hear, it mostly just looks like group therapy. You know, with a lot of talk about the mind and the body. It all feels very Eastern. Not especially sinister."

"Nah, it's all boilerplate New Age stuff, with a good dose of Greek mystery religion thrown in. That's your Eastern flavor. The Dionysian stuff."

"Well, they don't really talk about the ethos much. They pray a lot. All I know is that they're all about making this movie."

Karl set a cup of coffee down in front of Jack and stood across from him, taking his own tentative sips.

"Yeah, I can't quite figure that. I mean, you didn't give them that much money, right?"

"We're over-schedule and over-budget. We're all losing money on this thing," Jack said.

"Sounds about right."

"That's what Speck said. I'm a teacher, you know? I'm about getting stuff done."

"That Hollywood lifestyle will get you yet," Karl smiled. He was playing with a stub of a pencil.

"Don't think 'Hollywood' is quite the vibe up at the ranch. But the crew are all great."

"And when it's done?" Karl said, looking up, finally.

"Then it's done."

"And then?"

"What do you mean, and then?"

"What will you do? When it doesn't fix things. When Avery is still gone?"

Jack gave Karl a sad smile. "It's sweet that you're worried about me, Karl. But you don't need to be. I haven't lost it completely. Honest."

"That's not what I'm saying. Not at all. But I am worried."

"Don't be. Something bad happened and I've chosen to deal with it by throwing myself into other pursuits. What's so bad about that?"

Karl shook his head and leaned forward, placing a hand palm-down on the table before Jack.

"You need to get out of that house. I mean it. And not just because of the memories tied up there. It's not good for you. And this movie of yours? Don't try to sell that as some therapeutic distraction." He straightened again, keeping Jack pinned with his gaze. His expression was near pleading. "I know what you're trying to do, Jack."

Jack laughed, but it was forced, fake. He stood up and collected his things. Whatever Karl thought he understood, Jack couldn't talk about it. Not with him. Karl still lived in that other world, the world Jack had all but abandoned.

"See ya later, Karl."

He left quickly, with the weight of Karl's question pursuing him. *What will you do? When it doesn't work?*

At the door, he glanced back. From there he could only see Karl at his table, stubbornly reading the newspaper unfurled before him. He wanted to go back, to explain it all to his only remaining friend. Make him understand.

But Jack knew better.

He stepped out into a morning already grown hot, the sting of smoke in his eyes a trigger for all the memories of the previous summer. The fires had grown even more monstrous this time around. The smoke climbed down into his chest, and he relished the burning sensation like a penance.

In the car, when the stereo came on and connected to his phone, Avery's voice hit him with the weight of a year's worth of grief.

He'd found the folder on her computer, labeled Demos, with just four songs, Avery's voice and an acoustic guitar. The songs were different from her usual, gleeful garage thrash. It was still sharp-edged and aggressive, but melodic in a way that surprised him. The time stamps on the files said they were from two years prior. He'd had no idea she'd even written these songs, let alone recorded them. He wanted desperately to ask Em and Billy about the songs. Had they heard them? Had they worked them out as a band? Or were these something else?

Why make songs that no one would ever hear? Wasn't music an inherently audience-based form? It occurred to him that this music was a sacred place that Avery had kept perfectly private, even from him, and that gave the songs an even greater power.

He drove through the summer traffic that clogged downtown, and as he entered the shadow of the overpass—speeding out toward Jakob Speck's ranch, the distance smeared by wood-smoke—Avery's voice filled the car.

4.

Out at Speck's, they had a production meeting: Jack, Speck, and Dell. Dell wanted to green screen the new scene Jack had written. Speck wanted Jack to axe the new scene and just stick to the goddamned script. Jack wanted to do a night shoot—that night, down in Speck's north field.

Jack won, and they spent the day up in the attic again, getting the rest of the shots they'd need with the tunnel. It was hot and bright, with so little room that they were always bumping into each other, tripping over the legs of tripods, smacking their heads on the hanging lights.

Desh was a young East Indian kid with acting chops that elevated him above the whole project; thankfully, he was devoted to Speck and seemed to like the script. He played Jack's stand-in, Joshua: the desperate lover descending into hell to rescue his beloved. Like the old Giallo films, it was a mix of mythology and gore. The story didn't matter as much as the symbols on the screen—nonsense that accrued meaning through repetition. Desh happily crawled up and down the tunnel a dozen times.

When they were done, Dell set up an impressive dolly shot that moved slowly down the tunnel toward the blank space at the end, the track telescoping out beneath the camera. They all stood around and watched as Dell ran through several takes, silent, as if the camera itself was an actor.

After work, dinner.

The whole ranch ate in the big white kitchen. Jack looked around at the dozen or so faces, most of them young and beautiful, with Speck there amidst them all, and was surprised how at home he'd come to feel. Karl's remark about "being recruited" didn't seem like such a joke right then. He considered many of these people friends—even Speck, who was often quiet, a little standoffish, and frankly kind of spooky. But there he was, smiling down at his food as Tracy told a story, and Jack thought Speck was becoming a strange kind of father figure, which wasn't that weird, considering his real father was also quiet and a little standoffish.

He felt comfortable, almost happy.

And then he was crying into his bowl of soup. Silent sobs tightened his chest and constricted his throat. He pushed back his chair, stood, and hurried out onto the big covered porch before anyone could see his tears.

The sun was just slipping over the mountain, going out in a glaring red flare, with the wildfire smoke making the sunset somehow more spectacular.

The valley stretched out below; his house was down there, beneath that layer of smoke. And Avery. He knew it was stupid to feel this guilt, ashamed at his own brief moment of pleasure, but it didn't change anything. It was as if he could hear Avery's call all the way up there, drifting up from the basement, up the hillside, echoing across the tinder-dry woods.

The screen door screeched and slammed, and then Tanya was beside him, gazing out toward a sunset grown almost too bright to see. She looked like someone else out of her makeup. Olive-skinned and round-faced, with black hair standing out in natural curls, she looked nothing like Avery. He was grateful for that difference.

"You okay?" she said.

"Yeah. Sorry."

She placed a hand on his upper arm, lightly.

"Don't be sorry. Every one of us, every person in that house—we all know grief, Jack. That's what brought us here. You should really consider joining us for Circle. I think it could really help."

Jack pulled away, just slightly, but enough that Tanya lowered her hand.

"I don't want to talk about her. I want her back." The whole conversation was mildly embarrassing, and even after a year, Jack still didn't like saying any of these things out loud. Suddenly, he wanted to quit the whole thing, abandon the movie, maybe even leave town. Why shouldn't he? He'd grown sick of the place where they'd been so happy together, where he now was a kind of pariah. Talking about it was counterproductive. *Just do the work*, he told himself. *You stop thinking about the work and you have time to doubt.*

"Sorry," he said. "I appreciate the invitation. I really do. I'm just not quite ready for that."

Tanya nodded, still looking out from the porch.

"Well, when you're ready, we're here. A whole house full of people who want to help you."

Jack laughed through his nose.

"You're already helping me. You did hear that we're doing a night shoot, yeah?"

"I heard."

Jack could hear the smile in her voice, but he wouldn't look at her.

"Alright, let's get this show on the road," he said, turning back to the house and holding open the screen door. Tanya went through, and Jack followed, back inside where everyone looked up smiling as he entered.

5.

Jack's alarm woke him, his phone buzzing and chiming on the table beside him. He sat up slowly, raising his head from his folded arms. His shoulders popped, and he stretched his arms high above his head, unlimbering himself, before finally silencing the alarm.

He yawned and stared into the rough hole in the wall. It wasn't the first time he'd fallen asleep down here, but each time, the dark earth beyond the broken cement struck him as wholly alien, like it had been green screened in. He ought to repair it, just like so many things around the house. All those endless tasks, the fix-it lists they'd made. All left undone. He thought of Avery's plans for the backyard and then of all the turned earth out there now. The police had left string grids and tape around all of the fawns' shallow graves, ultimately disappointed that they were non-human remains.

After the investigation, he'd left the yard like that. He almost saw it as a badge of honor. It was a reminder of the ways he'd been misused and disbelieved. Each stake and tattered string was like a ribbon, marking the time that had been spent investigating *him*, when they should have been out looking for Avery.

He wasn't bitter, not at all. He was filled with rage. But like all of his rage over all of his life, he kept it tucked away—only now he had found he could let it out in incremental bits, pour it into the movie. Sublimation, Freud called it: the ability to transfer your neuroses into practical work. He remembered that from undergrad. Though Freud surely imagined architects and civic leaders when he described the outcome of a great creative impulse, not a low-budget horror flick.

He'd been seeing a girl at the time he encountered Freud's writings. They were both maybe twenty, and she'd told him that sublimation meant something completely different in the sciences. In chemistry, it described something skipping over a phase, like ice turning to vapor without ever passing through a liquid stage. He'd liked that idea and the poetry of the two definitions, their overlap.

Now, Avery was sublimated away, from living to ghost without ever passing through death. He was sure of this metamorphosis. Felt it with absolute certainty. He heard his wife's voice some nights and felt her nearby, always. He might even be able to live a normal life if he could only see her, talk to her.

If he could only see her. Know that she was okay. The idea that she might be scared or lost—or worse—it was too much. He felt it like a hot blade inside his chest. So, beyond all common sense, he pursued making this movie, hoping it would be a way that he could be with her, finally. But Tanya wasn't Avery, no matter how much makeup and imagination they applied. And the movie, so far, had done nothing.

Speck's information about how the *Red Witch* script was all supposed to work was vague at best. He couldn't even say for sure what Boorman hoped to accomplish. Bring Becca Mays back? Free her from the house? Nor could he say if Boorman thought it had worked.

"It's the process that matters, Jack," Speck had said. "The magic's in the making, not in the result."

"That sounds great," Jack had told him, exasperated, "but my wife is in there somewhere. The result is actually pretty damned important."

But Speck just kept telling him to hold on, to be patient. See the thing through. Though more and more, Jack thought that Speck knew nothing about real magic. Just a big mashup of religious mumbo-jumbo. Orphic mysteries, or some nonsense. Despite his doubt, Jack persisted. Going back was unthinkable. He could not even stop long enough to be concerned at his own disbelief.

Now, in the basement, he closed his notebook and the script opened beside it, stacking one on top of the other. Boorman's *Incantations* stood open to "Incantation XXIII." That was one of Boorman's persecution fantasies; laid-on Christ imagery, with the soldiers coming to pierce the speaker's side and gamble for his clothes. The whole biblical shebang. But it was also oddly beautiful, ending with the speaker singing as they dragged him down from his locust tree. As its thorns tore his flesh, the people all around heard his song and gathered. Jack liked that: the absolute faith in art to draw people together, even if it changed nothing for the person doing the creating.

He closed the book and shoved it into his bag.

He actually had some time. Night shoot. That field. The fog. Dell swore he could get it right on the first try.

Jack cocked his head, looking at the hole. Time enough to start, anyway. He'd been planning it for a while, this new project.

The roll of newsprint cost thirty-five bucks. He mixed it into paper-mache in the tub sink by the washing machine.

First, he made a neat lattice of duct tape across the hole, just to give it some structure, something to hang the paper-mache onto, leaving half-inch spaces between the silver strips. *Should work*, he thought, as he began tearing long strips of paper.

Starting at the top, he smeared the paper across the hole gently, not wanting to break the tape. Just get a first layer up, let it dry a little, make a base. Gray curds of the mixture dropped to the concrete at his feet and got caught up in the hair on the back of his hands and forearms. This was a different kind of work, and Jack found, to his surprise, that he was enjoying himself.

He'd made it almost to the bottom of the hole, when he stopped, looking into the shadowed space beyond. He thought of the bundled case he'd retrieved from back there, Boorman's papers and scripts. The writer had placed them there, not to hide them but because he thought it might have some effect. They were his spell books, his kooky little grimoires, and he'd used them to cast a spell on this house and on this space. He'd built a trap in that basement, and Avery had fallen in.

But now it was Jack's turn to try. But what kind of spell was he casting? His movie, *Red Witch,* was a spiritual sequel to *House on Blood Street*: Orpheus and Dante rolled up together and fed through the sausage grinder of old Italian horror films, with their dramatic coloring and surreal, meandering plots. And now, as Jack's team was approaching the end of shooting, he almost dared to believe they were making something kind of great. Something that people would actually watch.

Not that that had ever been the goal, of course, and he felt immense guilt at the thought of traveling the film festival circuit with the film he'd funded to resurrect his ghost-wife. The spirit of the project was irreconcilable with getting a distribution deal.

No, it was about Avery; this stupid hole in the wall was about Avery; and it was all some convoluted part of Boorman's plan. He'd built this fissure in the world out of his own worship. All those hours down here pasting cut up women onto the wall. That took something, didn't it? Boorman was, Jack now realized, just an obsessed fan. Something in Becca Mays's life or death had snagged Boorman's interest, and he'd worried it like a stone. Maybe the power of the mythology he'd built around Becca Mays's death was expressed in the film, or the hole in the wall. Maybe the whole perverted project was an embodiment of Boorman's pure will.

Jack stood beneath the bulb, paper-mache slowly hardening on his hands, and he smiled.

I can worship, he thought. *If I have the will for anything, it's this. It's her.*

He rinsed his hands in the sink, shook them onto the basement floor, and hurried upstairs.

In the bedroom, he dug through the small mountain of clothes he'd left unfolded on Avery's side of the bed. They'd never quite got the dresser situation figured out, but it wouldn't have mattered much if they had. Avery piled things up. It was her way. Clothes, mail, cardboard boxes broken down and stacked outside the back door. Build it up until it becomes an actual crisis, and then clean in a flurry of energy to erase the mess. Then start the process over again.

He extracted the oversized Sailor Moon T-shirt, the image faded to a ghost, holes near the collar. She'd had the thing as long as he'd known her. Slept in it constantly. He wadded it under his arm. Beside the bed, there was a little wooden box. Setting it on Avery's pillow, he flipped up the lid. A child's treasures lay inside: smooth stones; dimestore rings turned permanently green; a little plastic baby from a King Cake; a rubber finger puppet of a green monster with spindly arms, its mouth open in a toothy roar. Avery was a magpie, collecting anything that caught her eye, then transforming them into sacred objects. Jack lifted out the little woven bag and pulled open the top. Inside were three worry dolls made of wire dressed in colorful string. One had a miniature straw hat. One wore a blue dress. One was a baby, smaller than the others. A worry family.

Jack pushed the dolls back into their pouch, and carried it and the shirt to the living room. On the wall right beside the door, just above the rack where they hung their keys, was a framed snapshot of the three of them. It was at the aquarium in Seattle, and Dylan was maybe nine years old, smiling at the camera, blue light rippling up the wall behind them. A stranger had taken it for them, and Jack had felt something binding them together that day. Him and his worry family.

Jack took the picture down.

Back downstairs, he carefully worked Avery's shirt through the lattice of tape he'd made into the cavity beyond it. He rested the shirt on the hole's bottom, right where he'd found the scripts. He placed the photo and the little pouch of dolls atop it. He crouched there, looking at the collection. Three was a good number, but something was missing.

He pulled his wedding ring from his finger, taking flakes of dried paper-mache with it, and held it up. He kissed the ring and set it on top of the photograph.

Good.

Taking another strip of paper, he dipped it into the thick mixture and lifted it up, running his hand along its length, pushing off the excess goop. Maybe making things was magic, and maybe it didn't matter. What mattered was that he was doing something, and the feel of the cold paste under his hand was proof of it.

As he worked, he hummed; soon he recognized the music. It was the first song in Avery's demos. These tunes didn't have titles. Just timestamps. But he'd heard it more than the others since it always came up first. He listened to it each time he got in the car, and it had wormed its way into his brain.

Soon, he was singing, first under his breath and then out loud, his voice echoing off the concrete walls.

He worked and sang throughout the morning. Building something.

6.

At about four o'clock, Jack's phone emitted a long and constant buzz, rattling across the kitchen counter. He placed the plate he'd been washing back down in the sink, dried his hands, and reached for the phone. It rattled to life again just as he touched it. An alert. Usually, this meant a kid had been abducted—or, more likely, was being taken out of state by a non-custodial parent. The vibration meant, *everyone be on the lookout.*

Not this time.

They were evacuating everyone east of town, and people within the city-proper were advised to prepare for immediate evacuation. Travel on I-90 east of town was closed down.

"Fuck me," Jack sighed. He called the Ranch.

It rang three times, and Jack imagined the old white corded phone mounted to the kitchen wall, like at his grandparent's house. Someone picked up.

"Hello?" It was Tanya.

"It's Jack. How you guys holding up out there?"

"About like you'd expect."

"You being evacuated?"

"Jacob says we're staying, but we can actually see the fire from here. Some of the others are out spraying down the yard now, which is just useless, but you try to tell *him* that." He could hear the smile in her voice, but she was nervous, too.

"I've got a house in town, you know. If you all need a spot to crash."

A long pause.

"That's very sweet, Jack. I'll pass it along."

There was a rustle and pop, and then Speck's voice filled the phone.

"You want to get this shot, you better get yourself up here."

"You want to film? Tonight?"

"No. Now. Not sure there'll be anyplace to do it tomorrow."

"Forget it, Jacob. Bring everyone to my place. It'll be tight, but there's room for all of us."

A pause that lengthened.

Finally, Speck spoke. "That's a very nice gesture. Eventually, we might take you up on it. But right now, we have some unfinished business. Dell's already set up the shot. This is a now-or-never situation. Soon as the sun goes down, we're rolling—with or without you."

"Fuck, Jacob," Jack said, and he looked out the window into the yard, where a deer stood beneath the tree, watching him. "I'm leaving now."

Outside, the smoke was thicker and turning acid, burning his eyes and throat. He got in the car and closed the door against the choking fumes. It was approximately three thousand degrees in the car, but he quickly shut off the air conditioner, not wanting to pump smoke inside.

As he pulled away from the curb, he saw Mel on her front steps with her arms crossed, watching him. Hands still on the wheel, he gave a little wave with just his fingers. Mel didn't respond. Out of everyone, he was most hurt by Mel's opinion of him. Sure, Avery's ex Janie kept Dylan away, and that was a whole different kind of ache. He didn't actually care about Janie's opinion. He just wanted to see his kid. But Mel he liked, and he remembered Avery's hushed reverence for their neighbor that first night she'd come over. *Bad. Ass.*

Jack both resented Mel's suspicions and admired her for sticking to them. She was dedicated to Avery, just like he was. They were on the same side, even if Mel didn't know it. That would have to be enough.

There were barricades at the eastbound on-ramp, but Jack hung a left, going under the highway instead. The underpass guided him down through a momentary night and out into a world transformed by smoke into a darkened haze. He drove on.

Up the hill, the Ranch seemed to hover just above the smoke. Jack could almost see the sky. He parked his car, walked to the edge of the yard, and looked out over the valley. Below was just a layer of gray, like a hole in the world; off to his left, he could actually see a squiggly line of orange flame on the hillside, black behind it, as it marched forward, down into the valley. Tanya's description was right on the money.

This was end-times stuff right here. Terrifying. But he couldn't seem to summon the requisite terror. He watched the fire as if he were outside himself. Like he was just a character in a movie.

The screen door slammed, and Jack turned to see Speck coming down the steps, most of his face covered in an N95 mask. He pushed another mask against Jack's chest.

"Put that on before you choke to death," he said, his voice muffled.

Jack fit the mask over his face. The air inside it was instantly hot and damp, but the relief was glorious. He gave Speck a thumbs up.

Speck started walking, and Jack hurried to catch up.

"Dell's got us set up in the north field. We're gonna have to get it right the first time. Clock's ticking. We should be moving everybody out now."

"One shot," Jack said. "And we're done?"

Speck stopped suddenly in the deep shadows at the side of the house, the air outside of those shadows gray and thick. He turned to Jack, arms loose at his sides. With only his eyes visible, it was hard to read him, and Speck was always hard to read anyway.

"This is it," Speck said. "One last shot, and then we wrap. You and Dell can cut the thing, I don't care. But I took this on because I felt some measure of responsibility. Whatever Arthur did down there, he did it himself, for his own reasons, but I may have given him some tools, you know?"

Jack just nodded.

"So, this clears the ledger. I made the first film with Arthur, and now I'm un-making it with you. All balanced up. I'm happy to see this through, but when it's done, it's done."

If Jack didn't know better, he'd say that Speck was scared about more than the encroaching flames.

"I appreciate everything, Jacob. You know that, right? All you've done?"

Speck gave a little nod, reached out, and squeezed Jack's upper arm. Just a single application of pressure. Then he dropped his hand and turned away. They headed off toward the field, the smoke, the encroaching line of flame, and maybe—just maybe—a way through to whatever place Avery waited for him.

7.

Four people waited on the hillside, each of their faces hidden behind white masks. Dell fiddled with his handheld camera, and Tanya and Desh huddled close together further up the hill. Greg, crouching on his knees with his laptop open on the ground before him, adjusted the lights. He'd set up the lamps in four places along the hillside, with gels that cycled through various shades of red, adding more yellow at the far end. The practical effect of otherworldly color was enhanced by a thin smudge of natural, real-life orange on the next hill over: wildfire swiftly closing in.

Jack and Speck reached Dell, and Speck leaned in, said something into his ear. The words were lost behind his mask and the wide space, but Dell nodded.

"Let's do it," Speck shouted to the rest of the crew.

Nodding, Jack stepped forward, patting Dell on the back as he passed. The hill wasn't all that steep, but he still had to work to reach the actors.

"You two ready?" Speck shouted.

They both nodded.

"This is all you, cowboy," Speck said to Jack. "Your vision. Set it up."

Jack nodded. "Desh, I need you downhill a bit, and Dell is going to center your back in the shot. You're just moving forward, uphill. Don't crawl or anything and keep a steady pace. Tanya, I need you actually out of frame as you start your descent. Dell?"

Dell gave a thumbs up.

"Meet in the middle, and embrace. I won't tell you how that should look but we've only got one shot at this, so make it work. No pressure."

He smiled at them, even though they couldn't see it under his mask.

"Yeah!" they both shouted. They pulled off their masks and handed them to Greg.

"Places."

Everyone got into position, Speck standing downhill, arms crossed, watching. Greg cycled the lights down to a cooler pink. Tanya trudged up the hillside, her back to the camera. All they could see was her mass of dark hair, whipped by the wind. She looked nothing like Avery, but something made Jack want to rush after her, pull her back. When she reached her mark, she turned, giving them a little wave.

"Action," Jack called.

Desh moved forward, Dell keeping behind him, and Jack moved just behind Dell, watching in the lit rectangle of his monitor. Desh's dark shape almost filled the screen, but as he climbed, Dell subtly increased the distance between them, shrinking Desh in the frame, allowing the scale of the hillside to overwhelm the shot.

When Tanya came into frame, she appeared as a moving shadow over Desh's left shoulder, growing with each step. Jack felt more than saw the lights shift to a deeper red as the two figures approached one another.

The wind rose with sudden hot force that rippled across the grass like water, pulling at the actors' clothes and whipping Tanya's hair around her face. On the wind came gouts of gray smoke, ash, and glowing cinder that filled the frame, hazing out the two figures who had finally reached one another and were clutching each other as if it were the end of the world.

Another gust, and Jack could actually hear the fire's deep thrum, and looking up, he saw the top of the hill alive with orange flame.

"Oh, shit," he said, grabbing Dell by the back of his shirt. "We gotta go." Dell clutched his camera and ran.

Jack sprinted up the hill toward Desh and Tanya, waving his hands and calling out, but his words were carried away by the hot wind. When he reached them, they were staring dumbly up at the approaching flames. He grabbed at their bodies, pulling them and shoving masks into their hands.

"Run!" he shouted just as the air filled with a roar. He looked up to see a massive, double-propped helicopter passing over the hill, the sound warping away to nothing as it ascended. The firefighters would be here any moment. They'd stop it.

Looking down the hillside, everything seemed so far away. His eye moved swiftly up the far slope, toward the house. Greg's lights were abandoned with the rest of the makeshift set. There was a good chance the whole Ranch would be leveled tonight. He looked out once more at the valley below, the lights of the town stretched out before him.

Calliope Street was down there, tucked away in its little pocket, deep in the center of town, almost certainly out of reach of the fire. Avery would be safe, anyway. The wind pulled at his shirt, bringing darker smoke down around him.

He'd seen the final shot on Dell's monitor, captured just when the smoke rolled in. It was beautiful. The two figures, wrapped in billowing smoke, clutched each other in the red glow of an alien sky. That was it. That was what the whole project was about: that shot. The lights below prismed as Jack's eyes filled with tears. Even the mask wasn't doing much good anymore. He felt like he was breathing underwater.

Looking over his shoulder, he saw the jagged line of the fire. From a distance, it was hard to gauge the blaze's speed. It ate its way down the hillside at a shocking pace. The air was a whirling torrent of smoke and ash, and then he felt the wall of heat slamming against him, sucking the air away.

Coming uphill, through the smoke, was a figure, white gown and dark hair whipping, smoke almost rising off of its edges. And for the briefest moment, he was sure it was Avery, come back in answer to this spell he'd cast, out here in the summer night, while the world burned. For just a moment, it had worked.

But then he blinked his tears away and the figure resolved itself into Tanya, hurrying toward him, eyes wide over her mask. She stared beyond him at the jagged line of orange flame.

He wiped at his eyes with the backs of his hands and pulled his mask down so that it hung around his neck. Another gust, and a wave of oven-hot air struck him, sending him forward a step. Trying to take in a breath, he choked, and through his tears the world was divided into light and dark: orange light descending from the sky, swallowing up the darkness.

And rather than feeling panic, he felt suddenly at peace.

Tanya reached him, and he thought that she would pull at his arms and try to drag him downhill, away from the smoke and the rising heat, but she didn't. She was calm. Too calm.

"Let's go!" Jack cried. His voice whipped away in the wind, subsumed beneath the roar of burning acreage. He grasped Tanya by her arm, trying to pull her with him, away from the fire, but she rolled her shoulder back, pulling out of his grip, and shoved past him, up the hill.

Jack tried to call out again, but his lungs burned and he began to cough, his vision stinging. His eyes were so caked with smoke that they seemed to have stopped producing tears.

Tanya was well above him now, walking slowly toward the wall of smoke, the jagged line of flame. She looked over her shoulder, but Jack couldn't read her face. The smoke was too thick, his chest burning. He took a step toward her. Another. He must stop her, pull her back, but his legs felt leaden. Without knowing how or when it happened, he found himself lying in the dry grass, looking up. The air was a little clearer there, icy in his lungs, and there were no stars above. He squinted at the rafts of smoke that shifted over him, through the thick haze that covered the whole valley. He squinted at those pinpricks of light, hoping to see them one last time.

A roaring filled the night, louder than semis on the highway next to his childhood home. He could hear the interstate humming again, just as it had beyond the cinder block retaining wall as big trucks shifted down in the dark. The drone pushed him through time: ten years old, lying in bed on long summer nights, sheets sticking to his legs, streetlight casting its pale glow through his open window. He is unable to sleep because he is so frightened. He's spent his nights thinking about serial killers, unable to stop, fascinated and horrified in equal measure. He has discovered some truth about the world that he is not yet able to verbalize or even understand fully, but it frightens him more than he has ever been before. So he lays there, listening to the sounds of the highway, a jabbering radio down the block, and his parent's television, deeper inside the house. Occasionally, his father gives one of his sharp, barking laughs, and

Jack feels momentarily tethered to the real world again, or rather, to the false world of his childhood that has now been cracked open and exposed. More than once, he believes he hears footsteps on the gravel outside his window, only to realize that it's just the blood pounding in his own ears.

A couple of years later, he is walking to the bus stop a few blocks from his home. The moon hangs above the houses so impossibly large, that it must be a dream, but he knows it's real. It's a full, pale moon centered over the street, looking as if it might collide with his little no-name suburb and bring about some cosmic cataclysm. This moon could end everything: famine and the news of war and Derek Best, who makes Jack's life miserable, math homework and Sunday school and all of it.

But nothing ends. The moon hangs there, too large, filling up the whole sky, and the next day there is nothing to see. Jack's memory begins to take on the form of a dream, though it was no dream, just like his sudden hope for an apocalypse was not a dream but a fervent wish that was subsumed, finally, by shame.

He is swimming across the river. It is spring, and the water is icy cold. He swims to the far side and sits shivering on the rocks, his hands blue, but there's nothing for it but to swim back. No way out. He re-enters the water and his lungs burn; the uncooperative muscles in his legs seize and relax. The current pushes him further downstream until he slips under, choking and sputtering, chest a box of flame, and he feels how thin the line is between life and death. That line has always been there. No need for serial killers crawling through your window and cutting your throat, no need for Armageddons. Death is always at your elbow, a pale shadow, always waiting to catch you up.

Avery pulls Jack up out of the shallows and he gasps, air rattling in and out of his body as he's racked with shaking.

It hadn't been Avery then: someone else pulled him out of that river. But Avery is standing over him now, ringed with floating sparks and ash, and she is pulling him up into this hellish night, from water into flame, from death into life.

She wants him to follow, down into that valley. She's been waiting. She has a place all prepared for both of them on Calliope Street.

8.

Jack floated just beneath the dark surface of consciousness, a pool where sound came to him distorted, the edges rounded and echoing. He thought he heard the garbage truck on its five a.m. round: low beeping and the sound of hydraulics. He waited for the crash as the garbage fell into the truck's mechanical maw, but it didn't come. It just kept beeping and lifting, like a trace of song stuck in his head. If only he could hear that hollow thump and crash, it might complete the circuit and he could sleep again. A light from what must have been a passing car filled the room and was gone. He sank back down into the dark water, welcoming its weight and cold, thick pressure in his ears.

Time passed. He lay at the silty bottom of the river, grass waving around his face, light refracted into a million hexagons that shifted and rolled above. Little fish played through his waving hair. He felt skewered, as if a piece of river trash—a rusty metal bar, perhaps—had pierced his back and run through his ribs, and perhaps in the weeks or months or years that he had been down there beneath the river's weight the fish had hollowed him out, eaten their way in. His chest felt both hollow and heavy. Some fat bull trout was curled up in the cave of his ribcage, and it slept there, curled around itself, its gills working mechanically, filtering the water in and out. Jack drifted on the sound of the fish's respiration, the riverbottom cold against his skin.

Time passed.

Jack surfaced in a dark room with walls of glass. Directly ahead of him, through the first clear panel was a long counter, lit from above. Several figures lurked behind the counter. One sat. The whole scene made him think of the basement with its semitransparent plastic sheets and the light beyond. But this place was clean and sharp: the basement was just a scrawled storyboard for this, the real production. He couldn't move, and his chest felt as if it had been crushed. He opened his mouth to call out to the people behind the counter, but his mouth was full and his throat on fire. He watched his wounded chest rise and fall, and drifted back down beneath the surface.

When he awoke next, a nurse stood over him in maroon scrubs. A tall Black man with a bald head, he rested his big hands on the bed's rail and smiled down at Jack, showing all of his bright, white teeth.

"There he is. It's alright," he said.

Jack tried to speak again and choked. The nurse placed a gentle hand on Jack's arm.

"Don't try to talk. You've got a breathing tube in there, and some pretty severe swelling in your trachea. My name is Will, and you're in the ICU. You're suffering from some pretty severe smoke inhalation. They performed a bronchoscopy last night, and your lungs are inflamed, but there doesn't seem to be any other major damage. So we're treating you with good old-fashioned oxygen, waiting for the inflammation to go down. Do you understand?"

Will nodded his head at Jack and Jack blinked back, though he understood next to nothing.

"They called your emergency contact, but we haven't been able to get through. Anybody else you'd like us to call?"

Avery had been his emergency contact, and her phone was in a police evidence drawer somewhere, shut off and non responsive. Jack thought about Will's offer. Did he have any friends left? He couldn't imagine asking Karl to sit by his bedside, kind as he'd been. And Speck? Whatever he and Jacob were, Jack didn't think they were friends. Speck had helped him, sure. And it was true that Jack had never quite figured out what Speck hoped to gain from it all. Speck had said that the film cleared his ledger, that he'd helped Boorman. But Jack didn't know what that meant, unless he was delusional enough to think the movie would turn a profit.

He remembered the fire raging down the hillside. Tanya. The image of her silhouetted in the light of the fire, head turned to look back over her shoulder, face blurred by heat and smoke. Where was she now?

He shook his head at Will, who smiled, patted his arm, and straightened up.

"I'll tell the doctor you're awake," he said, and he moved away, sliding the glass door open and shut.

Jack watched as the nurse moved around behind the counter and picked up a phone. Then, he closed his eyes. In his mind, his lonely glass block floated in darkness, and he let it drift.

After two days of doctors and nurses prodding him, they declared he was going to live. Jack's body was cold from the inside out as they fed him through an IV, then removed his breathing tube. Extubation felt as if he were being pulled inside out. He was prepared to see large chunks of his lungs flop out onto the blue pad they'd placed on his chest to catch whatever the tube brought with it. Instead, it was just mucus tinged with blood.

They pumped him full of sedatives, anti-inflammatories, and antibiotics. They kept him on oxygen—though now through a face mask—and moved him downstairs to a regular ward.

Through all of this, Jack lay still, neither reading nor watching the television. He just watched *Red Witch* in his head from start to finish. Each time he reached the final scene, where the lovers reunite on the hillside as a bright line of fire divides the frame, he found himself crying.

Maybe his tears meant what they'd made was enough. The movie might be a very expensive brand of therapy or a way to process the impossible loss of Avery's disappearance. But he knew better. He'd moved beyond nothing. He was not getting over it. He closed his eyes and the movie started up again: the establishing shot, a house on a tree-lined street.

He tried not to think about Tanya.

The next morning, there was a soft knock at the door, and Speck was standing there in his usual uniform of short-sleeved western shirt, jeans, and boots. He held a straw cowboy hat in his hands, looking like he was there to pick Jack up for the prom. Jack waved him in.

Speck seemed smaller in the hospital room. Out at the Ranch, he'd seemed larger than life, but now Jack saw him as he was: an old man, not quite frail, but wiry, with bruises on the backs of his hands. Speck pulled a chair over to the side of the bed and sat down, placing the hat on his legs.

"How you feeling?"

Jack gestured with his hand. *So-so.*

"Well, you made it through intensive care. That's the trick. Any word on when they'll kick you out?"

Jack pulled the oxygen mask away from his face and spoke, his words coming out in a harsh whisper. "Thursday. Unless there's an infection."

Speck nodded.

"We'd better get you out of here, then. These places are petri dishes. Wouldn't be surprised if I caught something." He smiled, and Jack realized how mismatched the expression was on Speck's face. He looked like another man altogether: a man who spent his mornings at the diner on the east end of town, teasing the waitress and telling dumb jokes. Someone's grandfather.

"The Ranch?" Jack whispered.

"It's fine. Wind turned."

"The others? Tanya?"

"They're fine. Dell, too. Hell, they carried you out of there. Desh got treated in the ER and sent home."

"Carried me?"

"The old fireman's carry, with the flames practically licking their heels."

"Tanya's safe?"

"She's fine. Promise."

Jack couldn't quite believe that. He'd replayed that final memory so many times, over the last few days: Tanya walking calmly into the flames, even as Jack collapsed into darkness. He'd risked their lives. All for a stupid movie.

Red Witch was intended as a means of rescue, an Orphic quest into the underworld. The final scene, ambiguous as it was, was meant to be triumphant. Even if the lovers never made it back to the surface, they'd found each other. After all, the end of Orpheus's story was a tragedy.

But now, Jack realized that the characters in his movie had been made to save *him* all along. He'd been fooling himself. He never truly believed in Boorman's childish magic. He pursued the images and ideas in the script because he was trying desperately to find some way out, some way through. And then, the characters had saved him for real, in this world, carrying him bodily out of the path of the fire. He blinked. He was conflating his cast with their characters, all the lines blurred, or perhaps burned away.

He started to laugh, but it turned instantly into a choking cough. He put the oxygen mask back on, tears streaming from his eyes.

"Want me to call the nurse?" Speck said, starting to reach for the button beside the bed.

Jack held up a hand and shook his head; after a minute, the coughing stopped, leaving him panting. When he could control his breath again, Jack pulled his mask back down and turned to Speck.

"Why did you help me?"

Speck tilted his head to the side. "You needed helping, I suppose."

"Are you in the habit of helping every stray who comes to your door?"

Speck chuckled and leaned forward.

"Jack, it's the work of a lifetime. What do you think I'm doing out there? We're all strays, Jack. You, me, Tanya, Desh, and the rest."

Jack considered this, knew instantly that it was true. Before this moment, he'd always imagined there was some grand narrative or hidden agenda to the Ranch. Karl may have poisoned the well there.

"But, the movie."

"It'll be a good movie, I think. Once it's done. Dell's putting together a rough cut as we speak."

Jack squinted at Speck. "Can I ask you something?" he said.

"Sure."

"What's it all for? The Ranch, I mean."

Speck took his hat by the brim and leaned forward, elbows on his knees.

"You're just asking that now?" He gave another sweet, wizened smile, and Jack thought he might grow used to seeing this side of the old man. "Son, we're saving the world, one sorry son of a bitch at a time."

He stood, placed a hand on Jack's shoulder, gave a little squeeze.

"The others wanted to come. Are you okay to see them tomorrow?"

"Hopefully, I'll be home by then."

"Even better." Speck moved to the door, hat in hand.

"Jacob," Jack said, his voice almost working. "Thank you. For everything."

"Hell," Speck said, putting his hat on his head. "Everything ain't even happened yet."

9.

Jack took an Uber home from the hospital. His car was up at Speck's place, and he didn't want to call anyone. He just wanted to go home and climb into his and Avery's bed, in their own room. He missed the feeling of the cool sheets against his skin.

When the car dropped him at the curb on Calliope Street, he looked up at their house and then to his left at Mel's house, with its trim yard and brightly painted door.

Of all the people who had turned their backs on him, thinking he was a murderer, losing Mel felt the most personal. Most of their friends were really Avery's friends; what else would he expect. He actually admired the way they chose sides. He'd choose Avery's side, too, if he could. He'd tried.

Mel's coldness felt like an actual judgment, worse than being ostracized by the folks who missed his wife as much as Jack did. He hadn't felt this desire to be accepted since school.

He could write Mel a letter and drop in in her mailbox, but he had no idea what he would say.

He unlocked his front door and went inside.

The house was just as he'd left it before he headed to the last shoot at the Ranch. The vague smell of rot laced the air, from the garbage or the sink's ancient pipes, which liked to back up and not drain properly. Just one more thing on a long list of tasks he could not bring himself to begin.

Setting his phone and his plastic hospital sack of belongings onto the island, he dug out the sealed bag of cough drops they'd sent home with him. They were the only thing that kept his throat from being painfully dry. He unwrapped one, popped it in his mouth, and put a few into his pocket. With cherry-eucalyptus fumes filling his sinuses, he went out into the yard.

The deer was there again, far back at the end of the yard, where Avery had once envisioned a garden. Now, the area was overgrown with weeds and thistles that obscured the low chain-link fence. Deer roamed the neighborhood in gangs, eating people's flower gardens and blocking the roads. But Jack knew it was *her*. Their deer. The mother, seeking out her lost fawn.

He sat down on the concrete step and watched. It just stood there, looking back at him. The cups of its ears twitched and its dark eyes were wet and round.

Then it sprang away. One leap carried it over the fence, vanishing down the alley.

Jack was on his feet before he realized what his body was doing. He wanted to follow and to see where the animal ran. It was one more thing lost and gone away. No. Feeling sorry for himself wasn't doing any good, so he shook himself off and went back inside.

Down the steps, he flipped the switch, turning on the light above the laundry area. The far side of the basement was still dark. His plaster construction cast back the light in warped chunks. He moved through those broken beams, as if descending into the underworld.

But it was just a slab of concrete, and there was his table with his notes, a coffee cup, and his closed laptop. On the wall, the gray, lumpy product of his repairs. The hole was covered with paper-mache so thick that it was still damp in places, even after a week to set up. Perhaps its soggy surface would begin to sprout mold. Better than naked ladies. At the center, ragged and brittle, was the hole, staring back, unblinking.

He sat at the table and opened the laptop. As soon as he logged in, music blared out. The machine had paused halfway through the song, waiting since the moment when he had shut the lid and cut it off. Avery's song, one of the demos he'd found hiding in the download folder. Her voice was beautiful. As her acoustic guitar jangled and buzzed through the three-minute song, Jack sat back in his chair and listened. The light was still off above him, though the computer screen washed his face in blue light. He missed her so much in that moment that he felt it like a stone in his middle, a weight that would drag him down.

And then he sat up, opened his email. Nothing from Dylan. That ship had probably sailed. One more lost. He opened an email, typed in Dell's address, and then dumped all four MP3 files into the message.

He wrote just one sentence: *For* Red Witch, and hit send.

He sat in the hard kitchen chair and listened to Avery's voice. Her song went on, outlasting her as her voice drifted down the river of time to find him watching the ragged circle in the wall. He waited, and listened, and sang along.

10.

Over the next month, Jack fell into something like a routine. His Japanese students' school term would be starting up again soon, and he desperately needed the money, but somehow the thought of logging in to teach made him tremble. He wasn't sure he could face them, even over the video interface. What would he even do? Talk to them about language? Once, he'd been quite eloquent on the subject, happy to launch into rambling asides about the power of words. His high school students had heard it all. They would roll their eyes, sure, but Jack thought that some of them got it. Some of them heard.

But who was listening now? And what would he possibly have to say?

Radio silence from up at the Ranch. Not that he'd tried. That last conversation with Speck had felt somehow final. The brush-off. Jack had cost them enough.

So he puttered.

He woke late, traipsing down into the basement out of a kind of sad compulsion. He was hoping for some sign. Even pale things skittering in the dark. Dead things, cold on the floor. Anything. He thought back to those short crazy weeks when the house had woken around them, dreaming its half-formed images, and while it terrified him, it wasn't half as frightening as this silence, this emptiness, this silent dissolution.

So fucking emo. That was Avery's voice in his head. He welcomed it.

He headed back toward the stairs, stopping to reset the breaker for the washing machine, the thing roaring to life when he did. He went upstairs. A cold breakfast. A walk through the backyard, where the air was sour with smoke and the heat was oppressive. A slow circuit, his breath hot inside his mask, looking down into all the empty holes beneath the trees.

It would be a morning's work to fill them back in, throw down some seed, maybe plant a few flowers, but Jack's refusal to do so had all of the strength and vitriol of adolescence. He wouldn't do it because it was both easy and expected. He'd let another winter's snow fill the holes, let the excavated dirt turn to smooth hummocks, all out of spite.

Then, back down into the basement to stare at the computer screen, trying to convince himself he was writing something. Eventually, the screen would darken after a long-enough pause in his typing and he would find himself staring into that dark eye, willing it to swell, pulse, blink—do anything.

He was wounded by the house's refusals, and he didn't think it could go on much longer. He longed to be haunted.

11.

Full dark. The sound of traffic on the main artery two blocks over. Sharp smell of woodsmoke. He hadn't turned the light on above his makeshift work station, so it was just the filtered light behind him, fractured and caught up in the dirty plastic. Not even enough to cast a shadow before him onto the table, onto his hands or the nine millimeter pistol before him. No shadows. Just a colorless gloom that enveloped him, the table, and the wall with its staring eye. Above the patched hole was that little rectangle of pure night, not even the streetlight seeping down into the window wells.

Working the cough drop around in his mouth, he picked up the gun. It looked plastic and fake, but its weight was very real in his hands. He released the magazine, setting the gun down before him. One by one, he slid the copper-colored bullets out and stood them up on the table. Fifteen tin soldiers. Slowly, he fed them back into the magazine. He'd done this at least three times now, stalling. He didn't need fifteen bullets. Just the one.

He cursed at himself: he was a coward. This was a thing he'd known forever. The world frightened him; his own helplessness in the face of its terrors made him hopeless. The fact was that he had done everything he knew how to, and even some things he didn't. He'd made a goddamned movie, after all, which was so far outside his wheelhouse that he still couldn't believe it was real. Two weeks since the fire and the final scene, when he'd been dragged off the hillside by people who had been so intensely present in his life and then, as quickly, vanished. Having his life saved hadn't changed anything. Avery was still gone, and he still received wicked looks from the people at Orange Street Market. Mel despised him. He had no real family, certainly no one he could talk to about this.

What would he even say?

The house ate my wife.

It was true. The house had changed since that night. Grown still. His whole life, he'd wished that magic was real. He wanted to believe that there was some layer beneath the surface, a place without credit scores, student loans, and documents signed in triplicate. Something beyond the tedium of every waking hour.

Even if this magic was real, it was like every other kind of power in the world: not his to wield. He'd tried. They had the movie to prove it. Dell called just that evening, inviting him over to see a rough cut, up at the Ranch. Saturday. They would all sit in the big ranch house, watching the movie—his movie—projected onto the wall.

This should be exciting to him. Eighteen months ago, before they'd ever seen the house, it would have been a high point in his life. Him, Jackson Todd, the man who never finished anything, with a whole-ass movie to his name. Never mind that most of the heavy lifting was done by others; every project needed someone with vision. The market for horror being what it was, there was a good chance he could get the movie picked up by someone. Jack could work the festival circuit for the next year.

Exciting stuff.

Although, thinking about it, it would have been better if *Red Witch* had never been finished. He saw that now. It should have been like all of his other projects, like the house: a burst of creative energy that eventually faded away to 'a thing he would get around to eventually.' That was the way it should have been, because then he could have fooled himself a little longer and convinced himself he was doing something other than distracting himself while Avery was still missing. It could have been his life's work, getting her back.

Now, the movie was done and Avery was still gone, and he didn't know what to do next. There was nothing *to* do. Just the house, but he couldn't think of any reason to bother. Maybe fix it up and flip it, get out of town, and go somewhere where no one knew him. Start over. But all of that felt like a crushing,

Sisyphean weight. He couldn't do it. And he had no reason to try.

He pushed the magazine into the pistol's handle and pulled back the slide, chambering the first round. It would be easy. Not like all the other projects. This one would be finished the moment he started. One and done. And if anyone remembered him, it would be as one more ghost to haunt this house, one more unquiet spirit.

He raised the gun, pressing the barrel to his temple, then pushed it back a bit, right above his ear. He had to be sure. The shot had to jelly his brain as it burned through his skull. He felt this was the only way to turn off all of the thoughts and feelings, which were, in the end, just electrical firings deep within the mass of his brain. A house with bad wiring.

He slipped his finger inside the trigger guard, still not touching the trigger itself. His pulse was pounding in his neck, his hands shaking, and here was the final disappointment: he was scared. Even now, frightened at everything. Even this, which was meant to be the antidote to his fear. Just one more failure.

He rested his finger on the trigger, careful not to apply too much pressure. The last thing he wanted was to *accidentally* shoot himself. He couldn't explain why it would matter.

He took a long breath in through his nose, held it, and exhaled. That was the way to do it. Just one squeeze on the exhale. Calm and purposeful. He repeated the breath and repeated it again. *This time*, he told himself, but he did not pull the trigger. Another moment passed.

This time.

His phone buzzed on the table to his left, startling him. He quickly moved the gun away, heart hammering, feeling as though he'd been caught.

Jack set the gun down before him, took up the phone.

The text was from Dylan.

David got me a guitar.

Jack smiled at the phone. The kid was thirteen years old. Perfect time for it. David, that other stepdad, seemed alright.

Very cool. Send pics. Then he was wandering away from the table, toward the light, upstairs, where the house was still and quiet. He texted back and forth with Dylan, and eventually he put on a Depeche Mode record. The gun lay mute on the table downstairs. Later, he made a sandwich and went to bed, and the wheels kept turning. The world went on, even when he looked away.

12.

Three days later, Jack's phone rang. It was Dell, so he answered. Jack hadn't been back to the Ranch since the night of the fire, not even to collect his car. He felt happy at the loss; walking everywhere gave him time to think about how much more he could stand to lose while still functioning.

"Hey," he said.

"Jack. You coming up tonight?

"I don't know."

"We're doing a screening. Just the family."

"The edit's done? That was awful fast. Wasn't it?"

"A rough cut. Working around the clock. It's beautiful, man. So, you're coming?"

"What time?"

"Just come up."

"I don't have my car."

"Oh, shit. That's right. Well, you home? We'll come get you."

"Yeah. I'm here."

"See you about seven thirty," Dell said, and he hung up.

Jack meandered through the house, put on his shoes, and finally went up into what he would always think of as Dylan's room, though Dylan had never even seen it.

It was stuffy and hot in there, so Jack opened up the windows at both ends. A light breeze stirred, bringing a taste of smoke that tickled the back of his throat. He pulled a cough drop from his pocket, unwrapped it, and popped it into his mouth. He was becoming a fiend for the things. He sat on the edge of Dylan's bed and just listened.

He'd heard strange sounds up here before and felt strange breezes, and he wanted that sensation now as a sign of the fantastic, of magic. He wanted proof that Avery was not lying dead in the high grass behind some highway rest stop. A year ago, her death had been a certainty. He'd embarrassed himself in his statements to the police, his neighbors, and anyone who would listen. *The house took her.* That was the one thing he knew. But the longer this went on, the more distant that night grew, and the less real it felt.

He'd mythologized Avery's disappearance through endless rewrites of Boorman's script, slowly claiming it and making it his own. The movie was Jack's childish insistence that magic was real, but also that rescue was possible. In the end, the lovers meet on a dark hillside, wrapped in smoke and ringed by fire. *Shurpu.* Fire was the key, somehow, and he'd folded it right into the heart of the movie, even as the mountainsides raged and smoke choked the valley.

But the edit was nearly done. Dell called it a rough cut, but he was sure it would be polished; to anyone who wasn't in the film industry, it would look complete. That was Dell.

Then what? Jack had been stretching out what was left of his life with arbitrary goals. He wouldn't kill himself *until.* Until he knew Dylan was okay. Until the semester was over. Until they find her. *Until the movie was done.* That had been the big one. If it hadn't been for Speck and Dell and the whole crew, he might have tripped along forever, making *Red Witch* a lifetime project, shot on weekends like *Night of the Living Dead.* Jack could spend decades lost in editing limbo. He could live in that liminal space indefinitely. In fact, he'd always lived there.

But there was an eerie finality to this screening at the Ranch, and though there was the distant fantasy of the festival circuit and hope for distribution, or maybe getting picked up by a streaming service, all of that seemed outside of Jack, removed. At his core, he just didn't care.

He stared into the corner of Dylan's room where the shadows met, forming an odd rhombus of dark. The sunlight was that beautiful artificial pink. It was the smoke that did it. Gorgeous sunsets. As he watched, the shadow seemed to deepen, darken, and telescope inward, as if he might fall into it. In there was the final darkness and separation he so desired—if only he weren't such a coward. For just a moment, he half-convinced himself that Avery would be waiting for him there.

The sound of tires on the pavement interrupted his thoughts, and Jack looked away, standing to peer out the little window to see a red pickup at the curb. Dell got out, spinning the keys on his finger as he jogged up toward the house.

Jack went down to meet him.

When he opened the door, Dell nearly knocked him over with his embrace, pounding Jack on the back, the two of them doing an awkward crab walk as they rocked in the doorway.

"You crazy shithead. I thought we lost you," Dell said, and it took a moment for Jack to realize he was referring to the fire and Jack's near-deadly smoke inhalation, not his near-continual flirtation with suicide.

"I'm here," he said, and Dell finally let him go.

"You wanna see this thing? You're gonna shit yourself."

"Can't wait. Can we use that as a tag line for the poster?"

Jack collected his keys and phone, pocketing a few more cough drops and fitting his mask onto his face; Dell shadowed him, his face beaming.

"Let me grab my bag," Jack said over his shoulder, and he went down into the basement. He hadn't been back down in the last three days, and the gun still lay on the table. He let his eyes roll off of it and turned on the light.

He pushed his laptop into his bag and began to gather up his notes, dog-eared scripts, and battered copy of *Incantations*. So many words. Useless. Slinging his bag across his chest, he made a neat stack of the papers, setting the book on top. He placed it all on the floor beneath the hole in the wall, in that spot where the house had birthed that string of aborted deer. Here was *his* stillborn life, small enough to hold between two hands.

He could hear Dell's footsteps above, moving around the living room, and he knew he needed to hurry.

Back by the washer and dryer was a milk crate full of random junk; he thought he'd seen a barbeque lighter in there. He found it, gave it a click. A weak, blue bulb of flame rose from the opening. It was enough.

He moved back to the far end of the room and, kneeling down, clicked the lighter once more. He held the little blue flame to the corner of the sheaf of papers. They began to blacken and curl, and then the orange flame became visible, lifting itself up, already hungry.

Jack stood, watching the fire grow, and then quickly stepped away. Dropping the lighter onto the table beside the gun, he watched a thin stream of smoke rise up and fan along the wall, gathering along the beams at the ceiling.

Upstairs, he herded Dell outside. Dell was still talking about the movie; as they climbed into the truck, he was describing an early scene, but Jack just looked out his window at the house. He imagined gray smoke curling up from the open doorway.

But he never saw it. Dell pulled the truck away from the curb and they were off, down the shadowed tunnel the trees made of Calliope Street, out and away, leaving it all to go up in flames.

13.

They'd set up a screen inside the barn. The massive thing filled one whole wall, with a projector suspended from the beams above, white cables snaking down to the little nest Dell had made for himself, complete with a computer and mixing board. Jack followed the lines of cables to the speakers set up at both the front and back of the barn.

They'd done all of this, and the idea that they'd done it for him made him feel embarrassed and awkward. But had they, really? It wasn't just for *him*. He reminded himself that Speck had sunk a decent chunk of money into the project, but as person after person came up and hugged Jack, shook his hand, smiled at him and welcomed him back, this explanation became harder to countenance.

Tracy came up to him, holding him at arm's length to look him over.

"You look awful," she said. "We've missed you."

He looked at her face. She was young and beautiful and almost certainly damaged. Who wasn't? But she was also kind. Where else had he felt this kind of open, brazen kindness?

He straightened, pulling away and wiping his face with the back of his arm.

"Sorry," he said, sniffling.

"No apologies," she chided, and pushed him toward the chairs lined up in rows on the barn floor.

Speck was in the front row. He stood to shake Jack's hand.

"Looking much better," he said.

Jack smiled and squeezed the older man's palm, placing his left on top of Speck's.

"Thanks for this," he said.

"Sit down!" Dell shouted from behind them, and Jack waved up at the darkness of the loft.

They all found their seats.

Jack looked around, leaned toward Speck. "Where's Tanya? This is her show."

"Not here," Speck said, looking toward the screen, which was filled with blue light.

"Should we wait?" Jack said. "We should wait. This is her moment."

Speck just shook his head.

When the projector came on, its illuminated darkness was only a few shades lighter than the barn's interior. Were they descending or ascending? Jack's eyes adjusted. He clutched his knees with trembling hands. And then, there it was: the same establishing shot of the front of the house, but this time it was really the house on Calliope Street. The image gave Jack a little shiver. He thought briefly of the fire he'd set and wondered if the house was gone yet. He blinked the thought away as the movie cut to an interior shot.

Tanya moved through a kitchen that was not his kitchen, but rather a highly dressed set built inside the Ranch house. Jack tried to turn off that part of his brain that identified the film's props and sets as reality; he wanted to just see the movie as what it was: a made thing. He wanted to be submerged in the story, but it was as if he could see wires attached to Tanya's arms. His mind perceived what was happening behind the scenes, from the ragged frames of the flats that made up the far wall, to the tight crowd of people huddling behind the camera. He was painfully aware of the camera itself. He could not imagine Tanya alone in the kitchen because he knew the camera was there with her, watching. Jack had been beside it the whole time.

Red Witch was all wrong, and more than that, it was all a terrible waste. He'd spent the better part of a year on this, telling himself he was doing something important—saving Avery. But sitting in the barn, the whole project seemed like not just a waste but a heresy. Did he not even know how to mourn properly?

He felt suddenly sick, and he got up, crouching low, and went out into the night.

Outside, the air was cooler. He leaned against the outside of the barn with his hands on its rough boards, just breathing. He savored the way the wildfire smoke burned his lungs. He *should* feel it. It was what he deserved.

The hills stood black against the night, charred by the recent fire. The hills were just the ideas of hills, out there. The sky was a heavy raft of smoke, lit by no moon and no stars. Maybe there was nothing out there past the circle of the barn's light, nothing down the hill. Jack imagined that Speck's crew had struck those sets behind him, and now he was here, at the edge of the universe, with only the house looming behind him and the sounds of the movie spilling from the barn.

No. There *was* a world. He just had a hard time remembering that it kept spinning out there, away from his grief and pain.

He looked up at the house, half hidden behind shade trees, lights on the lower levels glowing orange through the drapes. *Where was Tanya?*

She was the lead, Avery's stand-in, and it was a little uncomfortable to admit how much he'd come to rely on Tanya, how her presence filled that Avery-sized hole in the world. He couldn't believe she would miss the screening. But then again, he would have said the same about himself and here he was, moving up the path, away from the barn, into the inky shadows of the trees.

He stepped up onto the Ranch house's darkened porch. Deep inside, a light burned, and Jack let himself in, drawn toward it. The door latching behind him seemed too loud, echoing through the house as if it were empty. The floor creaked beneath each step as he approached the lighted kitchen.

Halfway down the hall he heard movement ahead: someone was moving just around the corner, inside the kitchen, maybe by the stove. It had to be Tanya. Everyone else was outside. He stepped into the warm light, opening his lips in greeting, but his words died in his mouth.

No one was there.

"Tanya?" he croaked. His throat was so raw and dry. He sounded frightened, even to his own ears—of what? Tanya? Her absence? The house? That last gave him pause, and he looked around him, taking in the shabby wallpaper and the scarred countertops. It all seemed so real, so worn by time and use. So... *authentic.*

That insight rattled around in his mind as he backtracked down the hall, peering into the front room. Also empty. He passed through the little foyer again and climbed the stairs, thinking all the time of that scene in *Psycho*, when the detective goes into Norman Bates's house and the camera pans down from directly above. A God's-eye view, looking right down through the roof and the ceiling. Jack was no detective, and he had no reason to fear anything in this house. He certainly never had before. This had been a refuge for him, just as it had for the others.

Besides, everyone was down in the barn, watching the movie. Everyone but Tanya.

At the top of the stairs, right where Norman's mother would come rushing from the open door with her knife raised, there was just the familiar line of open doors.

He moved swiftly, peeking into each room as he passed, until he made it to the fourth one on the left: Tanya and Gracie's room.

The rooms were always sparse. Not quite Spartan, but close enough. Speck preached some kind of soul-body discipline about the body being only a container. Jack never really paid too close attention, just as he'd never participated in their Circles or their prayers and meetings. Too wrapped up in his own sadness, locked in his own head. But now, he looked closely at the square room with its one window, its yellowing lace curtains, and its two beds. The bed on the left was made up with near-military style precision, the pillow encased under the bedspread. Beside this bed were a few simple belongings: a hairbrush, a small, black digital alarm clock, and a bottle of ibuprofen.

The other bed was stripped bare, the old twin mattress showing faint stains.

Tanya was gone.

The room seemed suddenly too warm, and his legs went weak. He stepped forward, bracing himself on Tanya's naked bed, and sat on the mattress, waiting for his faintness to pass. Leaning his elbows on his knees, he hung his head low, concentrating on his breathing. Panic. That's what it was. No great mystery. Though he barely knew Tanya beyond their work together, her absence felt like the ground sliding away beneath his feet. He had that roller coaster drop feeling in his middle.

Tanya's absence resonated with Avery's absence. Jack raised his head, looking up at the ceiling, imagining, godlike, that he could see into the attic space above the bedroom that they'd used as a set. Was that tunnel into nothingness still there? Or had they already torn it out? He thought of the irregular circle of green at its narrowest end, a gateway to anywhere and nowhere. He imagined Tanya, wandering lost through an endless field of flat green light, and that image forced him to his feet.

He hurried, half-stumbling out into the hall, down past the other rooms, and grasped the plastic ring of the cord suspended from the ceiling. The attic ladder dropped down, accordioning out until it rested on the floor, and Jack did not wait, did not think, but simply climbed as a million reveals from a million horror movies flashed across the inside of his head. Clare in *Black Christmas*, face encased in a plastic bag. Norman's mother, spinning around in her chair as if on strings, to reveal her rotted-empty eye sockets.

Reaching the top, he stumbled the three steps to the hanging light cord, found it, and jerked it hard.

The attic space stood empty—conspicuously clean. They'd ripped out the set piece and swept every last piece of debris. The folding table and the kitchen chair, which had once done double duty as prop table and makeup station, were gone. There wasn't even any of the usual attic junk. No moldering cardboard boxes or broken lamps.

Someone dedicated to escaping the physical prison of their body to become pure spirit probably wouldn't have much use for knickknacks. Still, the emptiness troubled Jack and made him doubt his own senses. He searched his memory.

What if the movie had all been some sort of dream, some fantasy his mind had spun out while he lay in the hospital? He'd seen that reveal, too. A million times.

No. The others were down there now, watching *Red Witch*, which was the movie they'd all made together. If he'd stayed, he would have seen the scenes shot right here in this long, slanting room.

He backed away, moved down the ladder, leaving the light on, and hurried down the hall, the ladder still extended. He just needed to get away. Home.

Down at the first floor, he rushed through the door to find Speck standing on the porch, looking out into the night. Jack stopped, suddenly guilty.

"Where's Tanya?" he asked again.

Speck kept his face pointed away. His voice was flat, hollow. "She went home to Sacramento. Her parents came and got her two days ago. Sister's sick, I guess."

"Is she coming back?" Jack hung back, just outside the door. Behind his head, insects battered themselves against the porch light.

"Hard to say. Usually not."

"Do you have her phone number or something?"

Speck turned his head, glancing back over his shoulder, eyes narrowed.

"You know I don't. She made her choice. She comes back, and we'll welcome her with open arms.

But for now..." He let that thought trail off and looked away again.

Jack cycled through his internal catalog of horror films. They'd sacrificed Tanya to whatever gods they worshiped. They'd parceled out her flesh like communion. They'd burned her inside a Wicker Man.

That last thought stopped him. *Burned her.* He had a sudden flash of that night on the hillside when the smoke engulfed them, with a wall of flame approaching behind. Jack's eyes stinging and warped with tears, making it impossible to see more than a few yards in any direction.

"Did she make it back from that scene on the hillside, Jacob?" His voice sounded remarkably calm to his own ears.

Jacob gave a little shake of his head, and Jack could feel the older man's disgust.

"Her parents came and took her back to Sacramento. Now, are you going to come watch the rest of the movie? The others are waiting."

"No. I can't. I'm sorry." Jack hurried past Speck, down the steps to the path. He hurried through the shadows, still convincing himself that there was some immediate danger. In the movie in his head, Speck would chase him, or Dell would spring from the trees and grab him. His headlights would reveal the whole group lined up across the path. His whole mind was warped by too much time in front of the TV. He'd made it to the gravel lot when Speck called out to him, his voice bright and sharp.

"You're always welcome, Jack."

He reached his car, climbed inside, and locked the doors. The interior of the car, sitting closed for these last weeks, was oven-hot and the air smelled stale. Although he was trembling, he laughed at himself. Working himself up over an empty room. He started the car, switched on his lights, and turned around, pointing the headlights down into the tunnel beneath the trees, into the valley, toward home. He blinked, remembering his little offering at the basement shrine. The house would be gone by now, nothing but a loose lattice of charred timbers. But where else did he have to go?

14.

Somehow, his house was still standing, seemingly untouched. That seemed about right. That was on brand. The house seemed to stare back knowingly. It had his number.

He rested his head on the steering wheel, taking several long breaths, and then got out of the car. It was almost ten, the streetlights fractured by high branches, traffic humming a few blocks off. He stood on the sidewalk before his own house, suddenly frightened to enter.

A phrase from *Incantations* surfaced suddenly. "What is familiar turns monstrous." For the speaker in Boorman's book, this line described the poet's entire worldview. It was a kind of break with reality, in which the everyday world was recast as a labyrinth of horrors, dressed up in black comedy. But for Jack, it spoke to his experience of this house. It loomed over him, whole and horrible, like the killer from some old slasher, impossible to kill. It had taken his life from him.

He'd never suffered from anxiety, at least not in any clinical sense, but now, standing before the house on Calliope Street, he felt a rising dread and a certainty that he could not enter. He might never pass through that doorway again. He realized that his breathing was rapid—too rapid. He dropped his bag to the pavement and hunched over with his hands on his knees. Black spots. Sweat on his forehead.

I'm going to pass out.

He sat down on the strip of grass along the sidewalk, clutched his legs, and concentrated on breathing. *Stupid.* It was just a house, no matter what had gone on there and no matter what it had done. He raised his head and saw Mel watching him from her porch, hands on her hips. Her expression was cold, telegraphing indifference. Jack looked back at the ground.

"Mel," he said.

"Jack," she said back. "What's happening here?"

"Think I just had a panic attack. I'm good now."

"Are you?"

He looked up then, at Mel, whose face had softened almost imperceptibly.

"No. Not really. How are you?"

"Been better."

Jack laughed through his nose.

"Well, thanks for checking on me. I think I'm alright."

She came down and extended a hand to him. He looked at it for a long moment, surprised and touched, and then took it. Mel pulled him up with surprising strength, although he was almost a head taller than her. Once he was on his feet, her smile vanished. She arranged her face into a mask of indifference again.

Jack picked up his bag from the ground and started toward his own place, glad that Mel was there. He couldn't very well act terrified of his own front door while she was watching.

"Would you like a cup of tea?" she said as he got one foot on the bottom step. "I'd just feel better knowing you were alright. Not going to have a stroke or something."

He turned to her, saw something he'd never seen before: Mel, looking uncertain.

"Tea would be nice," he said.

While Mel put the kettle on the stove, Jack took in the details he'd forgotten over the past year. He was once again amazed at how a house with the same building plan as his own could feel so different, its kitchen so open and airy.

He watched Mel set out cups on the counter and pull down a tin of tea. She was so comfortable in her space, so welcoming, and he couldn't stand it any longer.

"I didn't hurt her," he said.

Mel looked up at him, tilted her head, and narrowed her eyes.

"Maybe not," she said, and went back to dropping tea bags into the mugs.

"I've just spent the better part of a year trying to get her back."

"And how did that go?" she said, putting the tin back into the cupboard.

"I think I did art therapy or something? Anyway, it was bullshit."

He turned away, looking out Mel's kitchen window at his own house, just across the narrow strip of yard, past the waist-high fence. He felt tears rising and fought to hold them back. He'd already almost passed out in front of Mel. He didn't need to weep, too. He knew his tears would appear fake, like a performance.

Mel opened the refrigerator behind him, taking out a carton of milk.

"Grief is strange. You never know what might help. Mostly, it's just time."

"I don't want to grieve for her. I want to get her back." The words came out more forceful than he'd intended, and he turned to Mel. Quieter, he said, "I don't think she's gone."

"Then where is she?"

"Still in there somewhere," he said, gesturing with his chin toward the house.

"Are you trying to tell me something, Jack?"

He laughed then, an actual laugh.

"No, Mel. The cops tore the place apart. One minute she was there, sleeping beside me, and then she was gone. She went down into the basement, but she didn't come back. It's fucking insane."

The kettle's whistle sputtered to life, rapidly climbing in pitch before Mel plucked it off the burner and filled the mugs.

"Look, for what it's worth, I don't think you hurt her. I *did*. At first. And more than likely I'm an idiot even now. Occam's razor and all that. But I think I believe you—about you, I mean. The rest just doesn't make sense."

He watched the trapped balloon of air make the tea bag float atop the darkening water. What could he say to that? Of course it didn't make sense. He knew that. Reason wouldn't help him anymore. Rationality wasn't Boorman's domain. In both his film and his poetry, there was very little thread to weave meaning out of. It was all vibes. Surreal scenes leading to even more surreal scenes, populated by characters who might as well be ghosts.

Jack tried to smile. It felt as if his face were twisted in some terrible rictus.

Mel put a hand on his arm, lightly, tentatively. She still wasn't convinced of anything. He didn't blame her, couldn't blame her. He didn't deserve anyone's trust, though somehow it kept being extended to him. Speck, Karl, and now Mel. Maybe they could all talk to Janie, convince her to let Jack see Dylan.

"Would you like to have our tea in the yard?" she said.

"That would be nice."

Mel collected the mugs, and Jack held the back door open, and soon they were seated at a glass-topped table, the only real light a long rectangle of window light projected onto the grass. The whole dome of the sky was filled with smoke, as if packed in cotton.

Mel carefully lifted her tea bag from the mug and flung it away into the bushes. She licked her fingertips and picked up her cup, holding it to her chest. Jack copied her, getting a weak smile from Mel when his tea bag slapped against the fence.

The two of them sat there, a part of the late summer night. The comfortable silence gladdened Jack. It almost made him feel sorry that he'd tried to burn his house down. Shit. He'd have to go see what kind of damage his little stunt had caused.

But not now. Now, he was sitting in the cooling night with a cup of bitter tea and a friend. That was something. Maybe not quite enough, but it was something.

A rustle and crack. They both swung their heads toward the sound. Jack heard the delicate crush of feet moving through the underbrush, and then she was stepping out of the shadows into that yellow patch of light. The deer stood perfectly still, as if suddenly aware of their presence, one ear twitching and turning like a radio dish, its big black eye shining with reflected light.

It was so close, almost within arm's reach, but if he stood, he knew it would bolt. So he sat perfectly still, steam wetting the underside of his chin, and watched. This was a visitation, and it calmed him, gave him a sense of peace.

The neighborhood was overrun with deer. Some people said they were a plague, eating gardens, cleaning the bark off of sapling trees, and standing in mute lines in the center of the roads. They were so common as to be invisible.

But Jack sensed something in the doe's nearness, in her silent regard.

The moment couldn't last. Three long, bounding leaps and it was over the fence and clattering down the alley. Jack let out a long breath, felt himself smiling. He looked at Mel and saw she was smiling, too.

What was there to say? They'd both witnessed something magic, and talking about it would only sully it, only lock it up with language.

He sipped his tea and thought about the frisson of energy that had radiated off of the deer. He imagined Avery, sitting on the basement floor, cradling the dead fawn in her lap, weeping; he thought of that basement room filled with fire. In his mind, it was a perfectly contained cube of flame, roiling and feeding on itself, an engine to fuel his sad and haunted dream house.

The tea was bitter. Wonderful.

15.

A black shape stretched up the wall, blackening the paper-mache not quite reaching the little rectangular window. It took the vague shape of a person, tapering upward, perhaps in a flowing gown. Jack imagined it carrying a candelabra. On the ground was a charred heap of blackened paper, the concrete stained dark beneath it. Not what he'd expected. That was the trouble with his life: it just kept going, and every time he tried to just burn it down, it turned out to be just one more job to clean it up.

He laughed to himself. His shadow played beneath the bare bulb. A little dance for his burnt offerings.

He went to get the broom and dust pan, and swept up what remained of the past year's work. Ash and flakes. Something, still.

Dumping the dust pan into the trash beside the clothes dryer, he looked back. There was only a thin wedge between the labyrinth walls, but through it, he could see the burned place, and within it, that tapering figure. The hole was not visible at all from this distance. From that angle, he let his eyes relax, and the shape became a tunnel, marking a low way through, out and up. He thought briefly of that wood and foam tunnel that was now gone from the attic space in Speck's house. Perhaps this was where it had always led: right back here, where it all began.

What is familiar is made monstrous, sure, but also the inverse, the equation working both ways. This monstrous house, haunted as it was, was home. And even if she was gone, Avery would always walk its floors.

Speck had called the death of Becca Mays an infection, a little abscess in the smooth surface of reality, nurtured and kept below the surface by Arthur Boorman and his obsessive care. Well, Jack had never worshiped at that altar. He had never fetishized his loss, however he may have wallowed in it. *Red Witch* was meant to be a means of rescue, and it had failed—just as he'd known it would fail, because a moving picture could never do all he needed it to.

Around him, the house creaked and settled, warming up for its night of noises. Come Monday, he'd make a list and set about finally getting thc place in order; when Avery came home, she'd be so surprised. It was all he could think to do now. Make these little gestures. He hadn't looked back. He'd never looked away. So, they'd live together, here between these walls singed by flame and steeped in blood, but that also held laughter and love, at least for a little while.

They'd haunt the house on Calliope Street together, for as long as it took.

He flipped the switch, killing the light at the bottom of the stairs and leaving just the single bulb back there, beyond the milky plastic sheets: a square of light, left on for her, down there in the dark, to guide her home.

ABOUT THE AUTHOR

Josh Hanson (he/him) is the author of *King's Hill*, *The Woodcutters*, *Fortress*, *Marshbank*, and *Minotaur: stories*. He is a graduate of the University of Montana MFA program, and is a longtime resident of Sheridan, Wyoming, where he teaches high school and college English and lives with his wife and three cats.

ACKNOWLEDGEMENTS

This book would not exist in its current form without FZ Boda and Amber Finnegan, and I owe them my deepest thanks for their tireless work, endless championing of the book, and regular ego boosts. Writing is a solitary pursuit, but editing is a collaborative effort, and I couldn't ask for a better team.

And, as always, I'd be able to do nothing without my wife, Amber Hanson. This book is yet another song to you, and your voice lends its harmony throughout.

www.ingramcontent.com/pod-product-compliance
Lightning Source LLC
La Vergne TN
LVHW031307150826
845672LV00010B/2658

* 9 7 9 8 9 8 8 8 1 5 4 7 1 *